Bedford Square 4

Bedford Square 4

New Writing from the
Royal Holloway Creative Writing Programme

Foreword by **ANDREW MOTION**

JOHN MURRAY

First published in Great Britain in 2010 by John Murray (Publishers)
An Hachette UK Company

1

Contents

Contents

Foreword

I began teaching Creative Writing at MA level fifteen years ago – for the first half of that time at the University of East Anglia, where I took over from Malcolm Bradbury after he retired, and since then at Royal Holloway, University of London. A lot about such teaching has stayed the same during that time – the emphasis on finding an authentic voice, paying a proper amount of attention to detail and to large issues of characteristion, dialogue, descriptive writing, and so on – and a lot has changed. For one thing, there's a new sense of the larger community: creative writing courses, which used to have a certain rarity value, can now be found in most universities. For another, there's a more precisely developed sense of expectation in students and in their teachers. The students quite rightly want more structured feedback on their work, and the teachers want a more discernible sense of wide reading and formal knowledge.

Why? Frankly, and due largely to changes within the curricula in schools and undergraduate courses at universities, it is no longer possible to make some of the assumptions about knowledge and expertise that could be made when I started this kind of teaching. And although this narrowing has certainly been offset by new additions of one kind or another, at Royal Holloway we have always felt it needed to be redressed. That's why, as part of the MA degree, our students are asked to take courses in 'Supplementary Discourses' and in 'Reading as a Writer'. And why, in the weekly workshops, we tend to spend a good deal of time talking about formal issues that might have been neglected in their previous careers. I have yet to hear a student say that their original writing didn't benefit from this complementary work.

Having said that, it has never been our intention to encourage writing which is dustily 'academic'. On the contrary, my fellow course tutors, Susanna Jones and Jo Shapcott, and I have always concentrated on the need for freshness, surprise and originality – arising from a sure but unshowy basis of familiarity with existing traditions and techniques. It is a great pleasure to see these qualities so apparent in this anthology. It is a heartening collection of pieces which are at once ambitious and achieved, and which are always vigorous as well as varied.

ANDREW MOTION

David Bausor

David Bausor was born in London. He worked as a City solicitor and as a Legal Aid immigration adviser before completing the MA in Creative Writing at Royal Holloway in 2008. His short stories have been published in Foyles's *Tales of the Decongested* and *The Edgeless Shape*. He is currently finishing his novel, *Ghosts in the Palace*, from which this excerpt is taken.

Ghosts in the Palace

Chapter Eight

[Conrad Fairfax is a solicitor with the Ministry of Justice in London. He is sent on secondment to a Tribunal dealing with war crimes committed in the republic of Balegule, a tiny state in the far north of the former Soviet Union. His first case involves the prosecution of a 'General Gradient' for crimes against humanity.]

Conrad arrived at Court Seven early. He loitered while the box of documents he carried grew heavy in his arms. Eventually, the custodian arrived. When the door was unlocked, Conrad pushed past into the dim room beyond.

When his preparations were complete, Conrad leaned back to check the clock on the wall. Time to spare. The courtroom was like a familiar machine, all of its parts in place. In the blocks of light from the tall windows, he could see the heavy counsel chairs and the judge's dais. The glass screen around the witness stand faced off against the dark wood of the defendant's box. The clock's tick was loud but soothing. He could have been back in the Royal Courts of Justice on the Strand, and only the Tribunal emblem over the judge's bench disturbed the illusion.

Hannah's brisk entry interrupted his reverie. She sat down close beside him, and began checking his paperwork. He noticed the crisply ironed collar of her white shirt, how it looked against her pale skin.

'Did you get everything finished?' she demanded. Her hands darted among his papers as swiftly as snakes.

'I did,' replied Conrad, trying to forget the misgivings of the previous night. 'I pride myself on always getting the job done.'

Hannah began to write out a checklist of their legal arguments, pausing only when a plump man bustled in carrying a bulging satchel. He wore a black three-piece suit whose waistcoat boasted a watch-chain draped across the well-rounded middle. He strode over, thrusting a hand out as if cleaving his way through an invisible crowd. Conrad rose to meet him.

'Mr Conrad Fairfax, unless I'm mistaken.'

'You're not mistaken,' said Conrad. 'This is Ms Hannah Kingdom.'

The man pumped his hand and released it. The gesture was as smooth as if it had been practised before a mirror.

'And I am Gerald Frobisher, of Cruickshank and Delacroix.'

'Pleased to finally meet you, Mr Frobisher,' said Conrad. 'I'm looking forward to our first day in court. Will your client Mr Gradient be joining us?'

'Now, now,' said Frobisher. 'Mr Gradient is not my client. You know that my client is Mr Ghrande. He will attend since he is still being held without bail.'

'My mistake,' replied Conrad.

They were interrupted by the entry of two blue-uniformed guards leading a man towards the defendant's box. The man wore grey overalls a size too big for his slight frame. Conrad studied him closely. In four months, it was the first time that he had seen the object of this case. The defendant was forty-ish and clean-shaven, his face nondescript apart from a puzzled expression. He did not look like a man who might have committed a crime against humanity. He looked more like a clerk, or the lawyer that Gradient was supposed to have been before he joined the army.

'My client,' said Frobisher, dropping his satchel on the defence table. 'Excuse me.'

The guards sat their charge down as Frobisher leaned over. Conrad eyed the heads bent close together, and heard the urgent whisper of conversation. The defendant began to shake his head.

'Almost time,' said Hannah. 'Are you nervous?'

'I'm fine,' replied Conrad, although a familiar slow churn was beginning in his stomach.

Conrad noticed that the rows of seats behind him were almost all empty. There were less than a dozen people here, including the translator. Three loud knocks on the far door announced the arrival of the court clerk.

'All rise for Judge Nicodemus!'

Conrad stood with everyone else, waiting until the figure in the dark grey suit was seated underneath the Tribunal emblem. The painted ruby of the torch glittered in the sunlight like a burning brand. Conrad was disappointed to see that Tribunal judges did not wear judicial robes: such robes gave proceedings a certain gravity.

'Case No. 1-600/95. In the matter of, ah, "General Gradient",' read the judge, enunciating each syllable carefully as he adjusted his glasses. 'I am Judge Kwame Nicodemus. I shall decide this preliminary application over whether to proceed to a full hearing. Who appears before me today?'

Conrad stood up. 'Conrad Fairfax for the prosecution.'

'And for the defendant?'

Conrad sat down as Frobisher stood up.

'Gerald Frobisher. I represent Mr Ghrande, the alleged defendant.'

'Alleged?' said Nicodemus. 'Oh, there is some issue about identification?' Nicodemus shuffled papers until he stopped to examine a page Conrad could not see. He guessed that it was the UN 'Wanted' poster with its smudged picture.

The defendant stood up. 'I should like to speak for myself,' Ghrande said in clear if accented English.

'Mr Ghrande, I recommend that you let Mr Frobisher represent you,' said the judge gently. 'It is in the interests of justice that you should have a lawyer.'

'I need no lawyer,' replied the defendant. 'Anyway, Mr Frobisher does not care to speak what I have to say.'

'What you have to say?' asked Nicodemus, pursing his lips as if he had just tasted something unpleasant.

'I shall say what I have to say. I am the one who can say it best.' The defendant turned towards the defence table. 'No offence to you, Mr Frobisher.'

Frobisher shrugged. 'None taken, I'm sure.' He leaned over and shook Conrad's hand, and then walked out without looking back.

'So,' said Nicodemus, with a sigh. 'This defendant will defend himself. If he later desires a lawyer, then one shall be made available. You may present your case, Mr Fairfax.'

Conrad began to speak, his sonorous cadences falling into a rehearsed rhythm. At this early stage, it would be enough to establish that there was some serious issue to be tried. What the prosecution had to demonstrate was not that Gradient was guilty of a crime, but rather that some crime had been committed. The point of the exercise was to illuminate the existence of a question, rather than provide a comprehensive answer.

Conrad began to sketch out the work of the 'Administrative Disposal Unit'. Incontrovertibly, there had been numerous disappearances in the disturbances leading up to Balegule's civil war. There was evidence that the Unit had been responsible. Gradient had been the commander of the Unit. Conrad implied that Gradient's Unit had been part of some orchestrated plan that had veered out of control. From the corner of his eye, he noticed Hannah ticking off the arguments on her list.

Conrad spoke in generalities, conscious of the gaps in the evidence and the difficulty of proving every detail of the allegations. He reverted to specifics when he discussed Ghrande's capture by UN troops, how Ghrande had tried to destroy his identity papers. Conrad pointed out the similarity between the defendant's appearance and the face on the UN poster. He closed by stressing how serious these crimes were, how destructive they had been for Balegule, and how critical it was for their perpetrators to be brought to justice.

Conrad spoke well. It sounded convincing, even to him.

'Do you have anything to add, Mr – ah – Ghrande?' asked Nicodemus.

Ghrande stood, adjusting his grey overalls. His bearing suggested both confidence and deference. Despite his shapeless clothing, he did have a definite presence.

'I am not this Gradient,' he began. 'I am a victim of the circumstances in my unfortunate homeland. In Balegule, there has been great misery and much confusion. Everywhere, uncertainty prevails.'

The defendant spread his arms, opening his hands to show empty palms. Conrad noticed the smooth skin and manicured nails, recalling that Ghrande's identity papers listed his occupation as 'carpenter'.

'Those who suggest I am Gradient are either misguided or mistaken. Even if I were – which is not admitted,' said Ghrande, waving a finger at Conrad, 'it seems evident from what the prosecution has to say that these charges are merely allegations without substance. Where are the bodies? Who actually says that they saw this Gradient kill anyone? So much killing in Balegule, yet no one can be found to testify that Gradient is a killer. Who can say that they saw him take people away, that they never returned? No one. There is no need for a hearing, because there is truly nothing to decide.'

'Thank you, Mr Ghrande,' said Nicodemus thoughtfully.

For an instant, Conrad saw a look of pleasure slide over Ghrande's face. *I win*, said that look, *I win every time*. Conrad felt a tightness in his chest.

'Quite impressive,' Conrad whispered. 'Ghrande might get off if he keeps this up.'

'Gradient. Not Ghrande,' hissed Hannah. 'You should think of him only as Gradient.' Her eyes glared as if she were trying to make him recognise some basic truth by force of will alone. 'You must think of everything that Gradient has done. You must know that the man over there did that. Or else we will lose.'

Conrad examined the defendant's box. The inhabitant gazed calmly back at him with his mouth creased slightly upwards. In that moment, he looked exactly like the grainy portrait in the UN wanted poster, that stippled mass of light and dark that barely resembled a human face.

Gradient. It was definitely Gradient. Hannah said so. Izhod said so, and she had seen him at his work in Balegule. Ghrande would know about her soon enough, and then the world would know him as Gradient. Hannah was right. From now on, he must think of the defendant only as Gradient.

Hannah began tapping her pen in a staccato rhythm. He wanted to tell her to stop. Nicodemus was writing notes and consulting his file.

Ten minutes stretched out until Nicodemus cleared his throat and spoke.

'After due consideration, I find that there is sufficient material for these charges to be heard. This matter will therefore be set down for hearing in six months. Mr Ghrande will be remanded in custody.'

Conrad felt a wave of relief. The first test had been passed.

'No,' said Gradient. 'I should like to be free until the trial.'

'I'm afraid that's not possible,' said Nicodemus.

'But I want . . .' began Gradient.

Nicodemus ignored the petulant tones, preferring to slip away through the rear door. The clerk loudly announced, 'All rise!' over Gradient's protestations.

Conrad and Hannah began packing the documents back into their box. The guards began to usher Gradient away.

'That went rather well, I thought,' said Conrad. 'Thanks for all your hard work, Hannah.' He felt elated, but also tired. Perhaps Hannah could be persuaded to take the afternoon off. It was only eleven o'clock, but it felt as if the day were done.

But there was one last thing; something that Conrad remembered when he tried to sleep that night. As Gradient passed the prosecution table, he seized Conrad's arm. Conrad stared at Gradient's hand.

'What do you suppose that you are doing here, Mr Conrad?' said Gradient softly. 'Do you imagine that you are fit to decide who is guilty? Do you presume to judge me?'

The pressure of Gradient's hand was steady.

'Take your hand away,' said Hannah coldly.

Gradient stared at her. The hand gripping Conrad's arm did not move. 'You do not tell me what to do,' said Gradient.

There was a certain timbre in his voice. Talking to the judge, Gradient had been quiet and always reasonable. Now the tone of his voice suggested something else, a demand for obedience or else consequences would be risked.

'No one tells me what to do,' repeated Gradient.

Gradient took a step forward, looming over the table, his hand still on Conrad's arm. The guard began to pull Gradient away.

Hannah spat in Gradient's face.

To Conrad, what happened next unfolded like a film in slow motion. Gradient lifted his hand from Conrad's arm and raised it to his cheek. His fingers traced the line of moisture they found there, an expression of disbelief washing over his face. Hannah drew her arm back as if in readiness for a slap or a punch. Conrad felt strangely removed from this unexpected stutter of violence. It was as if he were being told of someone else's dream, a jumble of images he had to struggle to understand.

Everything started again.

Gradient shouted, an inarticulate cry that brought out thick cords of muscle in his neck. The nearest guard swept Gradient's arm up behind his back with almost choreographed smoothness. Then he inserted his other hand into the right angle he had made of Gradient's limb, and pulled hard. Gradient took a couple of quick steps as his body was dragged sideways.

'Careful, careful,' Conrad found himself saying quietly, as though giving advice he were not sure would be taken. Suddenly the other guard was at Gradient's other side, and the two guards marched Gradient out of the door with practised efficiency.

'Are you all right?' asked Hannah.

'I'm fine,' replied Conrad quickly. That should have been his question to her.

Conrad began restacking his papers. Hannah helped him. He studied the swell of her lips. He had kissed that mouth with passion, and he wanted to do it again. Conrad could not imagine her doing what she had just done; pursing those same lips to spit at Gradient. The knowledge filled him with something like distaste. He tried to suppress the feeling. It was not right.

Hannah was almost at the door when she realised that he was not following.

'Conrad?' she said. Half hesitant, half impatient.

'Wait,' said Conrad. 'I'm coming with you.'

But the heavy door was already swinging back. He was alone again in the courtroom, with only the slow tick of the clock for company.

The wide stripes of sunlight falling across the floor looked like the bars of an enormous cage. A sense of foreboding was growing within him. Gradient might have a point. It was difficult to judge the correct meaning of everything that had happened. He shook his head to clear it. Conrad told himself that today was a victory, since the mechanism of bringing Gradient to trial had clicked on a little farther.

Time to go.

Conrad began to walk towards the exit. On his arm, he could still feel the pressure of Gradient's grip.

Thomas Bunstead

Thomas Bunstead is 27 and works as a translator. He reviews for the *TLS* and 3ammagazine.com and his prose has appeared in publications including *Text's Bones*, *Blueprint* and *Orphan Leaf Review*. He is finishing a short novel, and applying for funding to research a longer work with historical, bilingual and fictional elements, exploring the exile in South America of a famous nineteenth-century figure.

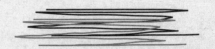

Offside

This story is just two people talking, I'm afraid. A boyfriend and girl-friend. There aren't any descriptions of them or where they are, so you will have to imagine it for yourself – perhaps the two of them just having left a pub, having stopped in the street. Perhaps you'll imagine them in West Street, in Dorking, Surrey, which has a large number of antiques shops, and is said to be the most polluted street in the South of England on account of the high buildings that line it and the town's one-way system. Perhaps it is quite overcast.

What? *she said.*
What? *he said.*
What? *she said*, I think you owe me an apology.
He said: I find it alarming you don't know I was joking.
She said: I don't care, it wasn't funny.
He said: Hold on a second.
She held on:
He went on: Do you consider me a chauvinist, sexist, a bigot who has experienced too little love and because of that hates woman?
No, *she said*, so that's why it is even less funny you making a joke like that.
But, *he said*, so you know it was a joke – and it was funny precisely because I'm not like that.
And, *she said*, you know I don't find that sort of thing funny, sexism. Why should I have to put up with it?
Hold on, hold on, hold on, *he said.*
She held on: *she held on*: *she held on*:
You're acting as if I was actually being a chauvinist, sexist, a bigot who has experienced too little love and because of that hates woman, you're acting as if that is what I am.
Hold on, *she said. But before he could do any holding on, she went on*: You acting surprised that I knew the player was offside in the stupid football match, and then you going on about how you'd taught

me what offside was once by using a 'female-friendly' analogy about women going shoe shopping and other women joining the queue at the front with their friends without having queued – the way you went on – why is that funny?

He paused before answering: What I find alarming is that you don't know the fact that that's not what I'm like.

She paused before answering: But the way you went on.

He went on: But we are already in that situation. You, a female of the species, are in the pub watching football. There's men, there's beer, there's a certain amount of grunting and scratching of testicles, every other word is F this – to me there's got to be some awareness of, of the sheer funniness of it. What worries me is that you weren't aware of the situation, the context in which the joke was operating.

And, *she said, nodding*, of the fact you're not like that.

It's alarming, *he said, nodding*, you don't know the fact that that is not what I'm like, exactly. The fact that that is not what I'm like is the only reason I'd ever make a joke like that. We comment on things, we play roles. A gap had been created by the fact that the two of us, well loved, well read, advanced in innumerable and important ways, were sat in a pub with men whose emotional acmes, the strongest connections they experience, are triggered on a weekly basis by beer plus football on the TV. By making that joke, I was commenting on the cliché that these kinds of men think women are stupid enough to not know the rules of a fabulously simple sport; I was making reference to the sad reality that these men might not think like that, had they spent all those overcast Saturday afternoons being attentive to their wives and girlfriends, shopping at Bentalls or going to the local Aquarium or to that cinema up near Waterloo where they give you 3D glasses or hiking.

She said: It wasn't even me you told that analogy to.

He said: It's not about the stupid analogy, and it's interesting you experienced me going on about it – it's just an extended analogy, it's stupid. I think I remember reading it in a supplement somewhere.

She said: It must've been some other girl you told.

But hold on, *he said*, I don't in any way believe women are inferior to men, or that anyone in fact would be stupid enough not to get what offside is. This is what's alarming. I am not a chauvinist, sexist, a bigot who has experienced too little love and because of that hates woman – I don't think you are stupid – you do know this? So why would I make a joke like that?

Exactly. Why would you make a joke like that, *she said*.

Perhaps, in a car park nearby, there is the sound of a lorry beeping as it reverses.

Andrew W. Campbell

Andrew W. Campbell was born in Raleigh, North Carolina, a town that embraces both sushi and collard greens, swing dancing and NASCAR, and which serves as the setting for his novel-in-progress. Before coming to the UK, he received a degree in religious studies, leased used trucks, hosted a late-night radio show, and performed as Santa Claus.

His or Her Cookie

Matt twisted and jerked the espresso machine handles. Holding one in each hand, he pounded out the used grounds from the last two lattes and rinsed them out under the hot water tap on the machine's right side. No sooner had he replaced them than Miranda called out the next order from her position at the register. 'Tall double skinny hazelnut!'

The customer wasn't at the counter yet. He had just appeared on the other side of the Joe Joint's glass door, but they knew what he always ordered. When he made it at the register she just asked him, 'For here or to go?'

The customer laughed. 'Man, you guys are good! To go, please.'

'Make that to go, Matt!'

'You got it!' said Matt. He had already tugged the third handle free from the machine and clicked out a dose of espresso grinds. With a hand press, he squeezed them down tight. Then he shoved the handle back into the machine and placed a cup underneath.

The whole process was music to him, a solo performance on that steam-powered Italian instrument. It was only a few months since he started barista training, but he had focused on it and made himself sensitive to the timing of the process and the sounds that cued it.

If the humidity was just right it took exactly forty seconds for the rich, brown liquid to finish burbling out. That gave him time to get the milk started. He poured a measure of skim into the metal pitcher and dipped the machine's steam wand into it. With a turn of the knob, steam exploded from the wand's tip, and he stirred the milk with it to create a thin layer of foam. It hissed and moaned, but not so loud that he didn't hear the click that came from inside the machine to signal the espresso had finished pouring. He left the steam wand shooting into the milk and grabbed a paper cup, into which he dumped the double shot of espresso and an ounce of hazelnut syrup. When the steam's roar dropped in pitch, he switched it off and double-checked the thermometer in the pitcher. Its needle slowed to a stop at 130 degrees

Farenheit – perfect. He poured the steamed milk over the espresso and syrup in one smooth gesture that left a crown of foam on top of the latte.

Each step he performed without thinking about what came next. He found joy in the motion and took pride in the results. And pride was something Matt really needed.

As last year's spring semester drew to a close, the principal called him in and told him that it wasn't working out. They were letting him go after only one year of teaching high school English. He wasn't too surprised. He had been awful. Hard to punish kids for skipping class with the number of absences he had. The week after finals, he drove around town dropping applications wherever he saw 'Help Wanted' signs. The Joe Joint hired him to work alongside kids only slightly closer to his age than the ones he had been teaching.

Matt set the drink down on the counter and announced, 'Tall double skinny hazelnut to go!'

The customer took a sip of the latte and closed his eyes to savor the caffeinated ecstasy. 'Aw, man. That's the stuff.'

In Matt's mind, the customer's name was simply Tall Double Skinny Hazelnut. At least four days a week he came in to get the same drink. Some Sundays he would show up with his girlfriend, Grande Double Mocha with Whip. They would sit for a couple of hours and do the crossword puzzle together.

Tall Double Skinny Hazlenut raised his cup to Matt in salute. 'Another masterpiece, good sir. My compliments, as usual.'

Then Matt felt Miranda lean her soft body in close to him, and it made him catch his breath. Her vanilla perfume was the only thing he could smell over the coffee stink. In a conspiratorial murmur, just loud enough for Matt and Tall Double Skinny Hazelnut to hear, she said, 'I think I ought to warn you, we seem to have something furry on the loose at two o'clock.'

A mouse? Matt looked up and to his right, and his eyes fell on a local character – a transvestite, a middle-aged man who dressed and spoke like a genteel Southern matron. The guy's skirt seemed a little short that day though. And his knees weren't closed. And then Matt saw in the skirt's shadows the 'something furry' Miranda had spotted – a pink-skinned critter curled up in its nest.

Matt tried to clench down his surprise. Only a startled squeak sputtered out.

Tall Double Skinny Hazelnut saw it too. 'Wow, she's going commando today,' he muttered under his breath.

'It's not fair,' said Miranda. 'I don't want to look. I just can't stop myself.' She looked at Matt pleadingly. 'Can you do something about it?'

A paisley kerchief kept her long, red hair tucked behind her ears, and she was wearing a faded, vintage Smurfette T-shirt. The blonde, blue-skinned cartoon winked at him from across the swell of Miranda's breasts. It was an inviting smile.

Miranda had been the first person to smile at Matt when he started working there. Everyone else made him feel old and fat and un-cool, like being on the wrong side of twenty-five he may as well have been fifty. He didn't listen to the right bands and didn't wear the right clothes. But Miranda had become his friend and she had been letting Matt crash on her couch since he lost his apartment the month before, so he said, 'Okay.'

'Oh, thank God. I'm going to go wipe down tables. Maybe I can scrub the image out of my mind . . .' She grabbed a rag and a spray bottle and went out from behind the counter.

'Good man,' said Tall Double Skinny Hazelnut. 'Earned yourself some boyfriend points there.'

'What?' said Matt.

'For me it's taking care of spiders. But between the two of us, I think you got the harder job.' He laughed and cup-saluted again before heading out of the store.

He thought Miranda was his girlfriend. Matt drew a breath to say that she wasn't, but then stopped himself. Why correct him?

And why wouldn't a regular think that? He and Miranda were always working together, always coming and going together. They laughed their way through their shifts, with those sort of playful, poking laughs. How often did Miranda give his arm an affectionate squeeze right in front of everyone? So, of course they looked like the happy couple, right? And if they looked that way to a stranger, how long before they started looking that way to Miranda too?

But in the meantime, Matt had a penis to cover up.

He didn't have a name in his mind for the transvestite who never ordered espresso drinks, just regular drip coffee. Sometimes he got a cookie too.

Wait, was that right? Did 'he' get a cookie? Or she? Both Miranda and Tall Double Skinny Hazelnut had called the transvestite 'she', regardless of that exposed bit of anatomy that Matt was coming to speak to 'her' about. How ridiculous was that? How could he say, 'Excuse me, *ma'am*, but could you please cover your *penis*?' A ma'am can't have a penis, that's the whole point of being a ma'am. Still, Matt tried to think of the transvestite as 'she' as well. Maybe that was what you were supposed to do.

So, *she* was reading the newspaper and had finished her cookie. A scattering of crumbs remained on its plate along with a few torn pink Sweet'N Low packets. Crimson kisses marked her coffee mug's rim. One manicured hand rested on the mug's handle, broad and big knuckled like it had grown up handling farm equipment. Maybe it had.

'Excuse me, ma'am?' he said.

She looked up. Her earrings jangled. 'Yehay'us?' she drawled, adding extra vowels to her 'yes'.

Matt realized he had never looked her in the face before. He hadn't wanted to stare, didn't want to make her uncomfortable. She was the only transvestite he'd ever seen in town, ever seen in person for that matter. Now, having avoided her so as not to stare, he was staring. He had never let himself fully take her in, and it was overwhelming him. And he could see that she knew it too. Of course she knew. She got stared at all the time. Whatever dumb-ass expression he was giving her was probably something she faced on a daily basis.

Her lips pursed and she raised her eyebrows. 'Can I help you with something?'

It wasn't that she possessed some strange mix of masculine and feminine that his brain couldn't cope with. She just looked like a man.

In women's clothes. With long, gray hair bobbed at her chin, styled like his grandmother's. Her face was ruggedly lined under the thin powder of her make-up. The only feminine thing about her was the Southern belle lilt in her baritone voice.

'Young man, is there some sort of problem?'

'I, um . . . I'm sorry . . . I don't want to embarrass you . . . but . . .' Oh, shit, he actually had to say it, didn't he? 'It's just that . . . I thought you should know . . .' He gestured at her naked knees.

'Excuuuuuuse me?' she said. He could hear her irritation.

Why had he agreed to this? In polite society, people aren't supposed to expose themselves, but if they do, the polite thing is to pretend you don't see it. Just get on with what you're doing. If you can't stop looking, that's your own problem.

But it was Miranda's problem. She had asked him to do this. She wanted something from him. And Matt wanted her to want something from him. He drew a breath.

'I'm sorry, I really hate to disturb you. I just wanted to let you know that we can . . .' He gestured at her knees again. '*See* you . . . from the register.'

She looked at him for a moment before she got what he was trying to say. Then her face went red underneath her make-up. She started muttering her apologies and folding up her newspaper. Matt could see her hand trembling.

'I really am sorry. I just . . .'

'No, that's faaaaah'ine. That's faaaaah'ine.' She didn't look him in the eye. 'That's just faaaaah'ine.' She rose from her seat and stood a little taller than him, actually. Matt was worried she was going to make a scene, but she just took a seat over at another table and pointed her crotch to the wall.

As Matt turned to go back behind the counter, he saw Miranda watching him. She mouthed the words 'Thank you.' He smiled, but then looked back over at the transvestite. Her hands gripped the paper tightly.

Taking his place once more behind the espresso machine, he asked Miranda, 'Want to get a movie after we close?'

'Oh, I'm not closing tonight.'

'I thought you were.'

'Take a look.' She handed him the schedule from its folder behind the cases of roasted beans. There was Miranda's name printed beside his, but it had been marked through and a new name written in – Krystal. 'You're going to be with the new girl,' said Miranda.

'Oh.' He kept looking at the paper. There was a faded splash of coffee on its corner, a tiny teardrop drip. 'Okay then. You want me to pick up a video on my way back?'

'I've already got plans tonight. Sorry.'

'You do?'

When did she make plans? They had hung out together last night and got up around the same time that morning. He had heard her in the shower when he woke up in the cocoon he made of her couch. While he completed his morning ritual of folding up his bedding, he heard the water stop and her hair dryer howl into life. The sweet smell of hot hair products drifted into the living room. When she came out, he waved a brief good morning before hitting the shower himself. They ate a quiet breakfast together while watching TV. Then they left for work.

'Yeah, I'm going up to Franklin Street with Toni and Bev,' she said.

'What about the car?' He had driven them to work.

'Bev's picking me up.'

'Oh.'

'Yeah, Toni wants to do the Chapel Hill bar crawl – celebrate exams being over, you know? Don't think they're going to let me come back till late.'

'Right. Cool.' It wasn't that she didn't invite him, it was that she didn't think to tell him. She just hadn't thought of him.

He looked back over at the transvestite. She wasn't crying, was she?

'I better take my break before you head off then,' said Matt. He came around to the other side of the register. 'Can you ring me up for a cookie?'

'Sure, what kind you want?'

'What kind did she get before?' He nodded towards the transvestite.

'Umm . . . One of the cakey smiley faces, I think.'

'One of those.'

Miranda started to ring him up. Then her face lit. 'Are you getting a cookie for her?'

He leaned over the counter and lowered his voice. 'Yeah, I think she was pretty embarrassed by that. So I thought . . .'

'Awww, that's so sweet.'

Matt made himself smile. It felt shaky. That was one thing he could do. He couldn't do a lot of things, but he could at least be sweet.

He carried the cookie on its plate, wearing its face of yellow frosting. The smile pointed towards the transvestite as he approached. Matt lowered his voice and spoke in the careful tones he probably should have used before. 'Excuse me.'

Her face looked weary when she turned to him. The mascara had smeared slightly.

'About before, I just wanted . . .' He held the plate toward her. 'You know, from me.'

The corner of her thin, hard lips curled as she took in the cookie's smile. 'Well, aaahren't you a dear. Thank you.' She took the plate that he offered. 'Thank you.'

Emma Chapman

Emma Chapman is 23. She is from Cheshire, and is now living in London. This is the beginning of her novel, entitled *Familiar Terrain*. Set against a bleached Norwegian backdrop, it is a book about a life shaped by trauma. Despite her best efforts to live in the present, Marta is plunged back into the past when her husband arrives home with a secret.

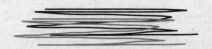

Familiar Terrain

Prologue

There was a room. It was underneath the ground, with no windows and no doors. The way out was in the ceiling, and that was rarely opened.

No matter how much noise we made, no one could hear us. I imagined the sound sometimes, bouncing off the metal walls like a ball in a computer game, programmed to change direction. We were playing alone.

We stopped trying. We threw things and shouted and screamed, tears trailing our faces and wetting the darkness, but no one was coming to find us. It was lost time: time we would never get back, time spreading never-ending ahead of us. A blackness soaking through tissue.

Sometimes, the trap door opened. It jarred awkwardly, where it had been cut into the metal. The light would trickle in like the first rays at the end of an eclipse. The room always seemed small then, smaller than we thought.

He would come down the ladder. Him, who must have been so ordinary in life, with his secret underground game. A torch would shine in our faces, which closed against it like the faces of pug dogs. With a nod of the head, one of us was chosen.

The time we lost may be gone, but it comes back to me in dreams. Dreams in the night and dreams in the day. I remember the smell of damp earth, the mildew, and the stories we told each other. I remember the darkness that was like a third prisoner, rocking us as if we were trapped in a ship's hold deep underwater.

I don't remember the worst. The moments he ripped from us, against our will. Those will never come back. I don't want to see them again.

Chapter 1

The letters arrive between eleven and twelve in the morning. I hear them hit the doormat. Then I know they are there, and that I need to collect them.

Usually, I am working on something in the kitchen. Preparing supper, the recipe book propped open on the book stand that Hector bought me for one of our early wedding anniversaries. Making bread: mixing the ingredients in a large bowl, kneading it on the cold granite worktop, watching it rise in the oven. Washing vegetables that I have picked in the garden, or bought at the market.

Today I am sitting at the kitchen table, a cigarette between my fingers. I am not really smoking it. There is a long tail of fragile ash hanging precariously from its end that I am aware of but don't shake off. I have put a saucer from Hector's mother's tea set down as an ashtray.

Eventually, I lift the cigarette to my mouth and take a deep drag. It tastes of earth, like the air underground. The bitter smoke fills the kitchen. I worry about it clinging to the curtains and hanging around too long.

I want to be a smoker. Just today, just at the moment. I try to enjoy the taste, but it lies heavy in my chest and makes me feel nauseous. It doesn't make me feel like I just don't give a shit. It makes me feel like shit.

Hector hates smoking. When we are walking on the street behind a person with a cigarette, he will cough his loud growling cough, almost as a warning. When he does this, I always see his vocal cords rubbing together and quivering, moist and pink like chicken breast meat.

My cigarette has finished itself. I put it on the saucer and go to collect the post. Mrs Marta Bjornson. Mr and Mrs Hector Bjornson. Mr and Mrs H. C. Bjornson.

The names on the letters do not seem familiar. I put all of them, including the ones printed with just my name, into a pile on the hall table, for Hector.

My apron strings catch on the door handle as I come back through to the kitchen. I stop and free myself, noticing a smudge on one of the panes of glass in the kitchen door. I go and fetch the polish from under the sink, rubbing it until it comes clean. You have to persevere when cleaning glass, mirrors and silver. The smudges cling on: they do not want to be removed.

I put the polish back, pick up the saucer from the table and take it over to the sink. I take the cigarette gingerly between two of my fingers, placing it on a piece of paper towel. I fold the paper around the butt, rolling it as small as it will go, and then wrap an elastic band around it. I sniff: it is still emitting the stench of stale smoke. I take it outside the front door, and put it on the window ledge. The air is fresh and cold, like plunging my face and chest in ice water. I will dispose of it later, when I go out to the market.

I return to the kitchen.

I decide to bake some bread, to fill the kitchen with the smell of rising yeast. I make the dough. Hector likes to have fresh bread in the mornings. I flour the counter. My fingers work at the dough, pressing it in on itself. It is cool, and a little sticky. I work to a rhythm, knowing just when to stop. I put it into a tin with high sides. It emerges like a pale breast.

I go to the sink and run the hot tap, adding the washing-up liquid. The smell of artificial lemons rises from the water. I wash the bowl and spoon, leaving the saucer until last. I do not want to contaminate the water with the smell of cigarette. It gets everywhere. I remember that from when I smoked as a teenager. I know all the tricks.

I sit at the kitchen table for a while. The bread will take hours. The kitchen table is made of glass, with a steel frame underneath. That takes some cleaning. It's not as bad now as it was when the kids were young. Their smeary finger marks were always there, like ghosts. I never had time to clean them properly.

I don't wait for long. I get up, hide my cigarettes in the teapot, pull on my red tartan coat and navy headscarf, and leave the house.

When I was younger, I would watch my sister play. Her white fists gripping the chains of the swing set. Leaping free and looking for fairies in the long, loud grass. Chasing the neighbourhood boys down the street. I was always holding back, never quite sure what to do. In the busy playground, I felt people were watching me, waiting to see what I would do next.

I couldn't run after her in the fading sunlight, tripping over the uneven road surface, not caring if my knees were grazed. I tried to, I wanted to, but my blood stopped me where I stood. There were too many eyes. At least that's how I remember it.

I must have been young then. This is what makes me think, so many years later, that I have always been the way I am.

I wasn't forced to set in a mould like so much uncertain jelly, I was fixed long before.

I drive into town. The greenery rushes past the car window: it has been a verdant autumn with plenty of rain.

The wooden houses pepper the roadside, some close and some further up the valley. They remind me of Swedish Brio toys, in reds, blues and yellows, painted garishly to counter the annual six months of darkness. On the horizon I can make out the beginnings of the fjord, glimmering as though swathed in cling film.

I park near the white wooden church. The grey spire stands dark and clear against the solid blue of the sky, so sharp I worry it might cause a rupture.

The market sprawls on the main street of the village. There is no access by car through the village on market days. Colourful fruits and vegetables organise themselves in front of my eyes: I am not sure where to start.

I walk up and down the stalls twice, smiling at some of the vendors. I know them all by sight, but their community is not fully open to me. I am a city girl, not a local, and as such I am only granted a certain amount of hospitality.

I go as far as the butcher's shop, ducking in and away from the market with its thousands of decisions. The butcher has a patchy red face, raw, like the slabs of meat that he works at all day. He smiles at me as I enter and join the back of the queue. There are two people ahead of me. I run through my purchases. Shoulder of lamb, diced. A kilogram. Four chicken breasts. That should do us for the week. Enough for two.

The butcher turns his attention to me. I tell him what I want as loudly as I can. He puts his hand up to his ear in a mock-deaf action and I repeat myself. He leans in further and I can feel myself begin to sweat. I tell him what I would like slowly and clearly. The other people in the shop shuffle their feet. He nods his head and busies himself preparing it. He takes some lamb from the window, weighs it, and tells me it is a little over a kilogram.

'That's fine,' I say.

'Medium pieces?' he asks.

'Yes,' I say.

'Without the bone?' he asks.

'Yes,' I say.

He hacks away at the shoulder, transforming it into manageable pieces for a stew or casserole. I am not sure what yet. The chicken breasts do not take long, and soon the ordeal is over. I pay the man and squeeze out of the shop, the carrier bag rustling against my legs.

I slip into the fishmonger next door. There is a big wooden fish stuck sideways on the wall above the young fishmonger's head, with a yellow eye that watches me. He is serving a young mother with a push-chair. The child looks up at me as he sucks on his fist. His eyelashes are like insect legs brushing against his cheeks. I feel the pressure rising again.

When it is my turn, I order a kilogram of halibut fillets for the *kveite-uer-suppe* on Saturday night. It is my speciality. He removes the glass-bodied fish from the display, weighs them, and then turns to the white counter to prepare them. I ask his white-coated back for 500g of char as well. I can hear the man behind me tapping his foot against the linoleum.

I leave the shop and walk back along the stretch of market stalls several times, considering which vegetables to buy. Eventually I have bags containing some onions, tomatoes, broccoli, and potatoes.

As I walk back to the car, I think about the fishmonger's hands. I wonder if his wife has become used to them over the years: to the smell of the sea as he leans past her to reach into a cupboard above her head, or places his hand in the small of her back. I wonder if she ever flinches. Perhaps they live inside the smell, no longer aware of its presence.

When I get home, wrestling with my bags to open the front door, I spot the rolled-up kitchen towel on the window ledge. I forgot to dispose of the evidence. I take the bags into the kitchen, pilling them on to the glass topped table. I pick up the paper on the porch, and walk out to the neglected barbecue, leaving a trail of misty breath. I take the lighter out of my pocket and light the paper, holding it there until the edge curls in light.

I return to the house, trying the back door but knowing it will be locked. When I reach the front door, I see I have left my keys dangling in the lock, the door ajar. Dangerous. When I was younger I would have checked every room to see if a murderer had entered while my back was turned, but I am not afraid any more. It's stupid to be afraid.

I walk through the hall. I stop. The letters I left on the hall table are missing. I remain still, suddenly frightened. I force myself to move towards the kitchen door. The back of a man, shrouded in a thick overcoat. It is Hector.

I open the door.

'What are you doing here?' I ask.

Hector turns and looks over his shoulder. His eyes are startlingly bright in the daylight; I watch the lines around his mouth steady. He turns back to the letters he is shuffling in his hands.

'Got off work early.'

I walk into the kitchen, and over to the bread on the counter. I can still smell the smoke.

'You scared the life out of me.' I try to giggle. 'I noticed the letters were gone, and . . . well, I was scared.'

'Why was the front door open?' Hector says, without looking up.

'I went into the garden.'

'Why?'

'I had the strangest feeling on the way back from the market that the back door was open. I had to check.'

'And was it?'

'No,' I say.

He looks at me, and raises his eyebrow.

'OK.' He puts the letters down, amongst the shopping bags. 'I'm going to have a shower.'

Hector walks out of the room. I stand by the kitchen counter. He stomps up the stairs and along the corridor. After a few minutes I hear the growl of the boiler as the shower switches on.

I turn on the oven. I check the clock, it is almost four o'clock.

I unpack the vegetables into the fridge. The carrier bags go under the sink to be reused.

I check the teapot. The cigarettes are not there.

I slide the bread tin on to the middle shelf of the oven. The mound glows in the warm light.

I clear the empty envelopes from the table and go to throw them away. The cigarettes are in the bin. Gingerly, I pick them out. The packet is damp: they've been run under the cold tap.

Kyo Choi

Kyo Choi is from South Korea. She worked as a Reuters corres-
pondent and as a banker in London where she has lived since
1991. She is nearing completion of *The Love Hotel*, a literary
novel about a man who manages a fantasy-themed love hotel in
London. The book explores the themes of memory distrust, loss
and fantasy surrounding a childhood trauma.

The Love Hotel

Tokyo, 1997

Halfway down the board a passage read, '*The purpose of Seikan massage is to refresh the body, mind and gun. Sometimes, the girl's index finger enter your back hole.*' I was sitting in a waiting room, as unremarkable on the inside as the building that housed it was on the outside. Keiko told me that sometimes the wait could be nearly an hour and advised me to take a book. She promptly handed me a collection of poems by Robert Browning. 'Very erotic,' she said primly and gave me instructions to take the underground and call *21 Seiki* (21st Century) from the station in Yoshiwara, an area in Tokyo not often found in street maps.

Between the short walk from Keiko's flat to the Metro station, perspiration from my brow pooled around my eyes and dripped on to my nose. The heatwave had begun early. June seared with the malice of an infernal summer. Even a brief seating in an unventilated place precipitated sweat that dampened one's underwear like ink on tissue paper. Japanese girls, still modest by Western standards, rose from their seats in the train and dislodged clammy garments that clung to, or more embarrassingly got wedged in between, their backsides with a sleight of hand so deft that only captured in slow motion would one fully appreciate the intricacies involved in the act. The heat was anathema to women who wore silk or delicate cotton for perspiration left behind the semblance of a fine cocaine-lined trail under their armpits or seeped through the V-point of their bras in concentric circles. It was a revelation to me that Japanese women sweat at all.

A smart black saloon with tinted windows arrived promptly after I called *21 Seiki* from a phone booth outside the station. The interior was cool and I tugged at my collar tips to allow the air to dry out my damp shirt. The driver, a small old man with a perky chauffeur's hat, smiled and bobbed his head in lieu of talking. When he did speak, I caught the words 'suck jack' and nodded my head judiciously. Later, I realised that he had said *soku jaku* which means to have oral sex without washing one's parts first; there is a respected etiquette amongst the exclusive soaps that one is clean before entering the establishment.

I had imagined kimono-clad women with ashen faces fawning gracefully over me but a surly young man in an ill-fitting charcoal suit greeted me instead at the entrance. Without looking at me, he pointed to a waiting room, one of several in the hallway. The sparse anteroom featured only an ebony-framed board on the wall written in English outlining services and fees. There were a few wooden chairs scattered over a grimy linoleum floor. The room was windowless. I settled into a chair and opened the book Keiko had placed in my coat pocket. She had stuck little yellow strips on the pages containing the highlighted verses that she wanted me to read:

> *Where is the use of the lips' red charm*
> *The heaven of hair, the pride of the brow,*
> *And the blood that blues the inside arm . . .*
>
> *Oh, that white smallish female with the breasts . . .*
>
> *Was a lady such a lady, cheeks so round and lips so red,*
> *On her neck the small face buoyant, like a bell-flower on its bed,*
> *O'er the breast's superb abundance where a man might base his*
> *   head?*
>
> *. . . There you stand,*
> *Warm too, and white too: would this wine*
> *Had washed all over that body of yours,*
> *Ere I drank it, and you down with it, thus!**

I had just started another Browning poem, 'Youth and Art', when the door opened abruptly and the same man who met me earlier

---

* Robert Browning: selection of verses from 'The Statue and the Bust', 'Fra Lippo Lippi', 'A Toccata of Galuppi's' and 'Too Late' (Wordsworth Editions, 1994).

appeared. My guess was that he was about my age, early thirties, and for a Japanese of my generation tall, around six feet. His hair was slicked back and he scrunched up his face in a scowl. He walked towards me gingerly with one shoulder almost leaning against the wall as if I was an object of suspicion.

'You want Japanese girl or something else?' he said with a squint out of one eye that seemed to size me up and exude hostility. In his hands was a small black velvet case.

The man stood before me whilst I remained seated, his arms extended and poised to open the case. For a moment I feared for my safety. I was a foreigner in the outskirts of Tokyo with almost no means of protecting myself.

'For twenty per cent more, I can get you Korean girls, very firm and fresh. Good at handring gun,' he said, pretending to shoot at my groin area. 'Or more cheaper, we have Filipina. Very good massagers,' he wriggled his fingers. 'You like farm girls? Then take Chinese. Choose from here.'

I looked up at him and then I saw it; his lazy eye, the left one, fraught with quivers and almost fully shut. His good eye was bloodshot clearly from the strain of working in an overloaded capacity. Perhaps I stared too long. There came an outburst from him.

'But no white girls. Too much probrem. Talk too much, eat too much, smoke too much. No stay fresh, no good.'

He sat beside me. The case in his hand turned out to be a portable album full of black and white photos individually tucked into plastic sleeves. They were all pictures of young women, their expressions bearing the kind of waxy smile one sees in school albums. He gestured at me to choose one.

I picked one who reminded me oddly of a secretary in our Tokyo office. She was a sweet girl who always wore frilly ankle socks with black plimsole-like shoes even in the cooler autumn days. My host, who now resembled a gentle Cyclops, shook his head. He repeatedly said the word '*mens*' and exasperated by the blank look on my face, he finally slapped one outstretched hand between his legs: 'Men-su, men-su.' Peering at me out of his good eye, he nodded in satisfaction when

I understood that the girl was menstruating and not *in situ*. So I chose another one.

'Mayumi, *Ano* . . .' He scratched his head. 'Good in the back.'

I was led up the staircase. A woman awaited us on the landing of the second floor. There was a flurry of politeness directed at me – the customary bows and smiles – in the form of a greeting from the hostess, a farewell from my one-eyed host. 'No Engrish,' were his parting words, glancing sideways at the girl. A pause ensued after he left us.

I found it awkward to look at the woman. She was older than her photo, although it was hard to pinpoint her age at first glance – perhaps late twenties or more. But it wasn't that; with her hair in two long plaits, wearing a grey pleated skirt and a white blouse of transparent material that revealed a dark bra underneath, she was dressed like a schoolgirl, even down to the white pull-up socks and flat black buckled shoes that members of English public schools wore.

She bowed at me again and walked ahead. We passed several rooms on either side. There were strains of music and perhaps I heard muffled laughter but otherwise, for a house of mirth, it was quiet. Our room was at the end. We entered a small vestibule that was sealed by sliding panelled doors with a middle partition. The lady knelt down and removed my shoes. Hers she replaced with white slippers. My coat was also hung up for me. She opened the paper-lined doors and ushered me in. This room bore no resemblance to the drabness I had seen so far.

The walls were lined with a shimmering textile imprinted with searing branches of cherry blossoms in vivid colours of fuchsia, magenta and violet. Their overpowering colours weighed down on the room making it appear smaller than its actual size. Mounted on the florid walls were long rectangular prints of erotic art, men and women in traditional garb fornicating in various positions. The room was coolly air-conditioned and I forgot about the heat that I had walked in from outside. A low square lacquered table that looked freshly dipped in blood stood in the middle of the tatami-covered floor. On either side of it were two large embroidered cushions. Their silken threads of elaborate designs depicting various flowers and birds sparkled at certain angles of the light. Tea set for two and a black lacquered humidor had already been placed on the table. Dark wooden cabinets in traditional style leaned against the walls displaying chintz urns, cloisonné plates and glazed porcelain vases featuring dragons and cranes.

We sat at the table, Mayumi kneeling and myself cross-legged. She poured me green tea and offered me a cigar from the box. I declined to smoke. We had not spoken a word to each other since we met. Her expression was impassive, not what one would expect from a girl in a prep school uniform. I was tempted to retrieve the Browning poems from my coat and recite some English poetry to her. She rose and walked to one of the cabinets. There was a stereo system inside and I was beckoned to come over. I examined the compact disc collection and found only one in English. It was a live recording of the Eagles in concert.

'Hotel Carifawnia,' Mayumi said in a mock croon.

The crowds cheered to the strumming of a lone guitar. Then came the slow beat of the drums – in this rendition they sounded like African bongo drums – throbbing harder and faster. Mayumi took my hand and led me to a door that I had not noticed before in the corner of the room. Inside, steps dropped into a sunken bath that spanned almost the entire room. The bath was partially filled already. The humidity infused with the stale fragrance in the room cloyed my senses. Candle-lit lanterns squatted on wood-slatted alcoves. Their flames flickered warily like serpentine tongues.

Mayumi helped me to remove my clothes and turned on the tap. I lay in the folds of the warm water and watched her. She removed her socks and slippers and walked into the bath fully clothed. As the water rose around her with every step taken down, she daintily lifted her skirt. The hemline lifted gradually like curtains on a stage until it was raised to the top of her legs. Mayumi stood before me, steeped in warm water, and removed her clothes.

She had no pubic hair. Her frame was slight, fine ribs protruding slightly, with merely a hint of breasts. The paleness of her skin lent her a hard statue-like quality. There was a dull look in her eyes. She lathered soap over me limb by limb with a towelled mitten. I reached out and loosened her long thick braids. I longed to cover that stony face with her hair. Instead, I lifted her and thrust her upon my hips so that she sat impaled upon me. Her bony legs hung limply. The bathroom door was left open. The music poured into the bath, drowning out the sound of the still running tap.

I closed my eyes. The crowd roared when the song reached its coda. It seemed to me that the room was filled with a noise distinct from the music and Mayumi's mechanical cries. I looked through the open door. The cherry blossoms bloomed so densely on the walls they looked like bloodclots. I imagined it was their distress call I heard, the shrieking of the masses of petals spread-eagled against the wall. The scream ripped through the piercing whistles of the audience as the song climaxed to its end. I closed my eyes again and put my hand on Mayumi's bobbing head below, pinning it down until the shuddering overtook me in convulsive waves. When she finished her task she bowed and glided out of the bath like a gorgon leaving her watery underworld.

Michael Donkor

Born in London to Ghanaian parents in 1985, Michael Donkor studied English at Oxford. *The Bandages*, his novel-in-progress, follows Belinda, 17, and her cousin Mary, 10, a pair of Ghanaian housegirls brought from their village to work in wealthy, suburban Kumasi. Here, while on a trip to the local zoo, Belinda struggles to tell her cousin that, after three years together, she has been given the chance to emigrate to Britain.

The Bandages

'And what about ostrich? It says here that you have young new ostrich. Where are you keeping that one?' Belinda pointed at a grainy photo in the brochure. The guide was not paying attention. She was sighing, surveying the lushness in front of them proprietorially, a wooden stick stowed beneath her arm. It *was* beautiful, if a little shabby in parts, Belinda conceded, considering that this was one of the only tourist attractions in the city.

The zoo was abundant with bright flowers, orchids. They shot out from dark bushes like eager painted hands, grabbing at the air, thickening it with syrupy scents. Cashew trees drooped low, heavy with suggestive, leathery fruit. Small streams cut across the landscape unpredictably, and when you bent down close you could see the water flashing as unknown fish zigzagged away. But Belinda had to move on. There were things to be done, or rather, *said*. She glared at the tour guide.

'The ostriches?' Belinda spoke firmly. The tour guide was still unresponsive.

Though the neat young woman looked 'professional' in her khaki uniform and gloves, there were things such smartness could not offset. Aunty had instructed her to walk on the other side of the road if she came across these people. Aunty had said that she wasn't 'prejudiced', but she was not completely convinced by the 'science' and did not know whether it was 'catching' or not. The disease covered the body in patches of peach and white. The tour guide had patches like this everywhere. The mottled skin made Belinda itch. The new beads on her waist suddenly felt restrictive. She twisted them round beneath her dress, brushing past the top of her knickers as she turned.

The tour guide cleared her throat. 'Ostriches. Good. Yes. If you will concentrate and revise your memory of the noticeboard encountered on your entry to this here institution, *Madam*, you will recall that we have sadly to inform you of this suspension of this ostriches, *Madam*.

They have been, I regret to inform you, removed from our due care and protection due to –'

'Due to?'

'Due to budget cuts,' the tour guide said, placing her hands behind her back. 'Me, I'm not supposed to be saying to you such things, Madam. I'm meant to tell you that ostriches have been *loaned* to a Washington Zoo, in United States of America, so that it gives a prestige and you feel proud that your nation's zoo is the envy of the world, oh, sharing animals with the West, hallelujah.' The woman spat on the ground. 'Sorry, but it is not true. We have *sold* our ostriches because how can you be keeping fanciness in country when people are not even reading or writing?'

'Cro-co-diles here!' Mary exclaimed, pointing to the words on a flaking arrow ahead. Belinda's arm suddenly felt lighter. Mary had dropped Belinda's hand and had run ahead.

Belinda had plaited Mary's hair that morning. She had tenderly rubbed pomade into the surprising paleness of her cousin's scalp. Belinda had tied the plaits with red and black baubles. As Mary sped up the dirt track in pursuit of crocodiles, brittle legs farcical in over-sized shorts, Belinda watched the baubles bounce primly, the hair shine.

'Careful, oh! We have not fed them for some four days – budget cuts!' the tour guide shouted, heading in Mary's direction. Belinda followed, biting her nails, spitting out shards as they broke on to her tongue.

Ostriches no longer a possibility, as they walked forward through the foliage, Belinda looked for the right place to sit Mary down. She needed somewhere empty and anonymous that could be theirs for that brief moment when, Belinda thought, she would show just how selfish she really was. When she would begin her seamless getaway with no thought for what was left behind. When she would make it plain she didn't care that Mary was losing another almost-Mother, or that they might send her back to the village where no one read to her, gave her extra meat from the stew, or even looked at her face unless it was the prelude to some instruction. Belinda removed her fingernails from her mouth, inspected them. They were covered in chipped half hexagons of Nana's red varnish.

She stopped herself. People were everywhere, preoccupied with their own intimacies, taking up valuable space. An Indian couple wearing matching baseball caps, necks identically adorned with binoculars, sat on a bench to her left. Near the porcupines, a father opened his brief-case slowly in front of three small children. By the water fountain, two nuns momentarily released their hooked arms so that one could stop to rub her hip. Belinda wished she could cast her hand through them all, make them run like so many frightened chickens. As if they weren't proving enough of a difficulty, the shoes Nana had picked out for her pinched her toes. When she took the shoes off, she doubted there'd be any toes left at all. Perhaps her feet would be compressed into fleshy triangles, edges puckering, threatening to bleed. Like sick pig's trotters, she thought.

The tour guide repeated that she could face 'the most severe of high recriminations and eventual dismissal' if Mary was not found. 'Hey! Hey! I have already been passing on the mention of budget cuts! This crocodiles will be bearing the most emptiest of stomachs, child. They will come, snapping for even this your little, no-meat ankles,' the tour guide yelled, signalling for Belinda to move quickly.

'Will you not disturb the animals with your shouting?' Belinda murmured.

'You think I'm having any consideration for the sleep pattern and well-being of a chimpanzee when you and your small girl may have brought the imminence of my sacking?' Belinda could not help but laugh. So did Mary, who presently jumped up from behind a palm tree.

'Why does budget cutting have to mean bad signs?' Mary asked the tour guide. 'How long have we been walking for and have I seen a cro-co-dile? No, Missus. Not even one of them to snap at my feet, like you are saying.' Mary, pouting, grabbed her right hip flirtatiously.

'This one has lip. This one has *lip*!' The tour guide, suddenly playful, extended a hand to Mary as she gambolled forward.

'You will take me?'

'I will take you.'

Mary began asking the tour guide what her name was, if she was married and what it was like to be married. Dawdling behind, wrestling with the layers of her long gold dress, Belinda remembered what women said about fat-cheeked babies who did not cry when they were passed between innumerable relatives: they said, 'Oh, he is such a good boy – he goes to *anyone*.'

Though Mary would hate to be compared like that, it was indisputable; Mary had that innocent ease too. For all her backchat, she was adaptable and happy enough to meet what she did not know with charm and curiosity. For Mary, Belinda reasoned, strangers offered the possibility of new games. Belinda wiped something sticky from her neck. It had fallen from the canopy above her, a great, glistening net of leaves.

Belinda considered beginning the imminent monologue by reassuring Mary she wouldn't really feel the loss: there would soon be a *new* Belinda. Another plain, respectful, frightened girl from some village would be found within weeks. All Mary needed to do was introduce herself to this one politely, show her where the towels were kept, and then they could play together. It would be that easy. Four butterflies darted towards Belinda. After flapping at their gaudy wings, she realised that Mary would ask if she herself was so replaceable: would Belinda also have a new Mary, she would want to know.

Something was happening ahead. Through the waves in the air made by the heat, Belinda could see the tour guide, Priscilla, lifting her staff, pushing aside foliage and ushering Mary beneath her raised arm. Belinda stumbled forward.

She had always imagined that a swamp would look like that. It was vast, ringed by bursts of tall, browning grass. Dipping dragonflies and midges fought one another. Large peaks of mud forced their way up through the water. Everything was silent, apart from the unlocatable sound of dripping.

The tour guide shouted 'Ladies, I am presenting . . . Reginald!' Mary bounced. Her smile showed the slightly splayed front teeth that

Mary had once said to Belinda were 'angry and trying to get going away from each other'. Mary began applauding.

'Reginald?' Priscilla tried again and encouraged Mary to clap louder. The water did not move.

'This animal is becoming more stubborn than my own Papa,' Priscilla hissed, moving closer to the fence around the sloped edge of the swamp. 'Reginald?' she said again, waving her staff above the water.

'I have never heard that name before,' Mary said, sincerely.

'Me, I hate. It is vestige of our colonial past.' Belinda was impressed by how meaningful the word 'vestige' sounded in Priscilla's throaty rasp. 'In fact, perhaps I should refer to him by his traditional name and then we will see if Reginald is responding,' Priscilla added.

'Perhaps Reginald is like your ostriches, eh? And you have led us on wild goose chase.' Belinda laughed at her own pun. She was surprised that she was able to make jokes. The others did not turn around.

'What is his Ghanaian name? On which day was he born?' Mary asked, sitting cross-legged on the wet soil. Priscilla retraced her footsteps, then squatted higher up on the bank with Mary.

'The matter is a complex one, for it is not in this zoo that he was being born, no. He arrived here when he was some nine years. Big strong men brought him in a truck all the way from Bolgatanga.'

'So you don't know for which day he is being named after?' Mary retorted.

'No, but I do know that he was delivered here on a Saturday.'

'So we will say that for his day. Yes, let us call for *Kwabena*. Come on.'

Belinda made her way to them, cursing the shoes. She squatted as they did, clapped towards the water. The sooner it was over, the better.

'Kwabena, come! You don't want to be gaining new acquaintances for diversions?' she said, raising her eyebrow and turning to Priscilla who looked distinctly impressed by her verbosity.

Nothing happened.

'There are tarantulas?' Priscilla offered to Mary. Her mouth and voice were limp.

'I am not liking the spiders, it's a boring.' Mary stamped her feet. 'Me, I have this spiders at my house anyway, isn't it, Belinda?'

Belinda nodded.

'They come into the bathroom. They don't care, they don't even be minding the cockroaches.' Mary spoke and shifted her gaze between Belinda and Priscilla with dizzying speed. Belinda could tell she was delirious with all the attention. Mary only babbled and blinked that quickly when she had drunk too much Sprite.

Then it happened. The water tore apart. At once, the three of them leapt back. Diamonds of liquid shot out and splashed on to Belinda's face. Kwabena dashed forward and made himself known. He snapped at the fence. Belinda gulped as it wobbled precariously, and shook to reveal its fragility. She saw his roaming, blank eyes: massive, dark planets. She watched his fat, knobbed tail whipping the water, sending up liquid again. Mary screamed. His long jaw mechanically flipped open and crashed shut with a sound of falling bricks, or breaking glass, something like that. He scuttled back. Mary began to cry.

'I didn't even get to be taking one single picture,' Mary moaned, redundantly pointing Nana's camera at the ripples Kwabena had left in his wake.

Belinda was not breathing. The fear was not that he would eat her, consume her in one gulp, although he looked as if he could. No. Belinda worried about what would happen if he simply *landed* on her. In her mind he was enormous and capable of anything. He had not yet leapt above the water's surface, but she knew that he could. He *could*. He could leap up and reach high enough to brush the trees, and then drop out of the sky, on to her, on to all of them. They'd be squashed. Mangled beneath his big, rough belly. Then it would be over. Everything done. God's only mercy? That she wouldn't have to tell Mary that –

'You see that bucket over there? Listen, do you see that bucket over there?' Belinda heard Priscilla trying to soften her harshness and say something maternal and soothing to Mary. It was not working. Mary, Belinda could see, had given free rein to her tears now. She was sobbing. There will be more of that, Belinda thought.

'In that bucket, there is meat – will you collect it for me?' Priscilla said, holding Mary by the shoulders. Belinda still could not speak. She said nothing as Mary shoved the camera into her pocket and ran up to a small hut not too far away, and returned with a dripping chunk.

'Good girl!' said Priscilla. 'Look at her, laugh, laugh at your Belinda, she is looking like she is a ghost, or in preparation for the vomits.'

Belinda tried to look amused.

'When he comes up again, you throw the meat at him, OK?'

Mary nodded.

'Kwabena, Kwabena –' Priscilla paused, tapped Belinda on the shoulder. 'Help me, Madam? It is you who clearly possess the special, Kwabena-getting power.' Quietly, Belinda added her calls to Priscilla's. The syllables came out of her mouth with increasing difficulty – each one somehow heavier, more unshapely, more alien than the last. Within seconds, that terrifying blur of grey, brown, pink and green rose again, moving more quickly this time, thrashing vigorously.

'Throw, throw!'

Mary launched the meat with a grunt. It hit Kwabena's snout. Belinda shook as he began tearing. He had such unrecognisable strength and purpose. It was masterful. He disappeared in an eruption of furious bubbling.

'That was the most brilliant and best thing,' Mary said to Belinda. Belinda looked at her cousin's cheeks. They were streaked with tears, sweat, water and blood.

Tom Feltham

Tom Feltham is 24 and lives in London. His novel, *The Inertia Reel*, tells the story of a fifteen year old's last summer with his severely autistic cousin, Doug, set in 1970s New York.

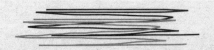

The Inertia Reel

Around four, as a new wave of boredom sweeps through the apartment, my uncle suggests I take Doug out for some fresh air.

'Can we get some ice cream cones?' I ask him.

'Okay,' he says, and without looking up he pulls some coins out of his pocket and places them on the table. I collect them and go over to Doug at the window, grabbing him by the arm and hauling him out of the apartment. Once we reach the stairs he starts moving of his own accord.

Outside the sky looks greased over; a few jet trails are smeared across it. Sometimes when we're out in the street Doug gets it into his head that he's a car alarm and emits a beeping noise with every breath; or that he's a police siren and wails constantly. Today he keeps quiet – he can go weeks without making any noise at all – but seems to be enjoying the sunshine. A few kids across the street recognize me and start to whisper. They're all stripped to the waist, some of them with T-shirts stuffed into the bands of their shorts. They're drinking from Coke bottles and their heads are gleaming with sweat.

Fat Craven is preaching alien abduction on the corner of Fifth and West 125th. No one except Doug ever takes any notice of him, except for when Fats gets into these kinds of comic scuffles with winos. Everyone has to take the long voyage around his stomach as he stands bewilderingly in the middle of the sidewalk.

I change my mind when Mount Morris Park looms above the traffic down at the end of the street. 'Come on, Doug,' I say, turning to him. 'Central Park?'

With a tug on his T-shirt I set him off in our new direction. We ride the subway from Lenox all the way down to Seventh Avenue and emerge from the station right into a blizzard of tourists. Holding on tight to Doug, I push past people, having to say 'Hey' every so often to get us both through. People seem angry or confused but then notice Doug and look away suddenly.

Back when Doug was much worse, I used to take him out in a

wheelchair. I enjoyed the responses he drew from people. They were non-responses mainly. Badly faked ones, guilty ones.

Clutching their cameras, swivelling their gaze anxiously like spot-lights striking random paths in the darkness, the tourists move about in little bursts of faltering confidence, like they can only trust the city or the map for so long. Doug and I walk past the fancy hotel lobbies, the stacks of newspapers on the sidewalks, and the people knocking into one another, stepping on each other's heels to get down into the subway or make room at crossings. People glued into their suits by sweat, big-bellied men with bunches of wiry hair bursting out from the hems of their New York Yankees caps. We stop to watch a man drawing with chalk on the sidewalk. Then we stop again for the crazy toys in the window of FAO Schwarz, and for the windscreen washers stepping out into the traffic and the guys selling pencils on the street corners. It always surprises me how Doug loves being in crowds.

I figure we can walk the whole park in two hours, be home by 6.30. It's funny, no one does it, walks south to north, takes in the whole thing. Central Park is just a short cut, a corner to miss on your way south, or a place to stop for a while before retracing your footsteps to the same entrance you came in by.

I hold Doug's hand when we cross West 59th to the park, feeling like I'm the baby and not him because he's bigger than me. Doug is typic-ally sluggish, but also capable of sudden bursts of movement. I've lost count of the times he's almost got himself killed by flying out into the middle of the street, gone after some invisible charm.

'You want ice cream, Doug?' I ask.

The park entrance unleashes a huge cargo of noise, from portable stereos, the gap-toothed mouths of little kids, the crunching wheels of rollerskates.

Doug follows me over to the refreshments stand, which gives out a sour smell of engines and food, both overheated. Doug becomes engrossed in rolling the skirt of his oversized T-shirt up and down over his flabby belly, so rather than trying to make him point out a flavour I leave him to it and get us a vanilla and chocolate double each.

'Ninety-eight cents,' says the guy serving us from up in the stand. He has to stoop down all the time for his face to be visible beneath the awning. He holds out the cones expertly in one big nuts-and-bolts hand and accepts a dollar with the other. He shows no sign of recognizing us, though I recognize him. He was working here all last summer too. But I guess he must get millions of kids recognizing him before he recognizes one back.

'Doug, take it,' I say, passing his cone to him. He accepts it, and all the features on his face make their way outwards so that it seems like his head has doubled in size with joy. He doesn't start eating it straight away, just stares at it like it might start talking to him if he pays it enough attention. I tug on his wrist and we go find somewhere to sit. The park is crowded; people are scattered all over, lying on the thin grass, missing shirts and shoes, like a refugee camp. Doug and I pick our way between them like war reporters or soldiers, my hand tight on his wrist in case he stumbles.

All the white people are suntanned. Some people have brought picnics with them, and the leftovers are still out on paper plates. We've never had picnics so much, but I don't really mind. I hate the way you turn your head for one minute and then your food is crawling with bugs or sprinkled with dirt. Other people look as though they must have made the decision to come to the park at the last minute. They've assembled makeshift pillows from their shoes with bundled-up shirts on top of them, and they've got newspapers or guidebooks tented atop their faces to keep the sun out of their eyes while they try to nap.

We find a clearing and Doug sits down without needing me to ask. We're by one of the long arcing tarmac paths, on uncomfortably hard ground, facing north so that we're looking out into the depths of the park. I watch all the different people as I lick the peak of my ice cream, mixing up the chocolate and vanilla with my tongue. It's melting already, building up at the rim of the cone, ready to plunge over the sides on to my fingers. Doug is combating this by getting it all over his mouth and chin instead.

'How is it, Doug?' I ask.

'Superb, Jim,' I reply for him. He looks up. 'Never before has ice

67

cream tasted this good. There come only so many times in a life when elements and qualities are so well matched.'

'Is that right, Doug?' He listens to me with apparent interest. Maybe he's thinking to himself, Yep, that's right, Jim. Don't you know it. In any case, he's not likely to interject or correct me any time soon, and he seems to enjoy having his side of the conversation taken care of for him while he eats his ice cream.

'Truly, Jim, I live for moments such as these.'

But Doug, if he could talk, would more likely speak the way my uncle does, in monosyllables, except when he's quoting from the Bible. Or he'd talk like the older kids from our street, like Tojo Mason or Jeffie Winton, like 'Fuck, this cone's the fucking shit, believe.' But I like to give Doug different accents according to my mood, make him talk like an NBC sports announcer or Abraham Lincoln or Johnny Carson, Lenny Bruce, Muhammad Ali, Martin Luther King or JFK. I don't know who he is today exactly. He's down to the end of his cone now, sucking the remaining ice cream from the little well in the middle. I look out across the park and see a couple of dogs firing broadsides off at each other while their owners yank on their leashes.

'What's your name, Doug?'

'Name's Jefferson Snack. Pleased to make your acquaintance.'

'What?' comes a girl's voice behind us, startling me. I twist around and look up and recognize Margie Thomas, a pretty girl from school who never so much as gave me the time of day when I sat next to her during science class every week last year. Now she's staring down at me with a big grin on her face.

'What are you doing here?' I ask, getting up awkwardly, pushing against the ground with my left hand, my ice cone still in my right. I let it hang down by my side, wishing I could be rid of it somehow.

'What arc *you* doing here?' she retorts. 'Talking to yourself, Jim. Really, you know that means you're crazy, right? I should have guessed. Is this your cousin?' At first I'm surprised but then I'm not. Everyone's heard of Doug.

She looks down at Doug keenly, and I look at him too. He still has chocolate ice cream around his mouth and the wafer cone in his hand.

He never eats that part. Usually I eat it for him. I feel embarrassment suddenly like a personal rainstorm opening up over my head.

'Yeah. His name's Doug,' I tell her. 'He can't hear you.'

'Really? Not at all? Look, he heard that.' She points at Doug. He's looking up at us.

'Yeah, he can hear things, but there's no point in talking to him. He can't talk, and I'm not even sure he listens sometimes.'

'Oh,' she says, and looks sorry.

'So . . . Who are you here with?' I ask her. I hope to God none of the other girls from school are hanging around. The last thing I need is a crowd.

'Oh, just my mom and dad,' she says. 'They're over there.' She turns and points down the path vaguely. I don't see anyone that could have given birth to her, or paid for her piano lessons for that matter.

'You know there's a concert later?' she says. 'We have to hang around for that.'

'Oh, yeah. In the Mall?'

'Yeah, they've started setting up already.' She looks at Doug again. I'm afraid to look with her.

'Well, we were gonna head that way next actually,' I say. 'It's so hot though.'

'Yeah, it's about ninety, my dad says.'

She's wearing a vest-type top that shows off the elegance of her long, bare arms.

'I feel like getting another ice cream,' I say, gesturing limply with the remainder of my cone. Then I remember that I only have enough change for the subway home. We'd have to walk all the way from here to my uncle's apartment, maybe missing dinner. But before I can tell her I've changed my mind, Margie replies.

'Oh, great. Wait, I'll get some money off my dad,' she says, and runs off, her heels kicking up high behind her.

I take the opportunity to finish my cone quickly, and then kneel next to Doug and wipe the chocolate off his face using the bottom of his T-shirt. He only panics when he loses sight of his cone for a moment, otherwise he's totally placid.

Margie returns with money and I try to get Doug to stand up, feeling her watching us curiously behind my back. I end up having to grab him beneath one arm, and then I'm shocked to find her appearing at his other side and taking the opposite arm. Part of me suddenly feels hatred towards her, and the other part swoons.

'Come on, Doug,' she says cheerily. He gets up with our combined efforts. I wonder if she told her parents about him. We get more ice cream and start walking together. Doug, dragging his feet behind us, looks a little confused to be eating another cone so soon.

'So what exactly is wrong with your cousin?' Margie asks me, her question broken up by licks of her ice cream.

'He's just insane,' I say, finding myself wanting to change the subject, not just to avoid humiliation but also to build some kind of mystery up, some danger. 'Yeah, he's just insane,' I repeat. But Doug isn't insane. If he were, it might be better for him. He could be one of those eternally happy-seeming lunatics. Margie looks back at him with renewed interest and nods thoughtfully like she knows exactly what I'm talking about.

When we've all finished our ice cones – I take Doug's away from him when it's clear that he's lost interest in it – we stop and sit down and watch a homeless guy as he walks around staring at the ground. Every so often he stops and inspects something lying in the grass and dirt. I imagine him living here in the park all year round, lying down on a bench, kicking back and resting his head on his hands like he's on vacation, walking in loops getting larger and larger then smaller and smaller, or just going back and forth between two points. I can see him taking a leak behind a tree, kicking up the first fall leaves, making snowballs in winter and sending them soaring, shaking his big threadbare coat out, examining it inch by inch and fussing over little items it's picked up without his permission, then attempting the *New York Times* crossword, using the pen he found one day in mid-May. I imagine him never needing to leave the park. I venture a look at Margie. She's sitting cross-legged beside me. Doug is sitting on my other side, kneeling with his hand shielding his eyes from the light of the descending sun. I notice we're all looking at the homeless guy and I wonder if they've been thinking the same things I have. I wonder if Doug's thinking anything at all.

Elisabeth Gifford

Elisabeth Gifford has three children. She has published articles in *The Times* and the *Independent*, poetry in the *Oxford Magazine* and the *Cinnamon Press Anthology*, and a short story in *Riptide*. She has been commissioned to write a book about China. She gained a distinction in the Oxford Creative Writing Diploma. She is writing a novel entitled *Darwin and the Mermaid*.

Darwin and the Mermaid

Chapter One

Ruth McLeod, 1982

We moved into the most beautiful cottage in the most beautiful place in the world. The first night we slept there, I knew it had a ghost.

I don't believe in ghosts. Not in any way. And yet, as I crossed the hall in the dark, my feet gritty on the new floorboards, and put my hand on the newel post to go upstairs, I felt her there: the blur of another hand descending on the painted wood. My heart jumped. She was so present I thought I was going to see her. I scanned quickly up the stairwell, around the dark hallway. For a moment, the walls flickered, seemed to double and shift.

I knew it was a little girl. I could feel her hesitating. I had never felt so afraid before.

And then it faded. I walked up the stairs. The landing was just the landing. The door of our bedroom stood half open.

I lay back down next to Michael and waited for my heart to stop thudding. But it was too dark in there, no slur of streetlights. The finish in the new mattress gave off a stuffy, chemical smell. I knew I wasn't going to get back to sleep. It was a relief to hear the waves in the distance, like soft breaths.

I got up and went to the window, lifted the blind and almost gasped. The moon was low, completely round and radiant in the blackness. You could see lines of its light along the ridges of the waves, continually moving through the darkness and then disappearing.

I felt calmer after that. When I woke next morning, the sun was bright yellow through the blinds. Michael came in with a mug of coffee. And it was stupid really, but I felt like I'd got through something. He sat on the bed with a bit of a bounce and I had to cradle my coffee so that it didn't spill on the new duvet – a wedding present from his mother.

'The wood's being delivered today,' he said, pulling on grubby jeans from the day before. 'So we might have a floor in the front room this evening. Donny's going to come and help pull up the rest of the old boards.'

'I'll come and help too.'

'I thought you were going to work on your paper.'

He leaned over and bashed my chin with a quick kiss. His arms looked different now, the muscles and veins more prominent. I thought how hard he'd worked to move us out from the old caravan we'd been living in at the end of Donny's croft. Donny thinks of it as his luxury caravan, even though the Tourist Board told him not to rent it out any more. But I always liked living there, right next to the deserted beaches and the wide Atlantic rollers that tower up like molten glass in the blue air.

Michael stood up and stretched his long torso. Combed his hands through his black hair. He smiled and slapped his legs, ready to get started.

'So, Donny'll be here in half an hour.'

'Yes, I'm getting up.'

'I wasn't suggesting . . .'

'Anyway, you're right. I need to get this thing handed in. I can't ask Dr Morgan for another extension.'

I could hear him whistling as he went downstairs. Michael's family used to live here on the island at one time, in this house. His grandmother was born here. He says there's a family story that her great-grandmother was a mermaid.

I always feel guilty that it's Michael who is doing all the backbreaking work, while I sit in the only good room and write about lizards. My PhD is entitled 'The Brain and Nervous System of *Podiarcis Erhardii*, commonly known as Erhard's Wall Lizard'. Michael has got used to living with my dry aquarium and its lizard family, and the faint acrid smell of waxy chrysalids that collect at the bottom of the tank.

I have a horrible cold wash in the sink in the corner of the bedroom and pull on my jeans and fleece. I look through the side of the lizard tank to see how they are getting on. There is a flick of a tail and a scuttle and the two lizards flash into a different position and then freeze. The thing about lizards is that you can never tame them. They have a very small, very ancient brain that operates on one principle: survival. They spend their whole lives on high alert, listening out for danger, scanning their surroundings with their lizard eyes, their toe pads picking up every vibration in the earth ready to send back messages to the brain cortex: to flee, flee now. They don't consider, or think, they simply reach a certain overload in feedback criteria and then run. They are a sleek little bundle of vigilant self-preservation; an evolutionary strategy so effective, you can find a lizard brain tucked inside every developed species.

I push back the sleeve of my fleece and carefully lower my hand into the glass tank. There is a flicker and they both scuttle to the other end in a flurry of sand and tiny sideways straggle legs. But there is nowhere else for them to go. I slowly move my hand towards the corner and there is another quick scuffle and my hand closes around one of them. I can feel the little whip of muscle working inside my hand and the scratching of its back legs.

I hold the chloroform bottle against my chest with the top of my arm and unscrew the top. Then I cover the opening with the wad of cotton wool and tip it over with my free hand. I hold the damp cotton over the struggling lizard, and then it stops. I put the lid back on the bottle, and sit down at the desk. The lizard is lying across the piece of card, its arms and legs something between a minute plucked chicken and a cartoon frog in its anthropomorphic arms-up pose. I pick up the scalpel and start to slit along the belly skin.

I realise that the banging and splintering from downstairs has suddenly stopped. I have an amazing ability to sit through noise and not notice it once I begin to work, but the sudden silence is unsettling. Something's come up, and I go downstairs with my arms folded. I hope it's not more problems. Michael's father has loaned us enough to get the Manse ready to take our first bed and breakfasters, but we need to be open as soon as possible if we are to keep up the payments.

Down in the sea room, where every one of the square sash windows looks out over the Atlantic, Michael and Donny are standing thigh deep among the floor joists looking at something. When Michael sees me coming in he does not look pleased.

'What is it?' I say. 'Just tell me the worst. Is it dry rot?'

Donny looks upset and serious. Michael is white under his summer tan and the grime from ripping up the rotten old wood. There is a sour smell of rot and damp.

'I don't want you to look,' he says. 'You won't like it.'

'What is it? Oh God, it's not another rat.'

I walk around the edge of the walls where there are some floor-boards still down and then lower myself into the floor space between the joists. The floor is damp and sandy and littered with dirt and debris. Michael and Donny are standing one each side of a small dark brown box, or a little metal trunk. It has evidently been dug up from the sandy soil.

I squeeze next to Michael so that he has to hold on to the joist behind him.

'Don't,' he says.

I squat down and look inside. The earth smells very sour and close here. I can see a jumble of tiny bones, although there is some symmetry to them; a tiny round skull, like a rabbit or a cat, in a nest of disinte-grating material. There are scraps of yellowed cloth still around the tiny skull. And then I stand up and put my hand over my mouth. I can see clearly what the scraps are now: the remnants of a tiny baby's bonnet.

Alexander Ferguson, 1885

As soon as I heard the news from my servant girl at the Manse, I hurried to Benbecula, but with the tides and the journey being difficult, I arrived too late. The locals were already settling into the wake. The fool of a minister from the dissenting church there refused to uncover the sea woman's coffin and raise it up again so that I might examine the body. I even took myself to the harbour sheriff in Lochmaddy, but he refused to go above the minister. He looked upon my request to disinter the mermaid – if such she be – with great suspicion.

It would soon be dark, and in this place the darkness is complete unless there is a moon. So I found lodgings at the inn next to the customs house. I walked around the harbour while my supper was being prepared and asked among the fishermen there if they had heard about the mermaid. They pretended they could not make out my poor pronunciation of Gaelic, but I saw some of the men cross themselves. They turned their backs to me, and worked at stowing their ropes and creels. The harbour was as still as a millpond, the water deep red in the setting sun, a second black inn and customs house perfectly inverted in the water. The silence grew long and I returned to the bare little room that serves as their hostelry.

I slept in my clothes between frowsty sheets, since, like most dwellings in these islands, the damp was cold and penetrated the bones. But I slept contentedly because during my supper I had persuaded the landlady, who was a compulsive gossip, and keen to help me improve my Gaelic by searching to explain herself clearly, to tell me all she had heard about the maid.

'It is the MacKinnons who found the poor lady on the shore, lying dead,' she told me as she cleared the table. 'And I heard that Annie MacKinnon touched her with her own hand, just as I am touching this plate now.'

It was most tantalising to think that soon I would be speaking with those who had witnessed this, as yet, scientifically unrecorded creature. I was awake with the first light and wrote off a letter to the University in Edinburgh requesting that the Dean of Science order an exhumation. I explained I had eyewitnesses who could attest to the existence of this half-fish, half-human organism; a completely new and previously undiscovered branch of the evolutionary chain. Here was the possibility of finding a new link in the transmutation of species, as postulated by that great scientist, Mr Charles Darwin.

I left the letter with the landlady with an entire shilling to get it to the mailboat, and rode out the happiest man in Scotland.

Of course, at that time I was not to know that the reply would be most discouraging. The Dean refused to order the raising of the mermaid's coffin. He wrote that I was too ready to give credence to 'the fanciful tales of fairies and legends held of the aboriginal peoples of the Western Islands in their state of ignorance'. He suggested that, now my health was improving, I should consider returning to Edinburgh where I could study once more alongside men of science and reason and continue with my classification of molluscs and crustaceans from the coasts of Fife.

By the afternoon I was back once more in Benbecula. By enquiring at some of the turfed black houses, which are surely some of the least civilised habitations in Europe, I was able to locate the women mentioned by the landlady. I rode to Traigh Mhor and left my horse grazing while I walked out on a vast plain of wet sand that mirrored the wide brightness of the sky. Two black figures were stooping to fill their buckets with periwinkles.

Once they understood my request, the women were very anxious to share their story. They asked for no coin. They appeared to be simple women of good character, and had felt deeply affected by the encounter. The details are as follows.

On the morning of the first Tuesday in June 1885, Mhoira MacKinnon and her mother, Annie MacKinnon, were gathering sea-ware from the shores of the island of Benbecula on the Atlantic seaboard when they saw a woman from the waist up, gliding along a little way out to sea, with her lower portion hidden under the water. She swam in closer, whereupon a huge tail could be seen wavering beneath the sea's surface. The creature spent a good hour travelling up and down the shore margin as the women worked, and since she had a cheerful face and voice, eventually they were not afraid. They were sorry to see her swim away and not return.

The next morning, after a great storm, they returned to their work and were grieved to find the mermaid lying dead on the white sands. She was of adult, human size, her face clearly a human face with long black hair, but they reported her naked body smooth and 'sleekit' like the skin of a seal. She did not have legs, but a tail covered in a thin loose skin. One of the women touched the tail, which felt smooth, as is a fish, but without scales.

As I rode back to the Manse, my mind was at war with itself, my intellect and education refusing to accept the existence of the sea lady. And yet are we not scientists? Are we not called to look at the evidence, not the theory? Could it be that I have stumbled upon a creature that sheds new light on the origins of man, a link in the transmutation of species as marvellous as any ancient fossil – *but which is not yet extinct*?

Carolina Gonzalez-Carvajal

Carolina Gonzalez-Carvajal has lived in so many countries and houses that she no longer remembers where she started. She has picked up a husband and three children in her travels. She was educated at Cambridge University, UCLA School of Law and worked in Los Angeles. She now lives in Cambridge. The following is an extract from a novel-in-progress, provisionally entitled *The Indelible Imprint of Ivo Andrada*.

The Indelible Imprint of Ivo Andrada

Caldillero, Spain 1905

Eugenia Andrada was mending a rip in her husband's shirt. It was his good shirt and she wanted him to wear it to the Semana Santa procession. He'd caught the sleeve on the handle of the bedroom door as he dressed that morning and then he'd thrown it on the floor when they'd started to argue. After he'd left, she had been so angry with him for going to work when he'd promised that he wouldn't, that she'd left it lying on the floor all morning. Now that she'd stripped the beds and shaken out the mattress, she was ready to mend the shirt. The tear was jagged and ran along the edge of the sleeve, more like a wound than a rip. She gathered the gaping fabric and pinned it back in place, then with tiny stitches she threaded her needle back and forth, back and forth along the line of the tear. Perhaps no one would ever know that it had been torn.

She ran her hand over her belly to feel for the lump of tiny foot that had kicked her ribs all morning. In only six short weeks, Eugenia expected the baby she was carrying to be born and today, as Lent was nearly over, it felt even more real. She put down the shirt and walked to the table where she'd been preparing a soup for lunch. She reached for the beans she'd soaked. Then without thinking, chopped a snippet of morcilla and popped it into her mouth. Rolling the morsel between her teeth, the fat globules melted on her tongue and she savoured the coppery taste of the blood pudding. Ever since the start of this pregnancy she'd craved unusual tastes and aromas, as if the baby was already reaching out to sample the world outside her womb.

In the late morning sun, patches of warmth and brightness seeped on to the chair by the window. It wasn't a bright room and in the winter it was damp and hard to keep warm, but the bubbling soup was fast raising the temperature and Eugenia was beginning to feel a little dizzy. She'd felt hot for the last month and her feet had swelled like plump little plums, purple and bruised by wearing shoes. She slipped them off her feet. Relaxing back into the chair, she moved a cushion into the small of her back to ease a dull ache and closed her eyes.

The nausea and cramps took her quite by surprise. She took a deep breath. The pain stopped when she stood but soon started up again. If she breathed through her mouth it was more bearable. Then it rose and fell, as she spooned a portion of the steaming soup into a tin container and cut a slice of rough bread to take to her husband at the dock. She took a deep breath.

'It must be the morcilla,' she thought; the lingering tartness of the blood made her teeth tingle. She clutched her stomach. Morcilla, meat – Good Friday was a day of fasting. She bundled the tin into her bag and hurried out of the door.

'You look a little pale,' said her husband, as they perched together on the sea wall, wrapped in the smell of low tide and salted fish. He dipped the bread in the still warm soup.

'Something I ate,' she said, wincing as another contraction swelled her, pushing baby, bowels and lungs taut against the blue of her stretch marks.

'We should stay at home tonight,' he said placing his hand on the drum of her stomach, letting it roll against his fingers.

'And miss everything,' she said, lightly kissing him on his forehead where the line of freckles from his nose petered out into the wisps of his receding hairline.

The harbour was large and full of small fishing boats jostled together. A thin strip of a railway line ran across the town to the edge of the dock and at the far edge, larger ships waited for coal. Beyond the harbour wall, the sea was very still. It was only a short walk from the edge of the sea wall to the centre of town but even from this viewpoint, the town seemed a negligible thing, a jumble of houses pasted on to a crack in the side of a hill with mountains rising sharply behind. Now clouds had rolled in off the mountains and were soaking up the light like a stain.

Eugenia moved slowly, climbing the steps that ran to the Plaza Mayor and on up beyond the church where two men were building a large bonfire. Flags and banners hung from balcony to balcony suspended off mooring lines. One thick black line ran from the top of the fountain in the centre of the square, drawing her eyes up to the single oak cross, silhouetted against the church, like a great sea anchor, holding the town firm against a coming storm.

She needed to rest, but with the aftertaste of the blood in her mouth and the rush of the blood in her ears, she couldn't concentrate. The pain in her back grew stronger with each step. Across the square, she could see through Palmira's half-open door that the furniture had been pushed back from the walls. Palmira was on hands and knees scrubbing and waxing the red kitchen tiles. Eugenia pushed open the door and lowered herself on to the nearest wooden chair.

'Can I have some water before I walk home?' she said, gulping her words in great deep breaths.

'Is it the baby?' said Palmira, handing her a cup of water and then stepping back to wash footprints off the floor.

'It's too early for the baby. It's something I ate,' said Eugenia blushing. She should tell Palmira, but Palmira was tipping the bucket of dirty water into the sink, squeezing the mop and wiping the counters.

'It's not the baby,' she repeated. Palmira looked unconvinced.

After a few minutes, Eugenia felt the pain easing and decided to start back. She wanted to sit in her chair at home and sip from a pitcher of barley water scented with almonds. The smell of ammonia and wax in Palmira's small kitchen was filling her nostrils and making her gag. But when she stood up from the chair, she felt a little trickle run down her inner thigh.

'Wait. I'll get my coat and we can walk together,' said Palmira as she placed the mop and the bucket back in the cupboard.

At that moment, Eugenia's waters broke and a yellowy-red tinged liquid gushed on to the newly clean stone floor, pooled in the scrubbed grout and puddled under the table.

Ivo Andrada was born the last minute of the last hour of that evening. A Good Friday baby. He was born in Palmira's son's small oak bed, tended by the midwife and watched over by a picture of the Franciscan saint, San Antonio, nailed above the headboard.

In the square, the rest of the village had clustered around, silently watching the hooded *cofradías* in their red and white penitential robes carrying the *Pasos* through the streets. The Virgin Dolorosa and La Santa Vera Cruz had been unpacked days before from the sacristy, polished and decorated with lilies and other white flowers by the pious ladies of the town. Now they sailed through the streets pitching like ornate battleships on the bent shoulders of the white robed men. Some of the brotherhood walked barefoot. Some had chains wrapped tight around their legs that chinked as they walked against the cobbled pavement. All wore the tall, black capirote hoods concealing their faces. Small boys marched solemnly beside them carrying lit, tapered candles, their white robes trailing on the floor. An older boy darted from candle to candle flashing a thin silver stick trying to catch the drips before the wax seared the younger boys' arms. A solitary drum beat the rhythm of the march. From time to time, a trumpet sounded. Husbands and wives wrapped their arms around each other, children tucked tight against their legs, fearing not only the cold air, but also that with the last roll of the last drum, the world would come to an end. A group of men, who'd been drinking since the afternoon, slumped against the pillars of the notary's house, half-heartedly sang a line or two from a Havana brothel song. As the final float with Christ carrying the cross entered the square, someone in the crowd started to sing a *saeta*. His crisp, sad voice pierced the square like an arrow. Otherwise there was only silence and the drum.

The Priest stood on the steps of the church to bless the crowd and light the bonfire that would burn until Easter Sunday. The crowd looked up to the bell tower ringed with the debris of a broken stork's nest. The bell ringers stood poised with the ropes threaded between their gloved hands for the signal to toll the bell. Small children, tired of standing still for so long, ran around in and between the legs of the people, and their teacher Señorita Mercedes didn't even try to stop them. Two teenage boys let off firecrackers in the fountain and an elderly couple dressed in their best clothes hung together like newlyweds and swayed to music only they could hear.

After ten hours of labour, Eugenia did not notice any of this. She could barely raise her head to look at the limp infant at her side. The midwife had caught him in a piece of sacking. The intricate blanket that Eugenia had been knitting for the last five months lay at the bottom of the drawer in her bedroom. The midwife plopped the baby by his mother's side. Raising herself, Eugenia looked down at the still, little figure. Crusty down ran along his forehead and across his distended stomach to the point of his tiny foot. She picked up his twiglet arm and studied the line of it. It felt both rough and soft as she stroked like the nap of her favourite velvet shawl. His long, delicate fingers and fully formed nails reminded her of a chicken foot on a string from the fair in Llanes.

'He looks like his father,' said the midwife, who always said this to new mothers. She was already packing her bag and hoping that the roasted bacalao would still be moist if her lover came to her when his wife fell asleep.

'He looks very blue,' said his mother. The midwife stopped her packing and glanced back at the child whose face was shading a purplish blue from the lips to the tips of his ears. She bent over the baby, felt his skin, then grabbed him up by his heels and turned his buttocks to the square. With her ruddy, chapped hand, she started to paddle him, not pausing until, with a sharp crackle of breath, the cries of the newborn filled the room. The baby's voice was then lost in the chime of the bells and the midwife's shout of '*Hijo de puta*' as she wiped a stream of urine from her left eye.

Much later, when someone had retrieved her husband from the bar and he was cradling his son, Eugenia recounted their son's birth. 'He was lying here limp and cold. I thought he was dead.' She shifted to find a more comfortable position.

'It's a miracle. He seems so healthy,' said his father, pleased to hear the strength of his son's cries but wondering if the boy would ever outgrow the conical shape of his head.

'The true miracle,' whispered his mother looking up above her head. 'The true miracle was that our son was born here in this bed where San Antonio, the patron saint of lost things, could watch us.'

His father looked up at the chipped painting that hung from a single nail above the bed. A rather portly San Antonio balanced a shrunken-faced baby Jesus at an impossible angle on his arm. The infant, who looked more like a slightly malign dwarf than the Blessed Child, was holding a wilted lily flower in his disproportionately large left hand. Señor Andrada fumbled in his pocket to see if he had any coins to give the midwife to thank her for her efforts in reviving the baby.

Ivo spoke at ten months old and by two years was asking the sorts of questions that no one in the village had thought to ask or knew the answer to. But even if he pestered people about why they had blue eyes when their children had brown or what colour was light and why was the sky up there and why was the grass green, they would ruffle his hair and send him on his way, thinking as little of his strangeness as they did of Tito's lazy eye, Pablo's red hair or Amalia's beautiful voice.

Ivo was his mother's pet. He always sat next to her in church and even taught himself to read by matching the sounds he heard to the symbols on the page. Yet, despite his mother's attention, he was a phlegmy, asthmatic boy, with a perpetual nasal drip. His dark shadowed eyes, set deep in his head, were like the pools on the beach at low tide; brown and matt on the surface, but if you stood quietly and looked closely, a whole world would appear. When the rapeseed blossomed and the yellow flowers dripped across the valley, he was forced to spend his days inside, peering through swollen red eyelids, drawing things he saw or imagined. His mother taped his magical land and seascapes to the doors of the furniture and propped them on the mantelpiece, until the whole of the house became a fantastical gallery.

'What sort of thing is that for a boy to do all day?' said his father with a worried frown, as he watched his son sketching a three-rigged schooner with vines for halyards. In the street, the neighbourhood boys ran ragged and riotous chasing a cloth ball.

'He's a delicate child,' said his mother, who when she looked at her son saw a young saint rather than a small boy with blue paint on his fingers.

Kat Gordon

Kat Gordon is from north London. She graduated from Oxford in 2007 and went travelling round the world to find something to write about; this extract is from the first section of her novel provisionally titled *Plum Jam and Mr Pickles*, set in north London. The extract begins with the protagonist, Tallulah, visiting her estranged father, who is hospitalised after a heart attack.

Plum Jam and Mr Tickles

The aunts are sitting in silence in my father's room, watching his chest rise and subside like a whisper. Aunt Gillian gives me an encouraging smile when I come back in; Aunt Vivienne arches an eyebrow.

'Does anyone want a coffee?' I ask. 'Or a water?'

They shake their heads.

'Well, I'll be downstairs,' I say. I'm suddenly exhausted.

I buy a coffee from the café by the entrance and sip it slowly. Even so, it's scalding and I burn my mouth. I wish my mother was here. Her father died of a heart attack when she was nineteen, not – as my cousin Starr once informed me – because my granny poisoned him, but because he drank like a fish right up until the day he keeled over.

My mother never spoke about her parents when I was younger. It was only a few years before her death that she first mentioned them to me, on a fruit-picking trip. My mother used to make all our jams and marmalades herself, and I loved helping her. I had a special stool to stand on, so I could reach the counter where all the fruits and glass jars were lined up neatly, freshly washed. I wasn't allowed to use the knife, so I stirred the pulpy, sticky messes in their pans. Every so often I would lick my finger then stick it in the bag of sugar.

The year I turned nine it was still sunny in October, so my mother and I went blackberry picking. Plum jam was her favourite, but my father preferred blackberry.

'You have to wrap up nice and warm for me,' my mother said. 'I don't want you to catch a cold.'

'I don't want to wear my scarf,' I grumbled. 'It's scratchy.'

'Hmmm.' My mother considered me for a moment. She turned round and walked towards her bedroom. She came back holding her pink cashmere sweater. It was my favourite sweater of hers; she looked so delicate and pretty in it, like the flowers she grew in her windowboxes.

'What if you put this on underneath the scarf and coat?' she asked. I stroked the sweater. It was unbearably soft and feminine. 'Then if the scarf feels scratchy you just concentrate on how the sweater feels instead.'

'OK,' I agreed. She slipped the sweater on over my outstretched arms and pulled it down; it felt like cream being poured over me. I rubbed my face with the sleeve. My mother handed me my coat and scarf and watched as I buttoned up. Now that I was only a year away from ten I insisted on doing the buttons myself, even though my mother was quicker with her fingers.

'Where are we going?' I wanted to know.

'To the woods,' she answered.

We walked hand in hand. It was autumn, and the air was cold enough to turn my nose and hands numb.

'How come I can see differently out of each eye?' I wanted to know. We were swinging our linked arms for warmth. My mother carried our pails in her other hand.

'What's the difference?' my mother asked.

'Things look more colourful out of my right eye than my left.'

'Really?'

'Yes. And when I look at something then shut my left eye and look at it out of my right, then it looks the same, but when I shut my right eye and look at it out of my left then it moves a little bit, like I've moved my head, but I haven't.'

'Well,' my mother said. 'That means your right eye is stronger than your left.'

I pondered that for a while.

'Does everyone have a stronger eye?'

'No,' my mother said. 'Not everyone.'

I took stock of my strangeness.

'Is it good to have a stronger eye?' I asked.

My mother squeezed my hand.

'There's nothing wrong with it,' she said. 'Your aunt Vivienne is short-sighted in one eye, even though she won't wear glasses. And your granny, my mother, was blind in one eye.'

I was intrigued. My mother never spoke about her parents. They died before I was born.

'Why was Granny blind?' I asked.

'Someone hit her,' my mother said. 'On the left-hand side of her face. Her cornea was damaged and she never saw out of that eye again.'

'What's a cornea?'

'It's the part of your eye that you can see.'

'Who hit her?'

My mother stopped walking and put our pails down. She took her hand back from mine and rubbed it against her cheek, not looking at me. I waited for a minute, then asked her again.

'Your grandfather,' she said, still not looking at me.

I tried to grasp this idea.

'Why did he hit her?'

'They fought a lot. And your grandfather grew up in a time when it was accepted that a man might hit his wife.'

'Oh.'

She picked up the pails and we tramped on. The woods smelt like earth and cold air. The leaves underfoot weren't crunchy any more, but stuck to the ground.

'Why did Granny stay with him? Can I ask you about her?'

'Would you stop asking questions if I said no?' My mother smiled at me.

'Yes.'

'Then I think you'd explode.' We stopped by a blackberry shrub and my mother picked some blackberries. She put one in her mouth. 'Open up.'

I opened my mouth obediently. She placed a berry on my tongue, gently. I brought my teeth down; the juice was sweet, just right. Not like some blackberries, where it was so sweet it made my mouth sing.

My mother was picking more blackberries and tossing them in her pail.

'She didn't leave because there was nowhere for her to go,' she said. 'Also because she loved him.'

'How can you love someone who hits you?' I asked. I was playing with my scarf, looking at it, at the ground.

93

She sighed.

'Sweetheart. It's absolutely wrong to hit someone, and most people know that. But sometimes you can love someone so much, that even when you know they're wrong, even when they hurt you, you still go on loving them.'

She handed me a pail.

'That's stupid,' I said. 'If someone hit me, I would stop loving them.' I kicked my pail. It tipped over and rolled away.

My mother cupped my face in her hands.

'It's not always simple,' she said. 'But you're clever and brave, and I'm so thankful for that. Every day.' She kissed me on the forehead. 'Now go and pick up your pail.'

Uncle Jack came infrequently, but the house always felt uneasy when he was there. He would go to my father's study with him and talk; they always closed the door. Once my father came out unexpectedly and caught me trying to listen in.

'What were you doing?' he asked me, frowning.

I thought he probably knew what I was doing.

'I was trying to hear what you were saying,' I said. I didn't know what to do with my hands, so I started playing with my hair, scratching my head.

'Evelyn,' my father called. My mother came out of the kitchen, wiping her hands on her skirt. Uncle Jack appeared behind my father, who stood, blocking him off, in the doorway.

'Perhaps you could find something for Tallulah to do,' my father addressed my mother. 'Then she wouldn't have to eavesdrop to amuse herself.' He stared down at me again. 'Do you have some sort of parasitic problem, Tallulah?'

'No.' I dropped my hands down by my side.

My father turned and ushered Uncle Jack back into the study. I saw a smile on Uncle Jack's face, and I thought I heard him say: 'Well, at least you've brought *her* up to be honest, Eddie.'

The next time Uncle Jack came round my mother turned off the cartoons I was watching and handed me an apron.

I didn't need a stool any more, so I leaned my elbow on the counter, cupping my chin in my hand and looking down at the jam I was stirring. Mr Tickles was at my feet mewling.

'Why does Uncle Jack have to come round?' I asked my mother.

She was taking the stones out of the plums.

'He's your father's brother, Tallie.' She kept her eyes on what her hands were doing.

'He doesn't act like a brother,' I said. 'Or an uncle. He never even brings me presents.'

My mother looked sideways at me and smiled.

'Other people's uncles bring them presents,' I pressed. 'Charlotte's uncle buys her fudge, and she brings it into school. It's pretty good fudge.'

'Do you want to take some of this jam into school?' my mother asked.

Mr Tickles pushed his empty bowl in front of him to our feet.

'No.' I turned back to the jam.

Mr Tickles rubbed himself frantically against my legs, my mother's legs, the table legs. He made the rattling sound that passed for purring with him.

I picked him up and hugged him.

'I've already fed him twice,' my mother warned. 'Don't be fooled.'

'He can smell food,' I said. 'He doesn't want to miss out.'

My mother picked up a plum and waved it in his face.

'Trust me,' she said. 'You don't want this.'

Mr Tickles eyed it eagerly.

My mother took a step back and put the plum down.

'I think he might just eat it anyway,' she said. 'This cat . . .'

I scratched his ear.

'It's just because it smells so good,' I said.

'It does,' Uncle Jack said from the doorway. 'The smell of plums always reminds me of you, Evie.'

I dropped Mr Tickles, who let out a yowl of displeasure and left the room. My mother put a hand up to her cheeks. She had gone red.

'Don't worry,' Uncle Jack said to me. 'I'm just returning my glass.' He walked round the table to the sink and put his glass down in it. When he walked back to the door he went the other way round the table; we had to squeeze to let him pass.

'See you later,' he said to both of us. 'Let me have some of that jam when you've made it. Every time I smell it I'll think of you.' He was looking at me, but my mother answered:

'Sorry, Jack, I'm afraid I'm only making enough for the three of us. We'll see you next time.'

He winked at me as he left.

Uncle Jack was right. Whenever I smell plums I think of my mother too.

It's not just jam you can make with plums. There's stewed plums, plum porridge, spicy plum crumble, poached plums with chocolate mousse. My mother was good at all of these, but she preferred to make jam. I know how she felt. There's something satisfying about seeing your handiwork safe in a small, neat container. Knowing it could last for years.

To make plum jam you will need:

6 lbs plums
1 pint of water
6 lbs sugar

First you cut the washed and drained plums in half, and remove the stones. Then quarter the plums and add the water, in the pan. Crack about 12 of the stones, remove the kernels and blanch in boiling water for 5 minutes before splitting them in half. Add them to the pan. Simmer until the fruit is pulpy, stir in the sugar and boil rapidly until setting point is reached. Remove the mixture from the heat, skim, pot, cover, and label.

This will yield roughly 10 lbs.

Aunt Vivienne appears before me, tall and unsmiling. She peels off her leather gloves and suit jacket. I wonder why she has kept them on till now. Probably in protest against the air of dinginess and neglect that the hospital seems to exude. I watch a nurse walk past, steering an old man by the elbow. He is wearing a regulation hospital gown, and there are stains all down his front; I can't tell what they used to be. I wonder, fleetingly, how my father found the strength even to walk through the doors nearly every day for the last twenty-five years.

'I've been sent to find you,' she says. 'Gillian would have come, but she's staying with our comatose brother, in case he wakes up and suddenly needs mothering.'

I gesture to the chair opposite me. Aunt Vivienne sits down. She's nearly ten years younger than Gillian, and I find I can't see a resemblance between them at all.

'I hear you've all but dropped from the family radar,' Aunt Vivienne says. She has folded her gloves and jacket neatly on her lap. 'What exactly have you been doing with yourself these last four years?'

'Nothing much,' I say warily. It strikes me as unusual for Aunt Vivienne to be asking questions about another person.

She arches an eyebrow again; it must be her trademark move.

'Darling, I do hate the way your generation seem to cultivate inactivity and boredom as if they're virtues,' she says.

I blow my cheeks out, and think that Aunt Gillian is probably right when she says that Vivienne could do with being taken down a peg or two.

'Speaking for my generation,' I say, 'I think we prefer to call it *ennui*.'

Aunt Vivienne inclines her head slightly in my direction.

'I'm glad you haven't turned out so *nice*,' she says. 'I was afraid you would, as your mother was the nicest person I've ever met.' She wrinkles her nose slightly.

'Fortunately,' I say. 'The Park genes seem to have overcompensated slightly.'

Aunt Vivienne appraises me, and takes a hip flask from her handbag.

'Fancy an Irish coffee?' she asks.

Alcoholism is definitely in the family.

97

I push my cup towards her. She gives me a generous splash; it smells like rum. Aunt Vivienne stops a male orderly walking by and orders a coffee. He's confused.

'I don't think we have a table service here, madam,' he says. 'But there's a café just over there – '

'I'm sorry,' I say. 'It's OK, I'll get it. Aunt Vivienne, I'll get it.'

The orderly smiles at me gratefully and leaves.

'Thank you, darling,' Aunt Vivienne says. 'That's very sweet of you.' She settles back further into her chair.

Jacqui Hazell

Jacqui Hazell was born in Hampshire. She has had a short story published in the Jane Austen inspired anthology *Dancing with Mr Darcy*. She has also had a range of humorous greetings cards published and worked at Buckingham Palace. She is a journalist and magazine editor and lives in London. This is the opening of her novel, *The Flood Video Diaries*.

The Flood Video Diaries

One

I was happy to hear Flood was dead, not as happy as I thought I'd be, but happy all the same. The inevitable had occurred – his demise both painful and premature, which seemed only fair. Things were as they should be. A correction had been made ensuring that the fine but precarious balance of the universe had returned, momentarily.

You see, it didn't last; it couldn't, because Flood stories sell newspapers. The press knew that, so their initial considered response – news stories and obituaries – quickly dissipated to virtual Flood hysteria. Art critics, columnists, even the business pages, everyone had to have their say and that's when I thought, enough.

You can take two or three hours or whatever it was, but you can't take my life. I never wanted to be an artist's model – never agreed to anything – I was young, stupid even, it hurts to admit that but that's how it was.

And now this, Flood's DVD, his diaries, or art film or whatever the hell it is.

I kicked off my shoes – as in the 'stunning' red shoes Marcus Harvey had admired. That's Marcus Harvey, art dealer, always in *Art Review*'s Power 100 list of movers and shakers in the international art world. 'Stunning shoes – girls get to wear such wonderful footwear,' that's what he said – not, 'Mia, what a pleasure to meet you – love your work – must represent you.'

I spread my toes, rubbed raw from walking too far, too fast in heels I wasn't used to – and for what? I sighed and reached for my bag. The DVD was on top. *Limited edition*, promised a red sticker. While the black and white cover photograph was of a woman's naked torso – model-girl thin and translucently pale with Celtic-style lettering like a tattoo round her navel. 'The More I Search the Less I Find' it said. Edgy, urban – things I am not, if I'm being honest.

I picked at the cellophane wrapping, my hands shaky. Get a knife.

Get a life more like. I crossed the old Kermit-green carpet to the kitchenette. We have one sharp knife and there it was half submerged in the greasy bowl – bloody Tamzin.

I knocked on her door. 'Tam, you there?' I peeked in. The double duvet was plumped and smoothed with the Zippy toy her stupid boy-friend bought resting between the pillows – funny how she made her bed but didn't bother washing up. WE ARE NOT STUDENTS ANY MORE.

Anyway, she was out – perfect opportunity.

I went to my room, straight to my desk and sieved through the sketchbooks, cuttings, pens and paints. I had a Stanley knife some-where. A blunt Stanley knife, there beneath a folder marked 'NEW IDEAS'. Must buy new blades, I thought, as I forced it between the folded and glued flaps of cellophane that enveloped the DVD's plastic casing. I had wanted a copy of this but no way would I pay for it. So that was something.

Back in the living room, I inserted the disk and pressed 'play'. The blue-blank screen turned black. No copyright warning. No trailers for forthcoming releases. It wasn't like an ordinary DVD. I should've known that. 'Watch this, if you can,' Marcus Harvey had said. 'It may change your mind.' I don't want to change my mind. And that's when his assistant, Amanda Darling, said, 'Trust me, it *will* help.' Never trust anyone who says 'trust me' – everyone knows that.

Words in white typescript began to move across the screen:

The More I Search the Less I Find . . .

And in the bottom right-hand corner, like a home recording, the date and place: Thursday 26 May 2005, the Merchant's House Hotel, Nottingham – a place I know, unfortunately.

I felt hot. I should change. I was uncomfortable in my only pair of smart, tailored trousers and a pin-tuck detailed blouse. But was there time?

Legs passed the barred window – an old man in khakis with a skanky dog. They couldn't see me. No one noticed me down there. I liked it like that. My first London flat, down a curl of slimy, uneven steps. Too hot in summer, cold and dark all day in winter, but it was private and the area wasn't bad.

I pressed 'pause', ran down the corridor to my room, and laid my clothes on the bed. They didn't look so smart any more. They hadn't worked – all that money – they didn't do the job.

I pulled on an old surf Santa Cruz T-shirt and shorts then back to the TV. My fists clenched, as the disk resumed from where I'd left off: a low-lit room and a figure emerging from the shadowy gloom. Slowly he walks towards camera – a hint of cigarette smoke and a pale face – *Jack Flood*.

My stomach tightened.

This is too difficult. I can't do this. I took a deep breath. Come on, Mia, you have to watch – have to know.

Jack Flood's dark hair framed an intense, inscrutable expression. He was dressed in chiffon – a black shirt open to his navel – fashionably thin, wasted even. And he was in a hotel room, that hotel room, the one with the bronze satin bedspread and crystal chandelier among the other empty trappings of a boutique hotel. To think I'd been so impressed by that place, by its look – its obvious statement of nowness.

I glanced back at the window – another pair of old, slow stranger's legs – but no Tamzin. When was she due back? I tried to think what shift she was on but all I could remember was her wishing me luck.

Jack Flood was looking directly at me. He was small and contained in the box of the chunky old TV but still it incensed me to see him like that, looking out, blatantly staring as he sucked on a cigarette. 'I never stop looking,' he says. 'Got to keep looking and seeing, really seeing – it's a lost art.' He gets up, walks round the room as if he's searching for something, then pauses and slowly turns his face back to camera. He is wearing eyeliner.

'My name is Jack Flood and I am an artist.'

'Yeah, a fucking shit one.' I was talking to the TV, saying something I didn't believe. Flood had won awards and made heaps of money. In fact he still does. What do I ever make? Call yourself an artist, Mia, you're having a laugh. It wasn't the best time for an artistic crisis in confidence but then again when is? I thought of that day, the morning-after when I had arrived at college, in my studio space, took one look at the layers of sketches pinned to my whiteboards and immediately pulled them all down in a silent frenzy before seeking out the large black bin to dump them in. But that was then and this is now and still I'm getting nowhere fast. I chewed at a hangnail, chewed too hard, ripped it off – shit, that hurt.

On screen Jack Flood is talking again. 'What is art?' he says. 'How can you tell? Is it all rubbish?' He curls his lip. 'These questions will more than likely go unanswered but what I can provide is an insight into the life of an artist: where I get my inspiration, what motivates me, how I make art. What do artists actually do? Is it the piece of piss you always suspected?'

He paces the room for a few moments and then grabs a leather jacket from the bed. He searches the pockets. 'Rough Guide to Nottingham – literally,' he says, unfolding a piece of paper.

'I asked the concierge, where's best avoided? Forest Fields, St Ann's, Mapperley, the Meadows . . . sound nice, don't they? But Forest Fields is the red light area and the Meadows and St Ann's are notorious for gun crime – they've all got territorial issues – it's the drugs, it's gang warfare. Then there's the binge-drinking in the city centre – the fighting, the puking and fucking in alleyways –'

Flood turns towards a side table piled with photographic equip-ment. He selects a small camcorder, turns and approaches the camera that's filming.

I moved further back from the TV – silly of me, I know, but I couldn't help it.

The film cuts to what must be Flood's hand-held camera. He films his route out of the suite, down a narrow corridor. He opens a heavy fire door and then makes his way down the hotel's winding backstairs and through the circular reception – decorated in Schiaparelli-pink, paisley-print wallpaper. He spins round the revolving glass door and out on to the cobbled street.

Daylight: his camera does a quick 360-degree scan taking in the Galleries of Justice museum across the road, the pub next door and a nearby church – the Lace Market area – streets I know well, streets I once loved.

There's a white car with lettering on the side.

'Taxi!' shouts Flood, then films the white saloon car as it draws up alongside. He points his lens through the open passenger window at the driver – a youngish man with sandy hair, a fat potato head and pitted skin.

Again my stomach tightens – *I recognise him*.

'I want to see Nottingham,' says Flood.

The driver stares hard. 'Why you film me?' His accent is deep and guttural – Eastern European.

'I film everything,' says Flood, 'a sort of cultural record, if you like. Anyway, I need a cab. Are you free or what?'

The driver nods solemnly and Flood climbs in the back.

The cab's interior is black vinyl – dated but spotless.

'I want to see the real Nottingham,' says Flood.

'I am sorry; what is it you ask of me?'

'The *real* Nottingham – not the city centre, the castle or the Robin Hood Experience – I want to see where people live, where real life happens. I have a shortlist if that helps.' Flood's arm moves into camera-shot as he passes the list over.

The driver looks at it briefly and shakes his fat, sandy head. 'Trust me, my friend, there is nothing to see.'

Two

I'd rushed back for this – really hot and pissed off – squished up against a suitcase, next to a man reading a thriller – *Dead Women* or something – and an older puffy lady in tweed fanning herself with a free paper. *Take off your jacket*, I told her telepathically. There must have been a good reason why she didn't but I couldn't think what it was. And *don't read on the tube*, I told thriller-man. My tutor always said that, 'Never read on the tube – a true artist never reads on the tube.' He was full of crap like that – the kind of crap you never forget.

I scanned the carriage – no one attractive. Sod it, I picked up a discarded copy of *Metro* and began to flick through it.

What a day. And yet it had started so well. In fact, I'd been on a high for days, ever since I got the call from Drake. I should've realised there was only one way to go. 'Drake Gallery want to see me,' I told Tam, my voice all high pitched and excited.

'No way,' she said. That's right, no way.

I sighed and curled my legs beneath me as I looked back at the TV screen.

Flood's video diary continued in Nottingham's Lace Market area: a place for tourists or partygoers – a museum, a church converted into a bar and restaurants in the old lace factories. Flood films blue sky and the church's honey-coloured stonework. An empty street – he cuts back to the cab's interior with its black vinyl seats and the back of the cabbie's head.

Flood begins to speak though he remains unseen, behind the camera. 'Look, I need a driver for a few hours, maybe more, I'm sure we can come to some sort of arrangement?'

'Have you not heard?' says the driver, his frown visible in the rear-view mirror. 'These places you want to go, they can be dangerous. There have been shootings; they are not places to go unless you have no choice.'

'Oh come on, this is England for God's sake. There are no no-go areas here.'

'They even shoot children.' The driver shakes his head. 'A girl was killed after Goose Fair – she was I think thirteen. And a few months back a boy was shot in Radford. It is crazy place.'

Flood films the silent street: sunlight on sandblasted stone contrasts with adjacent dark Georgian brickwork. The restored period buildings are immaculate and on the road charming cobblestones remain intact.

'Look, I haven't got much time, just drive me around; I'll make it worth your while,' says Flood. 'Where's best to start?'

The driver turns and looks hard at the camera. 'You make it double?'

Flood makes a comical choking sound. 'Sorry?'

'You say you make it worth my while. I want double pay and no filming me.'

'OK. OK, you're in luck, seeing as there's no other cab. Where do we start?'

'What is it you want?'

Flood's camerawork is shaky as he consults his list. 'Meadows, St Ann's, Forest Fields – actually, my friend, can we start in Forest Fields?'

'OK, I go to Forest Fields.' He checks his mirrors and pulls out.

The camera focuses on a blue, bejewelled elephant hanging from the rear-view mirror alongside an orange smiley air freshener.

'Where you from?' asks Flood.

'Poland.'

'Ah, great place – lots of vodka.'

'Lots of vodka.'

'What's your name?'

The driver glances in his rear-view mirror. 'Maciek.'

'*Magic*.' Flood laughs.

'To English it sounds like magic, but it's Maciek – say ma-check.'

'Well Ma-check, you like art?'

The driver shrugs. 'I not bothered.'

The camera is directed outwards: shooting shops, bars and restaurants as the cab loops round the one-way system. They stop at traffic lights and Flood focuses on a couple of teenage girls. They have long, yellow, straightened hair and matching black and white polka-dot, Ra Ra skirts.

'It's all art,' he says, quietly.

Lucy Hounsom

Lucy Hounsom is 22 and lives in Devon. Her work has been published by *Forward Poetry* and *Decanto* magazine, where she featured as Centre Stage Poet for the April 2006 issue. The following excerpt is taken from the end of 'Bearson', one tale from a collection of short stories she is currently working on.

Bearson

The contractions started on a milky afternoon when the sun was obscured by clouds.

The woodsman followed his wife's gasped commands and brought towels and hot water, tried to make her comfortable, but she thrashed around, clutching at the covers. He couldn't stand to hear her. She bared her teeth at him and bit her lips until they bled and at last, as evening fell, the baby came.

The woodsman held his wife as she screamed. He could see something dark between her thighs, the crown of the head. Her face was shiny with sweat and her smile a grimace of pain.

Something was wrong. The head didn't look right. The skin was dusky, not pink, the shoulders too broad. An arm came free, or something he thought was an arm, but couldn't be, for it ended in a small curled paw.

The woodsman backed away. His wife gave a final push and the creature slid on to the bed in a gush of fluids.

He saw his wife look down, saw the horror stagger her face. She scrambled backward, legs caught in the bedclothes. She gave a cry as another contraction pushed the afterbirth from her body. The woodsman felt sick. From opposite sides of the room, they watched as the creature struggled weakly on the sheets. Its body was entirely covered in a thin layer of black fur slicked down from the birth. It uncurled its limbs in silence and tried to open its eyes. Its face ended in a rounded snout and its cheeks were lightly flecked with white.

The woodsman's wife stretched out a timid hand, her knuckles pale against the creature's skin. It mewled and waved its legs again. She leaned a little closer. Its eyes blinked open and roamed blindly round the room.

'It can't –' the woodsman started. He took a step forward.

The woodsman's wife scooped up the creature.

'It can't stay here,' said the woodsman. There were spots of colour high on his cheeks.

'But he'll die. He's helpless.'

'It's an abomination.'

'It is still our child.'

'That is no child of mine.'

The woodsman's wife studied the back of her husband's shirt. Her eyes flicked to the dark window. The woodsman turned and followed her gaze. Then he strode across the room and pulled the curtains. She dropped her eyes to the cub that lay in her arms. A small fear fluttered in her stomach, but she brought the cub close to her face. It was a bear. Black like the wild ones that lived in the forest.

The woodsman made a sound in his throat and left the room.

When he returned the next morning, his wife was trying to feed the cub. He watched as she lifted it to her breast, directing its mouth towards her nipple. With a cry, he raced to the bed and snatched the beast from her grasp. It was the first time he had held it. Its fur was soft but fine, barely covering the skin. When it realised what had happened, the cub cried. It was a thin sound and throaty, not the healthy cry of a human child. His wife began to weep too. 'I must try,' she whispered. 'It's hungry. I'm its mother.'

'It's not right,' the woodsman replied. But he put the cub back on the bed and it bleated at his wife until she picked it up. He couldn't watch as she gathered it close and returned to her task.

The days wore on, but the woodsman's wife wouldn't leave her bed. She complained of nightmares that ruined her sleep. When the woodsman brought her breakfast, there were dark half moons under her eyes. They slept in different rooms now; he would not share his bed with the cub, and his wife wouldn't let it leave her side. The crib stood unused in the corner.

A week after the birth, the woodsman's wife awoke with a fever. She continued to feed the cub, but her hands shook, and sweat lay heavily on her skin. No matter how many blankets the woodsman tucked around her, she was always cold.

'I can't eat that,' she told him one evening when he brought her the last of their chickens.

'You must. You need your strength.'

'Please.' Her eyes brimmed. 'Take it away.'

So the woodsman ate it himself and used the leftovers to make a broth. It was thin; they always struggled for food in the cold months.

'Please.' And this time it was he who begged. 'For me.' She managed a few mouthfuls, but these grew smaller and smaller as the days passed.

He couldn't stand it. When he looked at his wife, he no longer saw the woman he married. Her hair had been thick, her skin clear. Now her cheeks had lost their colour; they had sunken in on themselves like the temple claimed by the mud in one of the arcanist's stories.

He remembered the face of Temperance. The card of shared troubles. Or so the arcanist had claimed. He never should have let his wife insist on the reading. A man mustn't meddle with his fate. But they had meddled. And now his wife was dying.

Tears choked him. The woodsman ran outside into the forest. Change had come. And it had travelled in the arcanist's bags. Hate balled his hands into fists. It was kindness that had let the arcanist into their lives. It was kindness that had doomed his wife. The woodsman couldn't stop the scream that rolled up and out of his mouth, a terrible roar of injustice. He clutched the pale bark of a silver birch and let his voice fill the forest. Then he slipped to his knees in the wet winter mulch and listened to his echoes.

His wife died in the early morning, when the light lay heavy in the sky. Her eyes were open; she stared at something he could not see. They were fixed on the window, as if she waited hopefully to see a face beyond the glass. The woodsman wrapped his fists in the curtains, drew the coarse material across his cheeks. He shouted and pulled, and they tumbled to the floor.

Then he gathered everything the arcanist had given them, built a bonfire, and burned it all. He threw the scarlet hat on last and watched its feather curl and crumble. When the sparks stopped leaping into the wind, he returned to the house.

He didn't think he could bury his wife. But when he saw her laid out, limbs stiffening, her face waxen like a doll's, he wrapped her in the bedclothes and carried her into the forest. She was so light; her body could have been made of twigs. He imagined he was carrying a manikin, a travesty of a human being. Her eyes could have been sparrow's eggs, her fingers thick roots of ivy, her once lovely hair withered bluebell stems.

He walked, hardly knowing where he was going. But some part of him knew where she should lie. Payment for what he had taken.

Dusk swooped on the wings of a raven around the arcanist's tree. It was no longer a sapling. Now it stood tall against the grim sunset, its girth ten times as wide as the woodsman's. With his wife in his arms, he was too numb to feel surprise. He knew he had interfered with something that went far beyond his knowledge of the forest.

He took the spade that hung from his pack and dug a shallow grave. He hacked viciously into the earth, hoping to sever some of the tree's roots, but they were buried deep underground. As he lowered his wife into the hole, his grief soaked the bedclothes that wrapped her. He looked up at the tree that towered far above him. She would lie for ever in its shadow.

It took him most of the night to return. When he opened the door of the bedroom, the cub was curled peacefully in the blankets he had brought to keep his wife warm. He screamed like a wild bird and grabbed the cub, blankets still caught around it. It struggled, but he held it tight against his chest. His wife had loved it, and he hated it all the more.

Outside the moon was dim, fading into dawn. The forest breathed odd and sultry breaths that chilled the sweat on the woodsman's neck. He tried to ignore the bundle that writhed in his arms. For the first time, he felt out of touch with the forest. Branches left welts on his cheeks and fallen debris tripped him. He had travelled through the forest in his indoor shoes and the day's walk had split the soles. Sharp sticks cut his feet; he ignored the pain. And though his feelings were muddled, he felt an alien hostility seeping through the membranes of the forest, searching him out, running through the veins of the ivy that twisted around each tree.

He had never felt unwelcome here; the forest was a life greater than his own, than all the things he could ever be. He thought of the streams, of the secret wells where water rushed by in the darkness, and the wild roses fell. He heard an echo of the lark's lonely song, the ruckus of the dawn chorus. And he felt the wind that swept the branches clean in autumn, the way it lifted the tiny hairs on his fore-arms, the way it made his shoulders itch, as if wings would break out there, and he could soar to the unseen melodies of the wilderness.

The creature twisted in his grasp. Cold stung his cheeks, or maybe it was tears. The woodsman plunged on through the trees, until one of the blankets snagged on a branch. The bundle fell to the ground and the bear let out a whimper as it rolled free of the warmth.

The woodsman watched the cub by the light of the weak moon. Its ears were folded back protectively and he could just make out the silver gleam of its eyes. A cold lump settled in his stomach. He thought of his wife pregnant and happy, her smile, the way she had danced in the summer. 'This is not my son,' the woodsman said, and the dead leaves shook their skeletons around him.

He turned his back. The cub mewled, a cry that shook his shoulders. He put one slipper-clad foot in front of the other and walked away. He imagined it writhing helplessly in a tangle of weeds, spiders clamber-ing over its sensitive skin, the cold that would creep into its blood and whisk it away into death. He never looked back.

The house was lifeless. The comfort had leached from the chairs and the walls closed in around him. Alone, the woodsman sat at the table and stroked the lock of his wife's hair she had given him when he first said he loved her. It was chestnut, a colour he had always liked. He stroked it, and wondered whether his wife had ever been content here. He remembered the way her lips curled upward when the arcan-ist told his stories. She had smiled at the thought of exotic places, of far-flung cities, deserts and oceans. Things which were not the forest. The arcanist's blue eyes held promises the woodsman could never fulfil. He only knew one story. He had never told it to his wife.

The story was about a man and a woman who lived in a forest. The man loved the forest, and one day he realised he loved it more than he loved his wife. He began to spend each day in the forest; he would leave at dawn and not return until nightfall. His wife gave him his dinner without complaint, but if he had paid attention, he would have realised she was not happy. One summer evening, a stranger asked to stay. Just for a night, he said, and he offered to pay them in stories.

He told tales of adventure; of the thieves who prowled city streets, of great deeds and the rise and fall of heroes, alchemists whose greed led them in search of gold, of beautiful but terrible women drunk on the blood of men. The woman listened avidly, dazzled by the promises in the stranger's eyes. As for the stranger, his words were solely for her. He never glanced at her husband.

He left the next morning. The woman wept in secret and when her husband went into the forest, she sat by the window and waited. She whiled away the summer at the window, convinced the stranger would return. But autumn came and he did not.

She lost all interest in food. She prepared dinner for her husband in a daze, sometimes slicing her thumb instead of the vegetables. She put her blood into the stew, unaware, and one night her husband tasted its bitterness on his tongue.

The woodsman tasted that bitterness now. The man in the story buried his wife too.

The cottage was cluttered. The walls continued to push inward. He had to get out. The woodsman stood up and reached for his coat. Outside, he breathed in deep and thought he smelled spring on the air, but it was only the snowdrops that nodded in the glade. The woodsman looked back at the place where he had lived for fifteen years. It needed some repair, he noted. The ivy had reclaimed the cottage's foundations and the chimney perched uncertainly on the slant of the roof.

A freezing wind entered the yard, catching the leaves, whirling them round the woodsman's legs. He watched a gust break like a white wave against the door. The wood flew back, bouncing on its hinges, and the leaves raced in, unchallenged.

The woodsman turned his face into the wind. It was a wind he had always run from, knowing its caress would freeze a man's blood. It blew south-west, so he picked up his stick, stripped off his ruined shoes and followed it north towards its source.

Dominique Jackson

Dominique Jackson worked as a journalist in Sydney before moving to London. This excerpt is the start of 'An Afternoon Procedure', a short story from her collection *The Cats of Australia*.

An Afternoon Procedure

Pru's overnight case was less capacious than she remembered. Reluctantly, she put aside the bed jacket, a white, crocheted affair with a pie-crust collar bought to receive visitors in when having Lily, almost eighteen years earlier. She had envisioned herself in it as a radiant new mother, propped up in the hospital bed, showing off a snug white bundle in the crook of her arm. But in the muddle of new motherhood it had come home unworn.

Bed jackets were old-fashioned these days, she decided. Besides, she was only going in for the afternoon. She took out her slippers and lavender pillow but left the facial mist for a refreshing pick-me-up at the end of it all.

Lily was leaving for the day, yelling goodbye. Neil was in his room, packing while talking on the phone. 'Make it happen or fuck off,' she heard him saying jovially. 'Good stuff. Alrighty, better push off.' He was zipping his bag. The awkward moment loomed when he would ask what she was up to for the day. Not that he minded or even really listened but whatever she had to say sounded inconsequential. And today she'd have to lie.

Pru slipped into her bathroom, eased the door shut and began humming busily. She commenced her morning routine, an involved process requiring a number of creams, gels and powders applied to specific zones of the face in a particular order. Some were tapped on, others smoothed in. Different treatments had different durations. Some were removed with a hot washcloth, some peeled off. She would drift into a reverie as she worked. Today, though, she kept an ear out.

'Pru?'

She turned up the humming.

Neil knocked.

'Just a minute!'

'I've got to get going,' he said through the door. 'I'm back Friday. Can you get those cheques off? And don't forget the car.'

'Rightio. Hope it goes well,' she shouted back.

'Yeah, me too. Rightio, bye then.' A moment later he added: 'You should take yourself out to dinner while I'm away. Go out with Jan. Or Pam.'

And he was gone, easy as that.

Energised by her successful evasion, Pru exfoliated with more vigour than the instructions specified before stopping to study her appearance, unconsciously sucking in her cheeks and pushing out her jaw almost to a sneer. She gently pulled up her upper eyelashes. Now *that* made all the difference. 'You're looking well,' she could hear Lorenzo from Il Piccolo Negozio saying while putting a heart in the chocolate of her cappuccino as he once had. 'Have you had a holiday?' one of the book group women might ask. She would smile enigmatically and offer up something about the benefits of sleep. Even – the worst-case scenario – if no one commented, she knew *she* would feel more confident, empowered by having done something about her situation.

At 9.15 a.m., Pru sent Janet a reminder of the pick-up time. Janet was the only person she'd told, over the remains of fresh mint tea at the end of a light lunch two weeks earlier. Janet had openly had a partial facelift.

'No, I won't tell,' she'd said. 'Though I am a bit surprised. I didn't think you were –'

Both women had tensed at the dangerous turn the conversation was taking.

'I just don't think you need it. *I've* never noticed your eyes.'

Janet was slim and – especially now – irritatingly smooth skinned. Therefore, Pru knew, Janet would never be able empathise with her plight. She might toss off the odd easy compliment, in the way women did ('Have you lost weight?', 'Your hair really suits you like that'), but Pru was certain Janet luxuriated in her aesthetic superiority. Take her outfit that day – tight trousers, loose top – which Pru half suspected was chosen to show off in a way that *she* could not (and would not anyway even if she could). So she chose not to tell Janet about 'the moment'.

The moment happened one morning a few weeks earlier. The mail had just popped through the letter box. Pru was standing in the hall, scrutinising the photographs from a fund-raising evening at Lily's school that she'd helped organise. Her eye had alit on a familiar jacket, one she also owned. The wearer – a smiling woman with eyes sunk into her face like currants into a bun – did it no justice. Three seconds later, she realised it might be herself. But something wasn't right. The photograph showed a weathered, substantial woman with the afore-mentioned curranty eyes. Wary, even. Whereas *she* felt herself to be a soft and delicate person, in some ways still more girl than woman. *Her* eyes were her best feature. Pru peered into the hallstand mirror, then back at the photo. She did this several times. Eventually, she had to acknowledge the likeness.

Pru knew she was not much to look at. At twenty, on friends' urging, she'd entered a holiday resort beauty pageant and come second, forever ruing the humiliation while gratified not to have come third. And that was the high point. She knew not to expect second looks from men on the street. Strangers had never asked her out, except for mentally unstable ones. No man had ever run up and pre-sented her with a bouquet, as happened to the women in the deodor-ant advertisements. Despite, or because of, this she took pains with her appearance. There is no such thing as an ugly woman, only a lazy one, was a line her mother trotted out whenever anyone complained about the amount of time she spent in the bathroom. Or *faut souffrir pour être belle*, while dragging a comb through Pru's knots. Pru took grooming seriously. She kept up with beauty innovations. Her visits to her hairstylist, facialist and nail technician were so frequent all had become close acquaintances. Occasionally, leaving the salon after an hour's attentive pampering, she thought herself nice-looking, in a soigné kind of way. Other times, faced with an incontestably attrac-tive woman, she felt painfully homely, which seemed unfair, given her efforts. Even after Lily's birth, Pru's happiness was tinged with secret regret at seeing her mottled exterior alongside the pale perfection she had produced. It reminded her of half-peeled lychees on display at the fruiterer's.

And Lily had grown into the sporty type who didn't fuss over her appearance, making Pru wish she hadn't waged war on her own. Pru's hair – once similarly lustrous – was now dull from years of perming and bleaching. Decades of tanning had wrinkled her skin prematurely, requiring laser treatments that left it strangely shiny. Relentless eyebrow plucking necessitated tattooed replacements that gave her a constantly surprised look.

Whenever Neil's gaze followed a comely woman, she didn't blame him (all men did it) but it stoked fears their days together might be numbered. Their marriage had reached a point somewhere between comfortable cohabitation and deep unease, on Pru's part anyway. Most nights they slept in separate rooms (his snoring) though this gave her the freedom to wear overnight beauty treatments.

For someone to find you attractive, you had to find yourself attractive, she heard people say. But what about when you *didn't* find yourself all that attractive, only acceptable at best? That's what she was taking steps to address.

'Oh, you know, I just want to look a little fresher,' she'd said, focusing on a fixed point just to the right of Janet's hair. 'I think I'm looking a little tired.'

'*I* don't think you are. What does Neil say?'

Pru looked down and smiled, half ashamed, half proud of her guile.

'He'll be in Melbourne till Friday that week.'

'Pru. You'll have to tell him.'

Pru raised her hands as if to say 'What can I do?' Easier to ask for forgiveness than permission, she had reasoned. Like when she had gotten her ears pierced at sixteen. Her father had been outraged, referring to 'self-mutilation' and 'looking cheap'. But he'd gotten used to it.

Janet put down her cup and looked at Pru doubtfully.

'What if – there's a complication?'

'It's an afternoon procedure!'

'What about Lily?'

'She'll be fine. I'll make sure the fridge is full of food. She's very capable.'

'Isn't it her do soon?'

For that was part of it too. In four weeks' time was their drinks party to celebrate Lily's eighteenth birthday and getting a place at university. Pru had looked forward to the evening, seeing herself and Lily as sort of representing the span of a woman's best years. Then 'the moment' happened. She wasn't, she realised, ready to be relegated to a supporting role just yet.

'Not till the 6th.'

'That's not far off. How did you find this guy? Did you get a referral?'

'He was on *Good Morning Australia*.'

The appearance of Dr Ricard Prendergast in Pru's life had seemed serendipitous to say the least. The morning after 'the moment', she was watching a chat show from her treadmill. After a segment about a new weight-loss shoe, Dr Prendergast, 'Sydney's A-list cosmetic surgeon' they called him, came on to talk about his afternoon eyelift. On the sofa beside him was a dark blonde, marshmallow-lipped woman about her own age, named Karen. They showed a photograph of Karen's old, tired-looking eyes then zoomed in on her new, dramatically open ones. Pru slowed the treadmill. 'She came in at two, was out by four and back at work the following week,' Dr Prendergast said, patting Karen's hand. 'It's made all the difference to her confidence, hasn't it, Karen?' Karen smiled shyly and all of a sudden looked quite approachable and nice. The clinic's phone number flashed on the screen. Pru ran to grab a pen. Panting from the sudden exertion, she scrawled the number on her hand then booked a consultation, before she could change her mind. Later that same day, she drove past a billboard for a cosmetic surgery clinic showing a beaming young woman declaring 'The best decision I ever made!' It seemed a positive omen.

Renew You Medical Spa had been in a surprisingly ordinary part of town, above a delicatessen, but its waiting room looked fresh and clean. Silk orchids on the formica counter tastefully obscured before-and-after photos of breasts, noses and eyes. Three middle-aged women sat reading celebrity magazines. Pru reread the fact sheet they had sent her, though she found it hard to concentrate. Instead, she discreetly examined the receptionist as a sample of Dr Prendergast's handiwork. But the girl appeared too young to need work. Or was she older but had had good work? Pru gave up. Under the table were neat stacks of brochures. One described an acid mixture that could be injected to plump the face. Of more interest was a vitaminic rejuvenation injective treatment with a lifting effect on the elastic-fibres of the skin. Then she heard her name being called.

An assistant took her photograph (smiling then serious) against a blank spot of wall in the corridor before showing her in. Dr Prendergast didn't look up from his computer. He was fleshier in the flesh, with an undisguised bald circle. Pru retreated into her shoulders as she waited for his attention.

'Now – Prudence,' he said finally, before swivelling around to give an open-mouthed smile. He had the slightest accent that made it Peru-dence, which she didn't mind. 'Nice to meet you. You can sit there. How are you?'

'Very well, thank you,' she said, discreetly arranging her waistband above what she called her midrift as she sat. 'And you?'

'Fantastic. Beautiful weather we're having, hey?'

Pru decided he was as nice as on the television after all.

'Now you're interested in' – he flicked back to the screen – 'rhinoplasty. Sorry, last client. Blepharoplasty.'

'That's right.' She looked at him expectantly.

'And you are – forty-seven. Any cosmetic procedures before?'

'Ah –' She raced through the vast catalogue of her beauty history. 'Not *surgery*.'

'Did you want upper *and* lower?'

'Just upper, I think. I mean, I think.' She paused. 'What do you think?'

'Let's take a look.'

Prendergast propelled his wheeled chair opposite hers so their knees were touching. Pru held her breath as he reached out to touch her face but ran out of air before he finished so it rushed out like a big sigh. She could see herself reflected in his dark irises. Her eyes began to feel dry from not blinking. To absent herself from the situation, Pru began pondering the nature of the doctor's appeal. He was quite swarthy. She didn't usually like such dark men but then again, she hadn't known any. What sort of women did he like? Would she be his type?

'I have to say, your eyes are lovely,' she heard him saying.

'Oh! Well, thank you. My husband says they're my best feature.'

Pru cursed herself for letting Neil invade her reverie as he so often did.

'You have a pronounced droop in your upper lids,' Dr Prendergast in fact said.

'And you're a little crepey here and here,' he added, dusting his fingers over her eye sockets. 'But your bags aren't too bad so I think you're OK for now. They talked to you about the fee schedule?'

'Oh. Yes.'

'You know it's not covered by insurance?'

'Yes.'

'We have a payment plan. And a multiple treatment discount. I'll get the girls to tell you about that on the way out.'

'Thank you.'

'Now, I'll talk you through the procedure. The surgery will take about an hour. We start by giving you a local anaesthetic and then make an incision –'

Was Ricard married? There were only photographs of children – two boys – behind his desk. Pru began building the romantic back-story for his singledom.

' – and there'll be bruising, like a black eye, which will last a few days. You won't see the results for several weeks but after that you will look – fresher.'

She snapped back to attention.

'Fresher. That's exactly what I want. It won't be *obvious* though, will it? That's my concern. I don't want people to tell.'

'It'll be very subtle. Don't worry. See you next Wednesday, no – Thursday.'

'But you'll be able to see a difference?'

'Of course.'

Dr Prendergast gestured to his assistant to usher her out. Another patient waited in the corridor. Pru hid her disappointment at the brevity of the consultation, smiling as she paid the deposit and left.

Liza Klaussmann

Liza Klaussmann is a journalist living in London. She received her BA in creative writing from Barnard College, Columbia University, where she was awarded the Peter S. Prescott Prize for prose writing. The following excerpt is from her novel, *Tigers in Red Weather*, about a family in post-war America, whose longing to be extraordinary leads to violence and betrayal.

Tigers in Red Weather

Daisy, 1959

It was only two weeks into the tennis program when Ed stopped coming. He would leave the house with Daisy every morning at eight and walk with her over to the tennis club. But that was the last she would see of her cousin until her reappeared at noon to pick her up and walk back to the house on North Water Street for lunch.

He didn't say where he went or what he did during the hours that Daisy spent skidding across the hot clay courts and working on her one-handed backhand. There was no point asking him; he would either say 'this and that' or nothing at all.

Daisy had mixed feelings about Ed's disappearances. On the one hand, she didn't really care. The only thing she really thought about during those three hours at the club was the singles match at the end of the season. As she crisped under the hot Eastern summer sun, as her thighs burned and her forearms hardened like the waxed rope bracelet on her wrist, all Daisy thought about was making her opponent cry in a practice match, making her move to volley invisible, making her step surer, making her swing move across her chest like a metronome. *Tick-tock, tick-tock, like a good little clock.* She wanted to hit the sweet spot every time. And not having her cousin there was just one less distraction.

But his absence was also a problem. He was always her partner for the end-of-summer doubles round-robin. Ed wasn't very good, but Daisy was strong enough to carry them, and while the doubles match was a bit of a joke, you had to play the doubles to qualify to play the singles. *Teamwork is God's work*, or that's what that shriveled prune Mrs Coolidge always told them in her lecture at the start of every tennis season. Normally, Ed feared not participating in the doubles match, because it meant an automatic hold-back the next year. But he suddenly didn't seem to care. But for Daisy, not having Ed around meant she was forced to survey the leftovers for a partner.

The only girl who wasn't a goof was a new girl named Anita. She had been giving Anita a mental tryout for a couple of days when she decided to approach her. The points against her included the fact that she had pierced ears. *Nice girls don't pierce their ears.* It wasn't that Daisy really had anything against it, but it was weird. None of the other girls had their ears pierced. And Anita looked a bit like a Beat, with her very straight black hair and bangs cut across her forehead. But she could return a smooth backhand from the right side of no man's land, and as far as Daisy was concerned that far outweighed pierced ears and the possibility of bongo-playing.

She had meant to approach Anita during their mid-morning break, when all the kids went to catch some shade under the back porch of the clubhouse and sip the cool lemon water put out by Mrs Coolidge. But as she made her way from the back courts to the large expanse of lawn that separated the front courts from the clubhouse, she spied her mother playing a match with Aunt Helena. Aunt Helena had turned the color of a red-hot poker with the exertion. But her mother moved coolly across the court, spinning up tiny clouds of clay in her wake. Her skin was brown and her hair, normally a glossy black, was taking streaks of honey after the weeks spent on the Island. But what struck Daisy most was how dispassionately she played the game. Daisy couldn't imagine how her mother could hold her racket so lightly, as if it weren't a weapon, how she could look at her opponent as anyone other than the enemy.

As she was contemplating this, her eyes moved to the spectators' bench in front of the court. On it sat Tyler Pierce, whose sea-grass hair had been accompanying her in her daydreams, watching the game with what seemed to be intense interest. She thought about going over and talking to him, telling him that the woman who played such a cool game of tennis was her mother, but she was afraid they would tease her later for fawning over an older boy. Reluctantly, she went up the steps to the clubhouse porch, and leaned over the white, painted railing, keeping her eyes on the scene beyond.

Her concentration was broken by something cold and wet being pressed on her arm. Daisy turned to see Anita smiling at her, a glass of lemon water between them.

'Hello,' Anita said.

'Hey,' Daisy said. *Hay is for horses*.

'She's beautiful, isn't she?' Anita said, scanning the court where her mother and aunt were now picking up stray tennis balls.

'Who?' Daisy said, confused by Anita's sudden appearance.

'The dark-haired one. She looks like Scarlett O'Hara, but more modern.'

'That's my mother,' Daisy said, squinting her eyes at Anita, but taking the lemon water anyway.

'Really? You don't look anything alike.'

'I know,' Daisy said, feeling irritable and crowded. 'I look like my dad.'

'Oh,' Anita said, sipping out of her own sweating glass. 'Well, I'm sure he's beautiful, too.'

'I don't know about that,' Daisy said, shifting her feet. 'Look, I've been meaning to ask you, do you want to be my partner for the doubles round-robin?'

'Sure,' Anita said, as if it was nothing at all.

'We'll have to practice a lot,' Daisy said severely. 'I mean, maybe every day.'

'We're already playing every day. But sure, why not?'

'Oh,' Daisy said. 'Well, good.'

'Can I come over to your house?' Anita asked.

'I guess,' Daisy said, looking closely at Anita now. Daisy had to admit that Anita's bangs, cut straight across her forehead, were glamorous, in some old-fashioned way. Like the photograph of that 1920s film star she had found in one of her mother's old scrapbooks. But she felt uneasy and wasn't sure she wanted Anita hanging out at her house. She wondered if she'd break out into some sort of strange poetry in front of her family. 'We should get back. Break's over.'

'I'll catch up with you,' Anita said, still staring at her mother.

As Daisy walked back across the lawn, her mother waved from the court.

'Hello, Daisy.'

'Hello, Mummy,' Daisy said, her racket like a sleeping weapon in her hand.

The next day, Daisy decided to hang back at the end of the session in order to avoid having to invite Anita over. She was leaning against the chain-link fence that separated Court 7 from the grassy paths and marshes that led up to the old ice pond, when her cousin rattled the metal behind her head.

'How's your backhand coming?' Ed cooed, mimicking the baby tones of the club administrator, Mrs Coolidge.

'Hell's bells, Ed, what on earth are you doing here?' Daisy said, spinning around and lacing her fingers through aluminum latticing. At his height, Ed towered above Daisy and she had to peer up into the sun to meet his eyes. 'If Mrs Coolblood catches you, you're dead meat.'

'You're supposed to walk me home, now,' Ed said. He was wearing the tennis clothes he had set out in from the house this morning, still pristine except for his shoes, which were muddy and scuffed.

'You're such a baby,' Daisy said. 'Why don't you just tell your mom you don't want to play?'

'Because I'd hate having to spend the morning with her,' Ed said, without any real passion. 'Come on, let's go for a walk. I found a good path to the pond, one that no one knows about.'

'I'm hungry,' Daisy said. 'Let's go back home. Mummy's making deviled eggs.'

'I stole two cigarettes,' Ed said. 'From Tyler Pierce, actually.'

Daisy imagined smoking a cigarette with Tyler Pierce in the shed next to the driveway, his hand in her short blonde hair.

'All right, but let's make it quick. I might starve to death.'

'Only the Chinese are starving to death,' Ed said.

'Hell's bells,' Daisy said.

'You should stop saying that,' Ed said. 'It doesn't sound grown-up.'

'As if you'd know anything about that,' Daisy said, joining Ed through a side door in the fence that led to the grassy corridor running the length of the tennis courts. 'Come on, hurry,' she said, pulling him toward the marshes in back, and out of the reach of Mrs Coolidge and her godly works.

When they had cleared the last court and were safely behind the tall marsh grasses and cluster of old oaks that made up the lush backlands of Sheriff's Meadow, Daisy slowed her pace and let Ed lead her, noticing that whatever it was he was doing during his mornings off had tanned the back of his neck.

'We have to go left behind the old shed,' Ed said, taking Daisy's hand and pulling her deeper into the undergrowth.

'There's nothing behind the old shed,' Daisy said, feeling cranky and hungry for lunch. 'I don't want to get my shoes all muddy tromping around in the marsh. Besides, there's hundreds of mosquitoes back here.'

'No, there's an old path I found,' Ed said. 'It leads to an old shelter. We can smoke the cigarettes there.'

'I thought you said cigarettes were for ladies of the night,' Daisy said. 'And anyway, how did you steal them from Tyler?'

'From his tennis bag. And the cigarettes are for you.'

'You have to promise to smoke one with me, or I'm going home right now,' Daisy said, catching her tennis dress on a raspberry bramble next to the dilapidated shed that belonged to a defunct camp house off the old ice pond.

'It's this way,' Ed said, carefully removing the cotton cloth of her dress from a thorn.

As they moved past the shed off the well-worn path leading to the pond, they passed an old stone marker whose face had been eaten by lichen. Daisy would have stopped and picked at it if Ed hadn't kept his grip tight on her wrist. He pushed through a cluster of bushes, pulling Daisy in his wake. Normally, she would have told Ed to stop yanking her around, but she wanted to know what he got up to on his secret mornings, so she let herself be led. Also, she liked him like this, when he was purposeful and had things to show her, instead of just mooning about staring at people and making them feel weird.

As they emerged on the other side, there was a small winding path, bordered on both sides by a wild, high hedge. The air was still and quiet, and only the sound of crickets purring in the heat broke the *hush-hush* of their feet in the damp grass.

'Hell's bells,' Daisy said before she could check herself. 'Ed, how on earth did you find it?'

'Just walking,' Ed said, but a slight inflection in his voice sounded pleased. 'I knew you'd like it. I knew you'd understand it,' he added, looking at her intently.

'Is there a clearing anywhere?' she asked.

'A ways up.'

'Well, let's smoke the cigarettes here,' Daisy said, putting her hand on his arm, feeling the ropy muscle underneath.

'Let's go a bit further,' Ed said. 'There's an old oak we can lean on around the bend.'

At the next turn stood an old rotting oak, its roots resurfacing like a winded swimmer. Daisy put her back against the tree's crumbling bark and slid down to rest on one of them.

'I hope you brought matches,' she said.

Ed handed her a cigarette and pulled a pack of matches embossed with The Hideaway. She put the cigarette to her mouth and felt the dry tobacco stick to her lips. Ed carefully lit the match and moved it slowly toward the end of the cigarette. It wouldn't light.

'You have to breathe in at the same time I put the match up,' he said.

Daisy did as she was told, watching the end hiss and then glow brightly.

'It hurts,' she said. 'It's sort of disgusting.' She felt a bit sick, like when she drank too much coffee. 'I don't think I can finish it.'

Ed was staring down the path.

Daisy tamped the cigarette out against the root, and sat feeling strange, and a bit sad about Tyler. Maybe she could pretend to like it if he asked her. She started kicking at the meadow grass growing up around the tree until she realized her white shoe was staining. Beyond the grass was what looked like a small clearing, but the dirt was tan and dark green, instead of brown. Daisy leaned her head against the tree and the clearing came closer into focus, until she realized it was a travel rug.

'There's a picnic blanket, or something, over there,' she said, nudging Ed with her other foot. Ed turned after a minute and squinted into the brush.

'Yes,' he said slowly, as if he were just waking up.

'What's it doing there?' Daisy shook off her nausea and stood up. 'Somebody's been having a picnic in your secret place.'

Ed was silent.

Daisy picked her way through the muddy grass until she stood a foot away from it. It was lumpy and stained with something that looked like chocolate sauce. Something that looked like a Man of War lay under one moth-eaten corner, its tentacles oozing out over the ground.

'There's something under it,' she said, her heart beginning to beat with some fear that had to do with quiet woods and faceless men with blankets. 'Maybe somebody's sleeping.'

'I don't think anyone's sleeping,' Ed said, walking toward her.

'Yes, I think so,' she said, feeling very certain that they shouldn't touch it. 'We should go. It doesn't belong to us.'

Ed stooped next to her and peered at the humped tartan wool blanket. He put his hand on a corner.

'Don't,' Daisy said, backing away until he caught her arm.

Slowly, he raised the rug.

Rebecca Lloyd James

After graduating from Cambridge, Rebecca Lloyd James lived in London for ten years and worked in publishing. She now lives in Wales with her husband and three daughters and runs a small independent bookshop. *Catch the Rooks Sleeping* tells the story of an unlikely friendship between two young girls, whose dangerous games open up the cracks in the lives around them.

Catch the Rooks Sleeping

The car was steaming up, so Mum had opened the windows. Now and then, as they turned with the road, wet mist stroked across Emily's face. The dampness seemed to be in everything and gave off a smell of soil, moss and something sharper, like cat's pee. It felt to Emily as if it had always rained here.

She was itching to stand up and stretch her legs. The space inside the car seemed to be shrinking. This was what the summer was going to be like – trapped, frustrating, boring. Emily wiped the condensation from the window yet again. Her sleeve was soaked and smeared the water into streaks so that nothing on the outside was clear. She slumped back against the seat, defeated.

She'd packed as many books as she could, even shoving some into the gaps between suitcases in the boot when her mother wasn't looking. There was a library a few miles away, apparently. But the house they'd borrowed was a farm way outside Llansansom, the tiny village that the buses left from. To get herself into the atmosphere, she'd reread *Carrie's War* along the motorway, until the twisting roads made her feel sick. She could see herself in Carrie – tall, and not really pretty. She wasn't really sure that she was as tough as Carrie either. She couldn't imagine leaving her mother and looking after a little brother alone in a strange, hostile place. All the way to Wales she'd been expecting to be taken back in time, to a world of mountains and greenness and an old language, where witches existed and magic was believed. But what little she could see through the car window looked much the same as England – just rolling hills, Little Chefs and shabby towns.

Carrie had gone to the Valleys, where there was mining and tight little houses clung to the hillsides. Where they were going the big attraction was the sea. But where was that? Hidden behind trees and smothered by this misty rain that didn't so much fall as hang in the air.

It had been sunny in London. Her father had ignored all their packing and preparations and was in the studio when they left, so he didn't say goodbye. But as they pulled away he came charging on to the pavement and waved ferociously, his eyes screwed tight against the light. She'd looked back when they stopped at the junction to see if he was still watching. He looked like a tramp, his painting cardigan stained and full of holes, his trousers sagging at the knees. And when he shuffled back inside he was hunched like an old man.

The house was called Sand, which had seemed promising to Emily, but it wasn't on the sea. The lane took them along the cliff then inland for what felt like ages. When, eventually, it came into view, it was bigger than she imagined, white with a grey slate roof, and Emily was relieved to feel a flutter of excitement at the sight of it. Heavy trees leaned all around the building, their branches dripping on to the roof. In the low light, they were blue-black, with a shimmer of clinging silver water droplets. On one side, the trees stood a bit further off and there was a wall that might enclose a garden. A thin sliver of grass, too meagre to be called a lawn, ran around the front. The small windows dotted around higgledy-piggledy gave it a wonky face. It looked asleep, though not unfriendly.

Emily looked across at Kate. Her sister's sleeping face was pale and serene, her long eyelashes curving away from her cheeks like a doll's. She seemed younger again with her eyes closed, not much older than Emily. She had been asleep ever since they had left the motorway, which must be hours ago. Emily wondered what Kate would think of it here. Last July they'd been in France while her father finished his commission and Kate had painted all day, or swum and sunbathed, and hung out with the local teenagers at the café at night, practising her French, she'd said. Emily, who was only eleven then, had had to stay with her parents. This year Kate said that tanned skin was past it, and didn't go with all her black clothes and Souxsie Sioux eye make-up. No chance of getting brown here, anyway, Emily thought. She leant over to say so to Kate but something about her even, shallow breathing and the careful way she rested her head on her arm made Emily hesitate before poking her. Perhaps it was better to keep her thoughts to herself for a while longer.

Mum was driving very slowly now. The engine was barely ticking over, threatening to stall. She gripped the steering wheel tightly. Her hair, which had been tied up, had come loose in chunks and pink circles had appeared on her cheeks. Her face was a little shiny and soft downy hairs stood out from the tight skin around her mouth. She looked like a more natural, tired version of Kate. Emily couldn't imagine being evacuated like Carrie, waving goodbye at Paddington, while her mother held back her tears. Overwhelmed, Emily felt a rush of protective love for her.

'Isn't this it, Mum? We're here, aren't we? You could stop.'

Her mother glanced round at her quickly, then braked too sharply and the engine shuddered and died. Kate groaned and uncurled herself, blinking and stretching, faking a yawn. She wasn't going to look like she was happy to be there. She shook her dark hair back into place and gave a quick smile to Emily. Her right cheek was imprinted with the criss-cross pattern from her cardigan. Emily smiled back.

Emily's legs creaked as she stretched them out of the car. As soon as she straightened, pins and needles rushed down from her thigh to her foot. She flexed it, grimacing, and then stamped it on the ground.

'Ow! Ow!'

Kate gave her a disdainful look from under her heavily kohl-rimmed lids.

'Great dance, squirt.'

'Ow! I've got pins and needles.'

'Girls, please don't fight.'

Emily fought the urge to point out that she wasn't fighting. That was the kind of thing Kate said. Anyway, Emily liked arrivals, even if they weren't glamorous. She could imagine them as the family in *The Railway Children*, only there was no train here. She watched her mother fumbling around in her floppy cloth bag for the keys.

'Got them. No. Yes. I think so.'

Kate sighed and walked towards the door.

'Looks like a really exciting place to spend the next six weeks,' she said. 'Bats and mice for company. It's a pretty desperate way to try to keep me from having fun.'

'Oh Kate. Come on. Let's not go through that again. I couldn't leave you with your father when he's working and you know it. It won't be as bad as you think. Let's get inside – if I can just find the key.'

Kate put her hand on the door. She looked small standing next to it; it was much bigger than doors in normal houses. Big enough to get through on a horse. Its black iron handle could have been part of a church. Kate reached out and turned it. There was a heavy clunk of metal and wood and when Kate pushed against it, the door opened. She gave a superior smile. It wasn't locked anyway.

Emily and her mother followed through a draughty porch and into a hallway. Emily was blind for a few seconds in the gloom. The hall was panelled in nearly black wood with a ceiling low enough to touch. Eventually Emily made out the shape of a staircase curving away from them at the far end. Across from that was a doorway edged with light. They made their way towards this, acrid woodsmoke catching in Emily's throat.

The doorway led to a kitchen, flagged like the hall. It was huge and square and almost bare except for a table that stood on squat legs in the centre of the room, its surface polished and pitted. Two windows were set into plaster-coloured walls that must have been two feet thick. Between them was a door out of *Alice in Wonderland* that didn't reach much above Emily's knees. In the far corner of the room was the source of the ancient smell – an enormous dark medieval-looking range with a vast blackened chimney. It was very cold. The only chairs were high-backed and lined up like sentries around the walls.

'Are we really supposed to live here?'

Kate's question hovered among them.

Emily went over to the tiny door and tried the handle. It opened smoothly to reveal a cupboard racked with wine bottles.

'Obviously Max does stay here sometimes then,' said Kate, turning and opening a dresser full of plates and linen. 'What does he eat?'

Mum ignored her and put down her bag on the table. As it sagged into a heap the keys, a lipstick and a chewed pen spilled out.

'Funny that the door was open. He gave loads of instructions about opening it and where to find the spare key. I suppose the cleaner must have been in and left it unlocked for us.'

'Do you think it's okay? It's miles from anywhere, isn't it? Maybe they don't need to lock up.' Emily tried to squash thoughts of cursed skulls and ghosts, though this was definitely the kind of place they'd haunt. 'Can we explore? Shall we go together?'

'Are you scared?' asked Kate.

'What about?' Emily tried to sound nonchalant.

'Old, spooky haunted houses with mad Welsh axemen lurking in cupboards.'

'Kate. Stop it,' said her mother, glancing at Emily.

'Stop what?'

'Oh, don't start.'

'Start what?'

Emily interrupted, 'Please let's go and look around.'

'You two look. I'll get the bags.'

'No, Mum. Let's all go. Then we'll get the bags together.'

'Do you think we'd better hold hands for safety?'

'Kate!'

Kate ran out cackling witchily and ran up the stairs. Emily and her mother followed, holding hands.

They didn't do this very often now, Emily reflected as they walked up the stairs. Her mother's hand felt small and dry, like a monkey's paw. They were both a little self-conscious, unsure how hard to grip the other's hand, and when they saw Kate's back disappearing through a doorway upstairs they instinctively let go. Her mother gave Emily's a little squeeze as she did so.

It was brighter upstairs. A long corridor had windows all along one side that looked out over the grass and the lane. A worn and faded carpet covered the whole length, patterned in red, gold and blue with swirls and mazes and exotic birds and beasts. The ceiling was striped with dark beams and on the walls were pictures that looked exotic and disturbing, of men with too many arms and elephant's heads.

143

There were loads of doors, all shut, except that Kate was charging from one to another, opening them and sticking her head inside, before declaring, 'Bedroom! Yuk! Bedroom you might like, Mum! Another bedroom! Oh, study! Em, come and see. Books!' She went to see. It was a room from E. Nesbit or *The Secret Garden* – the father's study, dark red walls lined with books, a huge leather-topped desk, a fireplace. Except that in those Victorian stories the study was downstairs and inhabited by a stern bearded gentleman with a stiff collar, whereas this one was upstairs, uninhabited, and presumably belonged to Max.

Kate shouted again.

'Oh God. You've got to come and see the bathroom. It's out of a museum!'

It was not very cosy, nothing like their little red bathroom at home. Freezing cold and almost empty, the one window was at ceiling height on the far wall, like in a prison. The walls and floor were covered in black and white tiles. Three chunky basins were lined up along one wall, each with its own towel rail underneath. But dominating everything was the enormous bath which sat majestically on claw feet in the centre of the room. The taps were attached to pipes alongside it and behind them a spaghetti-tangle of plumbing wound its way to a huge brass tank on a decorated stand. Another pipe came out from the top and ran along the ceiling to a shower head the size of a giant sunflower. The tank was covered with dials and knobs labelled 'hot', 'cold', 'building pressure', 'off' that made Emily think of the Inventing Room in *Charlie and the Chocolate Factory*. She went closer. Trying desperately to scale the bath's steep sides was the largest spider she had ever seen. She was transfixed.

'Kate, look!'

'What?' Kate was already bored.

'In the bath. It's horrible. Oh God. I can't move.'

Kate crept closer and looked.

'Ugh! Disgusting. We'll never be able to have a bath. Mum won't move that. It's miles too big to go down the plughole. We need Dad!'

There was an awkward pause.

'What are we going to do?'

'Let's get out of here!'

Kate grabbed Emily's arm in hers and they backed out slowly. Kate felt small to Emily now. It was weird not looking up at her older sister. Her own arms and legs felt too long, out of control almost. Kate was neatly proportioned, just right. It seemed ages since they'd been this close. Out in the corridor, Kate pulled back and looked at Emily.

'Haven't you grown!' she said, putting on a silly high voice.

'I can't help it.'

'I know. It's nice to be tall, though. You could be a model. You're skinny enough too.'

Kate had her head on one side, appraisingly.

'Can I draw you, while we're here?'

Emily was startled.

'Okay. If you want.'

'Right. Good. Now I'm going to get the best bedroom.' And she tried to dash past Emily, who caught hold of her arm, and held her back.

'Not fair. I'll race you.'

'I'll win.'

And they ran gasping down the corridor.

Ben Martin

Ben Martin was born in 1982 and grew up in Cornwall. He completed the MA in Creative Writing at Royal Holloway in 2008, having previously published short stories and freelance journalism. He has lived in Japan, Australia and London, and currently resides on the Gower peninsula where he is working on his novel *All the Right Answers*, the opening of which follows.

All the Right Answers

'OK. Look. What that is, it's you being that she has you be that way, yeah? Understand?'

'Yeah, I get it, Simon, all right?'

The girl huffs her lips big, drops back on to the futon with a thump that rattles the windows. She catches me looking and I blink my gaze to the carpet.

'OK, OK,' Simon says. 'Does anybody in this room think Sarah's complete about that?'

The heads on my left and my right both shake, barely perceptible movements that last no longer than it takes to wipe my palms down the front of my shirt. No one speaks.

'It's all right, Sarah. You can be complete about not being complete.'

'Well, that's what I am then,' she says. 'Complete about not being complete.'

She glares at Simon with her arms tightly crossed and her cheeks are a flustered red. She chews rapidly on the inside of her bottom lip. Looking at her – the bleach blonde spikes, the nose stud, the loud green T-shirt – it feels as though I've just learned a new rule in this strange game; no one that went before her questioned a single thing Simon said.

'All right,' Simon says. A smile teases behind his eyes and lips, not quite breaking the surface. 'Let's leave that one there for now.'

He shifts his position and blood shoots suddenly up through my body, sucking strength from my thighs, arriving on my eardrums with a crackling pulse. The feeling surprises me – I've been telling myself all evening that I'm not nervous.

'Will? How about you, mate? Got anything you need to say to be here?'

Simon is kneeling on the carpet facing me. His back is yogi straight and his palms rest flat on his thighs. That hint of a smile still plays on his lips and his dark brows are raised quizzically, pulling the eyes wide open. But for the slow blinks that come two or three at a time his eyes are locked unwaveringly on mine.

Earlier, closer up, I'd noticed how those eyes were different colours, that one was a flaky mix of blues and greens, the other almost entirely hazel but for a speck of yellow at one o'clock. From this distance – the width of his living room – the detail retreats, leaving just a vague sense of something unusual.

I decide to release the joke I thought of much earlier on.

'Right, so . . . this is the bit where you tell me I hate my parents, right?'

No one laughs.

'Dunno. Do you?'

I hear one or two muffled sniffs around the room but Simon's expression does not change. I try, pointlessly, to calm the tingling heat I know is turning my cheeks maroon, and inwardly curse myself for ever thinking this was a good idea. The frustration shows in my voice as just one note in a chord, made up also of nerves and chagrin and an attempt at indifference.

'No . . . I . . . I'm just not sure what I'm supposed to say here.'

'Anything you need to say to be here,' he says again, slowly, clearly, as if he's explaining something very simple. 'Like, just whatever's been going on in your life recently, or if there's something you wanna get off your chest, or something that's pissing you off. Or whatever.'

I look away, at the pale green evening beyond the window, look back and he is still staring.

I wish I wasn't here. How about that? You're a bunch of spaced out loons. I'm certainly not going to tell you what's been going on in my life recently.

'I'm not sure I do. Have anything to say.'

Simon shrugs with one shoulder and nods. The movement jostles dark licks of hair around his forehead and ears.

'That's cool, man. You don't *have* to say anything.'

The hand on my shoulder had surprised me. Instinctively I clenched fists, spun around to see a tall man in cut-off jeans standing too close behind me. My wallet was in my pocket. I shot my eyes along the beach, up the scrappy tide line, back towards the dunes. There was no one around. At the far end of the beach silhouettes of arms and legs flailed in the shallows and I could just make out the top notes of the children's cries. From this distance though there was little chance that anyone would hear me call.

A grin came over the man's face. He brushed a dark coil of hair away from his forehead and took a step backwards.

'Sorry, mate, sorry to disturb you. I was just wondering if I could take your photo? Just as you were there, sitting on that rock. All kinda . . . thoughtful like.'

Only then did I notice the solid black frame of an expensive-looking camera swinging by its strap from his left hand. He lifted it and removed the lens cap.

Relieved, my reply came out in a hurried breath.

'Yeah, of course, please, yeah, sure.'

He considered me a moment longer then nodded.

'Cool.'

I watched him take another two steps back in the sand and lift the camera to his face.

'If you could just turn around for me then, mate?'

I turned and tried, as best I could, to find how I'd been sitting before. Nothing seemed natural. The rock was suddenly hard and uneven beneath me; I felt aware of every muscle in my body. I could hear him shifting about on the sand behind me and then the camera started to sound, the electronic imitation of an old shutter clicking and whirring and sending prickly waves of self-consciousness through my limbs.

'Awesome, man, that's great. Just a couple more.'

I fixed my attention on the sea. Its great mass heaved in all directions, throwing tiny feathers of spray against the distant cliffs, hissing a foamy white fizz on to the steep sand in front of me. The steady breeze scored criss-cross patterns into its surface; way out on the horizon gulls circled and dived and behind me the camera made its grating electric wheeze.

'OK, nice one, man, thanks a lot.'

I turned around and saw him looking into the back of his camera. He nodded once or twice. I noticed a small black tattoo on his bare forearm. After a few seconds he screwed the lens cap back on and looked up at me with a smile.

'Nice one, mate. So you local, or . . .'

'No. It's my third day here actually.'

'Oh, you on holiday then?'

'No, no, I'm working actually. Hoping to stay for a while though.'

He pursed his lips and nodded approval.

'Awesome place, man, awesome place. You're gonna love it. Me and my wife just moved down here in May – setting up our own business.'

He gave the camera a little lift then looked around. I don't know how I didn't see her before – he must have been obscuring her – but perhaps a hundred yards behind him, walking by the dunes I saw a woman with long honey hair falling loose over her shoulders. A nearly naked, white-haired child hurried on unstable legs a few paces in front of her.

'Anyway, man. Cheers again, yeah. Maybe see you around.'

He took a step forwards, leant in and shook my hand. His grip was tight; I squeezed harder to match it.

'Simon,' he said.

'Will.'

And as I held the handshake, trying to meet his large smile with one of my own, I noticed there was something unusual about his eyes.

I'd tried sleeping on both the beds in my room and they were as hard and lumpy as each other. I lay back on the one nearest the door, staring up at patches of browned damp on the ceiling and following a long crack from one side to the other. I wasn't back from the fresh air long enough that I didn't still notice the room's cloying odour, a heavy perfume that seemed to be disguising something mouldy.

I'd left in such a hurry that I'd made no prearrangements but still, I hadn't counted on Cornwall being this booked up. Or this expensive. As it turned out I was lucky to get even the room I had – a last-minute cancellation from some insightful traveller had made this frowsty, floral-curtained twin available until Friday.

I'd decided not to eat – another evening being stared at by locals in the pub up the road was more than I could bear. I could have made a start on some work; as many times as I told myself internet access was essential I knew, really, that there was a lot I could be doing to *New World*: reading journals, drafting out structures for the early chapters, rereading my *Oxford Guide to Textbook Writing*.

One of the damp patches, if I focused my eyes in the right way, began to resemble a pig's head and body. There was, of course, another option for tonight.

I stood and walked to the window, leaning my weight into my hands on the sill. The view was across a stretch of fields, some quivering with tall green sweetcorn, some freshly ploughed in rutted brown lines. For six thirty the sun seemed high and shadows were still just squat dark puddles at the foot of trees or hedges, but the light had taken on a gentler, more golden hue, bringing out dust and clouds of midges in the air. Sevenish, he'd said. If I left now I could probably still make it.

It would be bullshit, I told myself again. Hippies and wackos and mid-life crises. Somehow though, this wasn't enough. Something kept knocking these rational objections down, as if they were as insubstantial as a paper house, all the while offering nothing as solid as an argument or even a worded thought to explain itself. It was purely a sensation, a gentle but persistent tug on my thoughts that, over the last two hours, had begun to feel physical.

I'd met Simon again only a couple of hours after he'd taken my photo. I was a mile into the hot trudge back to the guesthouse, up a steep, narrow road enclosed by two high hedges, when I'd heard several long and rhythmic blasts of a car horn. I stepped into the hedge, snagging my arm on a bramble, but the horn had sounded again. I turned, ready with a cross expression, and then I saw him, waving at me from the cab of a rusting white van.

It may have been just an offshoot of my embarrassment at being caught about to swear, but I was surprised how pleased I felt to see him.

He pulled up alongside me –

'You wanna lift, mate?'

I climbed in the front seat next to his wife and son and the van smelled of burning oil. He didn't introduce me to his family as we drove up the hill, just said something about the Cornish summer traffic being worse than London, and then fell quiet again until I told him that my guesthouse was just here, next to this lay-by.

'Excellent,' he said, pulling over. I thanked him and my hand was already on the door handle when he said:

'Hey, man – you got any plans for tonight?'

The stairs creaked as I walked down to reception. The phone was next to a rack of glossy leaflets advertising Cornish days out. In the van I'd waited as he scribbled his address down on a torn-off corner of envelope. Standing by the phone I pulled the torn-off scrap from my pocket and straightened it on my palm. If the taxi fare was more than ten pounds, I told myself, I would not go. I read out the address and the man on the other end of the line said twelve. I hesitated two or three seconds, then agreed.

'Right, 'cos it's Will's first meeting I thought we'd do Distinguishing Bernie again if everyone's cool with that? It's ages since we did it and it's always a good reminder,' Simon says.

'Oh absolutely.' The man on my left, Graham, speaks up and nods several times. This guy is exactly what I expected to find here. Fifties and dressed in a suede jacket and a collarless white shirt, almost certainly a divorcee. He shifts back on the sofa and the movement sinks me towards him. I correct this.

Simon turns to the A3 pad propped up on an easel next to him. I was wondering when this would come into play; it's been waiting like a patient assistant by his side since we started. The cover page is innocuous and blue, marked with the stationer's design. In the bottom-right corner the pages frill upwards, dogged and revealing shaded glimpses of the white sheets. Graham clears his throat and down to my right Kaz, Simon's wife, stretches her legs out along the carpet.

Simon is staring at the pad, very still. Positioned as he is he shows me an almost perfect profile, a strong Roman nose, the bumps of his thick lips. Amid the dark stubble that shades his chin and neck I am surprised by a patch of grey.

He snaps his head around, so quickly that it gives me a start.

'All right,' he says, decisively, but with an up note that makes me wonder if whatever decision he just made was spontaneous.

'Let's get present then. Everybody close your eyes.'

Hermione Pakenham

Hermione Pakenham is 24 years old and lives in London. After reading English at university she travelled and worked as a freelance writer for art, fashion and travel publications. She is currently editing an illustrated guide to propaganda and attempting to finish her first novel about the redemptive as well as the destructive power of memory and imagination. This is an extract from the second chapter.

Nine Days of Gloria

High above the river, in a stretching penthouse of glass and mirrors, eight people's chatter stops. Heads are turned away from the city's lights and all eyes but his are on the wall that runs parallel to the view. Dinner is over and the shiny, black table is busy with wax and napkins, spills, glasses and ashtrays, cloudy smudges, place mats and crusts, stray grapes, cigarettes and heavy earrings. The butt crackles as he drops it in the dregs of a wine bottle and finally, he looks up.

'Whoever guesses first gets a present,' says the man standing at the head of the table.

'What?'

'A kiss from Miles!' says the woman at the other end.

'Ink?'

Voices fall out again, the pause only working to encourage noise.

'I refuse to play until I know the prize.'

'Not ink,' says Miles. 'Trust me, it's something you'll like,' he says, turning to the woman on his right.

'Watercolour?'

'No.'

'Oil?'

'Ooh, ooh, I know!'

'Not oil.'

'I'm not sure Isobel should be allowed to play. Surely she's at an unfair advantage?' says a second man.

'I haven't even guessed yet,' replies Isobel.

'Drugs?'

'What?'

'Are we allowed to get up?' asks an American woman.

'No, you have to guess from here,' says Miles's wife.

'It wouldn't be much use disqualifying you after you've guessed,' says the second man.

'The prize is something powdery.'

'Poppy, shut up and guess what the mural's painted with,' says Miles.

'David, you're cheating,' says Miles's wife, who wonders why he must always win.

'Charcoal,' David states.

'Nope,' replies Miles.

'Mud?'

'Miss Isobel! Not just a pretty . . .'

'Miles!'

'Mud?'

'Um . . . not sure you weren't disqualified, Is –'

'Why? I don't paint in mud,' says Isobel.

'She doesn't paint at all,' says David, returning to his seat.

Twelve eyes stop and look at him. Isobel's face is frozen on the mural.

'She draws.'

'I paint too,' says Isobel, turning.

'I know you do, darling, I just wanted you to win,' he says.

Isobel smiles at her husband and the woman named Poppy feels sure she will never marry. Miles's wife wonders when it was Isobel got so thin and why on earth Miles is still standing.

'Love, sit down.'

'How much is it worth?' asks David.

'Independent of the flat?'

'Yes.'

'I have no idea,' says Miles, sitting.

'Any offers?'

'A few, though we haven't put it on the market yet. Clem won't let me.'

'Maybe I'll buy it,' says David.

'No, you can't!' says Clem. 'At least not until I've had a party and cycled around naked and . . . and let a red balloon float down the Thames.'

'The last thing we need is another roulette chip hanging on our walls,' says Isobel.

'Ah, but this time, darling, the roulette chip would *be* the wall,' says David.

The American looks at him blankly.

'Isobel thinks art should be free.'

'No, I think art has become an expression of how expensive it is.'

'As opposed to . . .?' asks the American.

Isobel smiles and with eyes cast down laughs, 'Well, anything else.'

Another silence, a flatter, shorter pause.

'I agree with you,' says the American's wife, too loudly. 'Art today is like buying a car or a house: it's about show.'

David's half smile has dropped and his eyes now look purposely glazed. He sits back in his chair.

'That's just the age we live in,' says Miles.

'Not all of us . . .' says Isobel. 'Some of us buy art for the experience it produces.'

'Who?' laughs Miles. Isobel throws the cork she has been picking towards Miles. He catches it.

'Hands!' says Poppy, lifting her head from cutting lines.

'So you don't like the mud?' asks Miles.

'No, I don't, I think its ugly and untruthful. I don't see –'

'*Untruthful?*'

'Well, if it's meant to be a reflection of this flat, of the river . . . I look at it and see circles in mud . . . The background should be black not white and the circles shouldn't meet, or at least not all of them. They should be different sizes –'

'Maybe you have to see it in the daylight at low tide. It really does feel like you have a little bit of the river sitting all the way up here,' Clem says.

'I think that would make me feel sad,' says Isobel.

'What if it's an ironic statement about the cost of this flat? Like . . . like you're paying through the nose to live on a muddy river bank that's going to be flooded pretty soon anyway,' says Poppy.

'But then you start reasoning with it; reason has its own ways of explaining life.'

David, having remained silent, ends the discussion he started with a definite: 'Well, if that's the case we might as well still be monkeys sitting in our trees pointing at bananas because they remind us of feeling full.'

Everyone laughs.

'Drugs up!' says Poppy, who will never note the urgency in her voice as being anything more than too much wine: David and Isobel will continue to stand for the loyalties, private jokes and judgements of a world she is not part of.

Driving home he thinks how late they had arrived at dinner, but if their parts were to be believed he had to allow the play to begin on the way there. He had ignored her defiant deafness at his shouts that there would be traffic. When she finally came downstairs he did not mention the time. He swallowed the fire and said she looked pretty. He made sure his tone was of a certain pitch; but he knew he had to say it: that that would hurt her more. She did it of course to make him hate her. The game was his too; he relished their nightly successes of hiding the skeleton, but the dress, the hair; those were directed at him alone.

But now the night is over and his blood is running warmer. For a moment at dinner he loved her even: a perfect painting of elegance against a night of indulgent red and white mess.

'Clemy seems happy,' he says.

He looks across at her but she is facing away from him, staring into the night or her own reflection.

'The American girl . . .'

'Lisa?'

'Yes. Boring?' he asks.

'Not especially, no.'

Silence. Her movement, or lack of it, is too conscious now.

'Good looking.'

'Really?'

'Yes. In that American sort of way,' he says.

'Healthy.'

'Symmetrical, balanced.'

Silence.

'Well, you do love symmetry,' she says.

The audience has left and the lighting backstage is too bright. God forbid that one night she should keep her costume on.

'And you find it boring?'

'Yes.'

There is a pause whilst he manoeuvres into the drive. He turns off the engine and places his hands back on the wheel. Slowly he exhales and leans his head back.

'So I was right.'

She turns to look at him but his eyes are shut. She gets out of the car and lets herself into the house, softly shutting the door behind her.

He had watched from a bench on the quad. Four of them sat engrossed as the figure wrestled its bike to the post. The bells sounded across the cobbles, and he thinks they must have been smoking. Her bag kept falling past her head and knocking the front wheel and handlebars round at impossible angles. She was bending lower and lower, trying to join the lock, until she stood up, flushed and angry, only for her bike to crash over and for the books and slides to spill from her satchel. Her eyes fell across them with embarrassment and he felt overwhelmed by tragedy. Helping her pick them up he handed her back pictures of the Colosseum and the Parthenon, Pantheon and Pyramids, Acropolis and the Hippodrome.

She seemed untouched by it all – even then – the drinking and the smoking. When he saw her at parties she moved as if wrapped in a film. She was clean in a space where mascara had run. Against a sheet of high-pitched voices and darting eyes, she was quiet and still. But her voice was steady and her gaze direct. Her movements were accurate but unconscious. Aged twenty he could not conceive that anything so young, so beautiful would not be coherent, simple, open. Getting out of his car, picking up a leaf on his otherwise clean drive, he thinks how grace had been her greatest trick.

A light from the landing above catches her shoes kicked off at the bottom of the stairs. He double-locks the door behind him and turns on the outside light. Walking over to the stairs, he contemplates the shoes; he bends, picks them up and carries on down the hall, past his study. Turning on the kitchen lights, he opens the cellar door and throws stiletto after stiletto into darkness. Before the clattering stops, he shuts the door. He pours himself a glass of water and stands with his back against the sink. The fruit in the bowl is washed and stacked, the tea towels hang in line with the fridge, the granite is clean enough to show another world; a green, star-sparkling, light-reflecting world. Even the drip of the tap seems organised. All of this softly hums of his cleaner: a woman he pays to keep order, a woman he rarely sees but who, just now, he is sure he loves most in the world. Money well spent.

His mother had warned him. Not outwardly, but in her own way. A mother who drank tea from a pot at four-thirty and who found roses excessive; a mother who made her life his and saw weakness in shut doors; who thought fruit juice common and triumphed at not crying, saying 'Tears are vulgar' to a ten year old whose father had died; this mother fell back to noticing 'what a wonderful observer' Isobel was at every opportunity. His mother. He should have seen past the snobbery.

It is late, past two, but his nose and throat are burning and his jaw is tight. He switches off the kitchen lights and stands at the French doors with his glass of water, staring into the garden. It used to paralyse him, not being able to see anything but the lights and reflections of the room inside. Curtains were for people with things to hide: he knew that, but in his own house, he swore he would have shutters and blinds. Older now, the shapes in the night still look foreign and he wonders when he last saw the garden in daylight. Even with the lights in the room turned off he cannot see enough to stop a drop of sweat fall somewhere between his shirt and skin. There is something at the back, right at the back. He cannot remember there being a bush there. He thinks it looks like a crouching figure. Hands poised on the lock he is ready to examine for himself, to explain away the night's uncertainties, when a green square appears on the black lawn. The figure turns to nothing but empty space at the edge of a lawn, his wife in the bathroom above him, her trickery, his mother's unheard warning. He waits for the green to turn black and goes to his study.

Rebecca Prestwood

Rebecca has worked in education and human rights and lived in many exotic locations, including Hong Kong, Thailand, Indonesia and Cleethorpes. Her first novel, *Agency*, is supposed to be about a group of cool young people dealing with sex, violence, guilt and betrayal during the 1997 handover of Hong Kong. Unfortunately, their mothers keep turning up and Rebecca can't stop them.

Agency

Ashley

Hong Kong, January 1997

In the dead light of the Arrivals lounge, I scanned the people, packed in Escher-tight behind the barrier. I was looking for my mother.

Instead my eyes caught a ripple at the back, a Filipino woman unzipping the crowd with her hips. Petals from welcoming bouquets spiralled in her wake. Knotted fingers undid as she ploughed through family groups. A pockmarked taxi-driver found himself back in the second row, hidden from potential customers by a sudden bosom. Centre stage, the woman paused, stared down her scowling enemies. She pulled a sign from inside her jacket and held it above her head, Manchester United top riding up over a narrow roll of brown belly fat. My mother-ready smile crusted over.

The sign had been ripped from a cardboard box and one end had split as it ripped, exposing the corrugated inside so the last letters were shaky. *Arsly*. *Arsly Ceding* it said. She had spelled my name wrong.

Mimi, my mother's maid. She stood in the entrance, ignoring the tuts and looks of people behind her. 'Mum got big do,' she said by way of explaining why Lauren hadn't come. She pulled her top lip up, flashing pointed incisors, and shook my hand, hers rough and dry. She put the sign behind her, then allowed it to fall from her fingers to the floor. A sideswipe with her foot and it was litter, under someone's heel.

She lifted my rucksack off me, grasped my case and began her twisting progress through the crowd. The small of my back felt cold without my rucksack's weight. Mimi turned. She flapped a hand at me, fingers down, a go-back-where-you-came-from kind of gesture, but I guessed it must mean follow me. Looking back, my sign, or Arsly's sign, had been kicked again and lay bent up against the barrier, like an ice skater after a fall.

The space Mimi cleared closed behind her and I pinballed through the crowd. Every thirty seconds Mimi would turn and shout at me

'You want drink?' or 'You want toilet?' and I would shake my head but look into the distance so that people wouldn't know she was talking to me.

She held open a glass door and tipped me into a taxi outside. Two breaths of Hong Kong and I was in the back seat, car air drying the inside of my nose. Mimi organised my bags in the boot and then got in next to me, placing her plastic handbag lovingly between us. If I looked at her she made intense eye-contact, flashed her crocodile smile, waited. So I looked out of the window, my fingers making greasy prints on the cool glass.

The night was slung with neon lights and riddled with Friday-night partygoers, winding their way slowly round the car bonnet whenever we were stuck in a bottleneck. Then we began to climb uphill, leaving the lights and people for trees and tall pink buildings and a blackness somehow thicker than I was used to; a night done in oils.

When we stopped, I waited outside for Mimi to pay. I was still soaked in plane sweat, the Vaseline version of perspiration. I shivered. I wondered if Hong Kong was like the Sahara desert which we had done in geography; hot during the day but freezing at night. Though I was pretty sure that had something to do with landmass. Continental something or other. I wasn't sure it could apply to islands.

Inside, a marble lobby, a bored fat guy half asleep at a desk, a carpeted lift. Silence grew in the sunlight of Mimi's expectant smile; I could feel it coiling, triffid-like, into every corner. 'Have you worked for my mother long?' I asked. My voice cracked, the last word a bird screech.

Mimi flashed teeth, nodded. 'Nineteenth floor,' she said, pointing upwards.

I couldn't tell if she had misunderstood my question or was now making her own bid for conversation. I raised my eyebrows in a show of interest and surprise. 'Ah, nineteenth!' I said.

At the door Mimi exchanged her shoes for flip-flops. She offered me some but I shook my head, unwilling to reveal airplane feet; pale wet grubs, the birth residue of black sock fluff.

A brownish hall, polished wood sticky under rubber soles, a bright white kitchen. Cling-filmed bowls on the side, a jaunty packet of Jaffa cakes. Mimi peeled off plastic, shook it from her fingers to lie on the work surface like a discarded chrysalis.

'I'm not that hungry.'

Mimi began transferring wet meat from the bowl to a saucepan.

'Just tired, really.'

Mimi laughed, switched on the hob.

'If you could just show me my room.'

'Mum said make sure you eat. Airplane food made of plastic.' She shrugged. 'I think is fun, you know? Trolley. Wrapped up food. I say thank you like a party.'

A nose-wrinkling smell drifted towards me, citrus and salt. Mimi skimmed a full bowl along the breakfast bar to me, like a barman in a Western. My first spoonful set my mouth on fire. I ate the next by rolling it between my teeth, throwing it to the back of my throat like a dog with a bone.

When I had eaten enough to satisfy Mimi, she showed me to my room. I got into bed fully clothed, clutching Jaffa cakes. Normally I eat them sponge first, then chocolate, sucking it off my fingernails to be left with a sliver of shiny orange. But tonight I put a whole one straight in my mouth. It's 9 a.m. in England right now, I thought.

I woke before seven, my eyelids snapping open like roller blinds, the flat heavy with sleep. In the bathroom, cut-glass bottles, ruby, emerald liquids shot through with gold sparkles. I opened a pearl-coloured one and sniffed it. It smelled of holidays, like I imagine hope smells. I screwed the cap back on and instead found on top of the cabinet a sliver of soap, marbled with age. I washed at the sink, bending over to do my hair, staggering on one foot to get the other in the bowl, soaking the fluffy bathmat. I dried myself with a hand towel like a wisp of cloud. I thought of towels back home which were baked hard in the tumble-dryer and sometimes smelled funny, like that fake Parmesan you get in a shaker.

Shorts and T-shirt, ready for sunshine. I left my room on tiptoe, hearing every sound through Lauren's ears. The hall walls were covered in a fibrous beige material. I pulled a stray strand and it came away, hairy and sectioned, like a miniature sea rope. In the far corner, a vase on a small curved table. I touched the rim, thin enough to snap like a biscuit. It wobbled and I backed away, hands held out in supplication until it settled into stillness. I peeked in the living room, at a mahogany cabinet peopled by butter-fat porcelain men, cross-legged, their right hands palm outward in greeting.

In a kitchen cupboard, I found a nest of bowls, matt black and square. I levered one out, wincing at the scrunch of china. Special K looked dirty floating in milk tinged grey round the edges.

Then, in my room, I unpacked the stationery I bought on the school trip to France. I picked and pushed new pens out of packets and organised them in drawers. I kept out a pencil and one of those silver pens that you shake and they smell like pear drops. In each of my notebooks I wrote my name, in pencil first and then, when it was neat, in silver, pressing down to release slidey blobs of wet metal. *Ashley Ceding, Miss Ashley Ceding, A. Ceding* of *Bonham Drive, the Mid-Levels, Hong Kong*. I decided on the purpose each book could have for a grown-up and wrote titles, *Diary, Chinese, Quotations, Recipes*. I stacked completed notebooks on my desk, their edges neatly aligned.

I was blowing on *Quotations* to dry it when I heard three taps. My mother, Lauren, in a pink silk dressing gown.

'Ashley! Such an early bird. May I?' She padded in on bare feet and leant against my desk. She picked up one of my books. '*Chinese?*' Her eyes went wide. 'Wonderful. You'll have to teach me.' She put a hand to her chest. 'Still hopeless.'

It was the first time I had seen her in three years.

Mimi came in next in the same football top as the night before. She was carrying a tray and had an empty bin bag over her arm. She ducked her head as she walked between us.

Lauren hadn't changed, except maybe there was something brighter about her. Her hair was no longer honey but pale, like shortbread. Or a Labrador. She was tanned and, despite the dressing gown, already made up – her lips a muted red, her eyes framed by darkening shades of grey.

Mimi pressed the plunger on the cafetière, poured out two cups.

Lauren sat on my desk chair, one brown leg gracefully bisecting the pink silk. 'Now. How was your flight?'

'Fine,' I said. 'How was your party?'

'Oh, so-so.' Lauren glanced round. 'We girls won't be needing milk or sugar, Mimi.'

'Okay, Lauren, ma'am.' Mimi handed us each a cup. Bitter. My mother considered the taste, smiled. 'You are so the best, Mimi.' She put her cup down, carefully, on the desk. 'Did you sleep well?'

'Yes, thanks.'

'I'm so glad. I picked out the bedclothes myself. Egyptian cotton.' She smiled, scratched a forearm, raking up white marks on tanned skin. 'Now. Do you have plans for your first day?'

I wriggled a bit. 'Unpack, I suppose.'

She waved a hand. 'Mimi and I can do that. Adore to in fact.' She smiled. 'You go play. Explore. You must be longing to!' She turned her head, indicated with her chin. 'The bin bag, Mimi.'

Lauren reached over and patted the bedclothes next to my knee. 'For school clothes.' Her red nails looked like ovals cut from a car bonnet. 'We'll do a proper shop.' She sat up again, yawned behind a thin hand. 'Dear me! I simply cannot do late nights any more. Now. Do say if you'd rather keep anything. You're probably thinking, "Silly Lauren, what does she know about fashion?"'

I shook my head.

She glanced at my T-shirt. It said Vaseline on it. 'Oh yes, I know what I must look like to you. And we should anyhow leave you out something warmer. It's quite cold here, in the winter months.'

I shrugged, aware suddenly of my knees, white and bracketed by lumps of fat, poking out of my shorts. I pulled the hems down to cover them.

I watched Mimi shaking out my clothes. She held them up for my mother's nod or shake before flicking them into shop-sharp folds and placing them in a pile to keep or in the open bin bag. The pile to keep didn't get very big.

I stiffened as my T-shirt from my last day at school, covered in biro signatures, went in the bag.

Lauren turned, eyes wide. 'Do you want that? Though if it reminds you of school . . .' She shuddered. 'Eugh, school. Who's not happy that's over? I remember burning those dreadful navy pants the day I left. In the science lab. Imagine. Would you believe they smelled of burning plastic?' We smiled at teenage Lauren burning her pants. I wondered if she had already been pregnant then. If not, it was hardly a good omen. 'And then tomorrow we can go shopping. A whole wardrobe. Like Julia Roberts.'

There was an appeal to the idea, a new me. I looked down at my shorts. They were tie-dye. 'Maybe we could go today?'

'I wish, but I've a silly meeting. For the Children's Fund. We're planning a ball, Handover week! We must be mad.' She leaned in. 'I don't think David is ever going to forgive me, he hates it when I fill the flat up with our ladies.' She pulled a face and turned to Mimi who was putting the small pile of approved clothes in a cupboard. 'I often hide out in the kitchen with you when the ladies are round. Don't I?'

'Oh yes, Lauren, ma'am.' Mimi smiled her swift crocodile smile but her eyes slid away from mine.

My mother laughed. 'We eat the cake, don't we, Mimi?'

'Yes, ma'am.'

'Saving them from themselves, we call it.' She held up a finger as if testing the wind. 'You won't want to be here, will you? Talk talk about nothing very much.' She raked at her forearm again. 'I'll call Sarah, see if you can go round there.'

I felt my cheeks warm. 'Don't bug people for me. I can stay here.'

'It's only Margaret's daughter.'

I shook my head.

'The cellist? Margaret from the Homeless?' She sighed. 'I've talked about them. Sarah is taking a year off from her degree, she's at Cambridge.'

'She's older than me?'

Lauren pouted her lips, coaxing. 'Only two years, Ash. Pash. Dash. Splash.'

'She'll feel like she's babysitting.'

'Don't be a silly. Sarah needs a friend.' Lauren looked at me with raised eyebrows. 'Aren't you going to ask why, you social philistine?'

'Why?' I asked.

'Because Margaret won't be around much longer.'

I thought she meant Margaret was leaving Hong Kong, then I twigged. 'Oh.' I looked down at my lap.

'Do it for me.'

I shrugged, smiled.

'Cool. The black bag, Mimi?'

'What's wrong with Sarah's mum?'

Lauren pulled the corners of her mouth down. 'She has something wrong. Down there.' She inspected her face in my mirror, pressing a line next to her eye and sighed. 'Sarah's a brave little soldier.' She smiled, close mouthed. 'You're here! I just can't believe it!' She held her hands out as if inviting me into the space between but I didn't move and she adjusted her robe collar, opened the door. 'You're going to have such fun. I really feel it.'

Mimi stood up too, the knot of the now full bin bag in her fist. Eyes down, she moved cups to the tray, picked it up, balanced it on her fist. Before following Lauren, she looked back, flicked up lacquer-black eyelashes. I started to smile but she was gone, shutting me in with a nudge of her hips.

Suzanne Ramadan

Suzanne Ramadan was born in Sydney, Australia. She studied Economics and worked in the finance industry before staging a timely exit and moving to London. The following is the first chapter of her first novel, *The Floating Boater*.

The Floating Boater

Chapter One

Naima Ikram's birthmark prickled. She firmly believed that there was pleasure in the deferral of relief but the hot and itchy sensation from her birthmark had intensified over the afternoon, and now she could think of nothing but her desire to rub it. As the wind whipped through her hair and the car radio crackled with poor reception, she looked sideways at Fawzy. He kept a firm, two-handed grip on the steering wheel and a lop-sided smile at the road ahead.

She delicately patted her neck with a handkerchief, intending to manoeuvre her hand to her chest and scratch it, but lost her nerve. The risk of Fawzy noticing any such movement, she decided, was too great on this momentous day. Oh brother, it was unbelievable, how much she wished to scratch it. She unfurled her cramped legs and shifted her weight awkwardly on the seat, taking care to avoid jostling the cardboard box that sat by her feet. Two weekends ago, this very box had carried two dozen mangos home from Mario's fruit stall in the Haymarket. Today it carried pickled lemons, jars of green olives, and sesame paste, to a house that she had never seen before, in a town that she knew nothing about. Like it or loathe it.

The back seat of the car was stacked with similar-looking boxes that heaved with her favourite dried pulses: borlotti beans, cannellini beans, fava beans, black-eyed peas, chickpeas.

'This is entirely unnecessary, *ya butta,* we will find everything we need there,' Fawzy had insisted when he saw her preparing an assortment of ground spices into glass jars. He repeatedly assured her that Burraboo would be bountiful in all respects, '*ya butta*, why so much?' but these confident assertions had made her even more anxious and inspired a secret, final visit to her favourite deli yesterday, for even more olives and salted pumpkin seeds. Just to be sure. Who knew what they would find when they reached Burraboo?

Sweat streamed down Naima's back as they drove through a slash of blue gum forest. Sitting below her collarbone, her birthmark sprawled over her right breast like a puddle of spilt soup. During episodes like this, when her birthmark prickled and seared with heat, it would turn a slightly darker shade of claret; and her right nipple would become as hard as a lemon pip. This had been a constant source of embarrassment to Naima over the years and required her to fold her arms against her chest for long periods, a posture that many misunderstood as arrogance.

'The car smells like a falafel shop,' said Fawzy, his voice rising above the radio static and the din of the clunky motor.

Naima stopped humming and stared at him, delight and surprise twisting her mouth into a wry smile. The hot January afternoon had punctured nothing of his enthusiasm, and even in the woozy subclimate of their car, sticky with spilt cola and reeking of unidentifiable burnt plastic, his voice shimmered with happiness. She was quite unaccustomed to this new unclouded manner of his.

'We could be on Safia Zaghloul Street, queuing up for lunch at Mohammed Ali Ahmed, don't you think?' said Fawzy. As if to reinforce his point, a gust of hot air through the open windows discharged a fragrant blast of cumin and coriander from deep within the boxes to the front of the car.

Naima chewed her bottom lip, reluctant to dent Fawzy's good mood with her misery.

'You know I prefer the one in Moharem Bey,' she said. 'I could eat a plate from there right now,' and she smiled at him with a deceptive show of pleasure when, more than anything right now, more than her desire to stretch her legs, or eat a falafel from Moharem Bey Street, she wished to scratch at her hot, prickling birthmark.

'You've bought enough supplies to make your own falafel for a year,' continued Fawzy.

'Everyone in the Paprika Triangle tells me it will be difficult to find macaroni in a small town like Burraboo. They say that even in parts of Sydney it's hard enough to find spaghetti that doesn't come in a tin,' she said.

'This is nonsense talk. It's 1974, not 1904. Who tells you this nonsense talk, anyway?'

'Lots of people tell me. Jehan and Leila . . . even Nabil warns me about this.'

Fawzy pulled a face but his eyes remained fixed on the road. 'You shouldn't listen to Nabil. He is all talk and no trousers.'

'I'll miss my friends,' she sighed, after a long silence.

'Ah. You'll make new friends,' Fawzy said, nodding his head rapidly. He swerved to avoid a brown muddle of fur from the shoulder of the road.

'It won't be the same as the Paprika Triangle.'

'No, it will be much better,' he said. 'Everything will be better, believe me. And after all, I have my hearing back.' His voice boomed with triumph.

'Yes, of course. Your hearing,' she said. Unbelievable, how his spirits rose with every kilometre taking us further from Sydney, she thought.

'And I will earn a good wage now, no more rubbish jobs for you or me. I think we should buy a new car soon, how does that sound?'

She looked out of the car window. Sprawling grey-green coloured treetops sat beneath the blue of a sky like a crumpled sheet.

Naima turned to face her husband's profile. His dark sideburn fanned low and wide on his cheek and revealed the odd white hair. When he pressed his lips together, as he did now, dimples grazed his cheeks. *Yo-oh, here we go.* All discussions about Burraboo inspired in Fawzy this maddening lip movement.

'But it must be an Australian car. Holden. What do you say?' said Fawzy, his voice rising enthusiastically.

Naima leaned back heavily into the car seat, wearied by this Burraboo talk. Their friends in Sydney had all laughed when they announced that they were moving to a coastal town called Burraboo. 'Eh? Burraboo? What is Burraboo?' they had teased. The men had hooted and slapped Fawzy's back and took turns shouting various mispronunciations of Burraboo. Nabil suggested that it sounded like a type of fish, best eaten fried.

179

The breeze from the open windows was cooling, but even so, the crisply ironed clothes that she and Fawzy wore had started to crumple in the heat. She patted her hairline around her forehead gingerly with her fingers. *Yo-oh.* The stickiness of the afternoon had destroyed the elegant, clean sweep she had created this morning and replaced it with frizzle. All that twisting and straightening, and for what? For this? Tchh. She checked her hair in the side mirror. Frizz sprouted around her face and over the coil of hair she had meticulously arranged at the back of her head. Ruined. Her hair was a madman, and every day was full moon. She attempted a few feeble pats over the top of her hair. But the damage was done, her misery complete.

She pulled out a handful of salted pumpkin seeds from a plastic bag on her lap and concentrated on extracting the seed from the shell. With her teeth she made two deft crunches per seed. Always two, for good luck. She offered some to Fawzy, who shooed the bag away. Between crunches, she listened to him talk about the miraculous feat of construction that was the Pacific Highway. Each new acclaim of engineering prowess presented by Fawzy reminded Naima that they were moving a little further away from her Paprika Triangle.

Oh, she knew she could make a go of it in Burraboo. She could make a go of it anywhere. Anywhere, she told herself. They had agreed on two years. And what is two years anyway? The two years they had lived in Sydney had whirred by as quickly as the hands of an accomplished drummer on a tabla.

A strip of hard, burnished light slanted over the passenger side of the car and on to Naima's left cheek. The car radio hissed into a new frequency of static. Why, today, must everything be so unbearable? Queasy with dread and nerves and too many pumpkin seeds, she lunged impatiently for the radio dial.

'*Yo-oh.* I can't find a station,' she huffed, a few seconds later.

'Keep trying, my duck. You'll find the right frequency.'

'You think there is a right frequency? I tell you, there is nothing to tune into at all,' she said, and swung the dial quickly as though she were turning a stubborn door knob.

'You won't find it like that. Let me do it.' Fawzy hustled for the dial and after a minute or so the static made way for the vague semblance of music. 'You see?' he said smugly, and settled back into his seat.

When finally they turned off the highway and on to the narrow, poorly paved road leading into Burraboo, it was almost 3 p.m. Flanked by stringybark woodland, the Valiant bounced and rattled on the uneven surface for a few minutes, and when the road suddenly smoothed out, there was a large signpost that read: *Welcome to Burraboo*.

Fawzy whistled and honked the horn and raised both hands joyously off the steering wheel for a few seconds, making the car swerve and Naima yell at him. He laughed and squeezed Naima's knee and larked about the car's clutch having survived the journey from Sydney. As they approached the town centre Naima twisted her body towards the cluster of roadside shops to gain a better view.

'Look, Fawzy, look!' She pointed her hand out of the window. 'There's your pharmacy.'

'Not mine yet,' said Fawzy, slowing the car down and peering over Naima's shoulder to stare at the *Burraboo Pharmacy*. There was giddiness in his voice, something more than excitement, that Naima had not heard before.

A few cars were parked on Main Road. A woman and a child on the street stared at the dusty Valiant as it crawled towards *Ted the Butchers*. Under the faded green awning of the *Royal Hotel*, a dog barked at them. A clump of woodland was followed by a petrol station, then more woodland. All this empty land, Naima thought, so much space.

In Sydney, they had lived in an apartment block in Petersham that sat below the flight path. It was red brick, as was every apartment block that surrounded them, and for this reason Naima had named their neighbourhood the 'Paprika Triangle'. It was the golden mile of Petersham because there was always something to remind her of Alexandria: old women with arthritic ankles who wrapped their scraggly hair in black scarves, Nino who roasted his almonds in such a way as to rival Emil's on Ruml Street, and the men who congregated for hours on the sidewalk, smoking and chatting on warm nights. In the

Paprika Triangle, the apartment balconies were lined on top of one another like a stack of dirty dishes. The drone of traffic from the nearby Parramatta Road rose and fell like a wheezing troll, while train lines to the rear of their apartment block made a rattle that snaked through the belly of the building. In the flat above the Omars' and next to the Faraks', they were swaddled by the songs of Abdul Halim Hafez and scents that lingered: fried garlic, chilli and tomatoes. There was a tiny deli a few blocks away that sold olives out of large barrels. Aniseed, cloves, nutmeg and sesame seeds were sold by weight from large casks. Lebanese bread came three times a week from a bakery on the other side of Sydney; Fawzy refused to eat the Lebanese loaves, insisting that the only bread he would touch would be white and fluffy, pre-cut and sandwich ready. 'No need to cling to the old ways. What is the point of coming here?' he would scold.

Fawzy made a sharp left-hand turn into a small street, a cul-de-sac, and cleared his throat before announcing, 'Hungerford Place. This is it.' The Valiant croaked to a crawl as Fawzy scanned the letter-box numbers. 'Look for number six,' he instructed. At the end of the street was a mass of uncleared land, which stretched into the back of the block and beyond. Bush bled into bush.

He brought the car to a sudden stop. 'Where is number six?' Fawzy muttered in confusion. He stepped out of the car frowning and surveyed the street. Number six was inexplicably absent, with the house number sequence presented as two, four, eight. Turning to the entrance of the street, he squinted at a large three-level sandstone house situated well off the road and up a steep hill. It was the only property without a street number. It wasn't quite on Hungerford Place, but rather on the T-section where it crossed the street perpendicularly.

'Maybe it's this one,' he said hesitantly.

'Are you crazy? It's the biggest house on the street, Fawzy.'

'Well, maybe it is, but –'

'What exactly did they say to you?'

'They said to go to number six.'

They took another look up at the majestic sandstone house.

Fawzy drew a deep breath. 'Wait here, I'll ask,' he said.

He bounded up the steep lawn with sprightly steps. Naima scratched her birthmark hard with her fingernails as she watched him speak with someone at the door. A dull throbbing began to emanate from her chest as her skin started to swell.

She stepped out of the car. Beyond the curve of the street, beyond the mass of uncleared bush, an exquisite finger of deep blue sat above the distant treetops and below the pallid sky. It was startling to see that wedge of blue so unexpectedly close.

When Fawzy jogged back to the car he was panting a little. 'Did you see how near we are to the sea? Your father would approve,' he said, speaking in short breaths. 'Can you believe it? We are here. This is home.'

Naima looked at him, uncertain, her hand placed casually over her chest. The two well-dressed strangers in Hungerford Place stood still for a moment; the neat, slender man with the dimpled cheeks and the anxious woman with the intricate hair arrangement, as the briny air thickened around them.

Ayndrilla Singharay

Ayndrilla Singharay is from north London. She completed her BA in English literature at University College London in 2004, her PGCE in 2006 and since then has been teaching in a secondary school for children with severe learning difficulties. Her writing concerns the Bengali community in both London and Calcutta. This is an extract from the opening chapter of her first novel, provisionally titled *City of Old Demons*.

City of Old Demons

Chapter One

Manik was a few steps ahead of Kamala, skipping his way through piles of lifeless leaves. He was a boy entirely swallowed by his coat; his sister's old red duffle coat, which Kamala hoped would last him until his ninth birthday. He was growing so reluctantly that this seemed ever more likely. The small satchel on his shoulders jumped, as he stirred up the leaves and the sound of waves rolled along the pavement. Kamala gathered up the end of her green sari and waded through the dry sea to catch up with her son.

A handful of leaves still clung to north London's branches. They fluttered heroically in the sharp wind, but soon even they would leap to earth and in their defeat they would mark the real beginning of winter. Kamala smiled; she preferred the colder months of the year, the ceremonious act of wrapping herself in layers made every outing seem like an adventure. The cupboard next to her front door was a medley of scarves, hats and gloves and it was with a quiet rapture that she unlatched the wooden doors and selected the items according to her mood. Before she left the house to collect Manik from school, she chose black leather gloves to go with her long, sturdy coat, and draped her neck with a deep green scarf to match her sari. Green and black made her feel instantly glamorous; from a distance, she considered herself quite attractive.

Manik began to take deliberate two-footed jumps along the pavement and on the third jump, an alarmed pigeon arose like grey fire from a leaf-pile. Manik turned his hooded head and a pair of dark, bright eyes looked to Kamala for a reaction.

'Walk nicely, please,' she called, tilting her head gently. Manik nodded, turned back and was all coat again.

Lately, Kamala had counted many more birds in the trees, although she soon realised that they must have always been there. She could see them, because the walls of their homes had fallen away. Pigeons, magpies, sparrows: nests on display for admirers and predators alike. This was the tragedy of the animal kingdom: to have their lives laid bare, never to know privacy.

Kamala and Manik turned the corner into the familiar rhythm of semi-detached houses. From the outside, they looked irresistibly uniform; red brick doll's houses and tidy front gardens with clean, painted white gates. Their symmetry pleased Kamala now just as it had sixteen years ago, when she and Abhik were first shown the house by a young man who grinned energetically to apologise for its small-ness. That man could have saved his smiles. For while Abhik hoped for a home with high ceilings and never-ending floors, Kamala knew from the beginning that this was not Calcutta. Life here meant a life without servants, and if she alone would be preserving cleanliness in the house, it would have to be of a manageable size. Number sixteen became theirs in a matter of weeks and now, every time Kamala turned the corner into Beresford Road, she relived the enduring satisfaction of a decision well made.

Manik pushed the gate open and stood patiently facing the front door; a coat-shaped patch of red on royal blue. Kamala turned the key and he rushed inside, climbing out of his coat and shedding half his volume. Manik's body did not reflect his eight years of living. Smaller and narrower than the rest of his classmates, he sometimes made Kamala fear for his health. But his hair, a solid, metallic black, and his eyes, endlessly searching, were enough to convince her that Manik was in tip-top condition. Arms and legs could be fleshed out over time; hair and eyes you were stuck with.

Manik kicked off his trainers and shut himself in the downstairs toilet. Kamala folded her gloves and scarf and put them back inside the cupboard. She stood in front of the mirror to smooth down her wind-blown hair. It was black, like her son's, but a few pale strands had appeared over the last few years so that her head was partitioned by shiny silver veins. The rest of her hair hung over her right shoulder in a dense rope, tightly plaited together by strong, determined fingers. Her face, small and flushed with cold, was clean of make-up except for a thin layer of black kajal that framed her round eyes. She rubbed her cheeks, blinking. She did not look forty-three, although she could not tell if she looked younger or older.

As she reached to hang up her coat, a warm contentment flooded Kamala's body; it started from the tips of her nails, the colour of cinnamon, down through her wrists, weighted by gold, under the invisible hairs of her pale brown arms; it poured down her neck, like a drink, filling her chest and trickling down to her abdomen; it washed over her stretch marks, silver snakes wriggling down her hips, it swam along her heavy legs, and finally settled in her feet and toes.

She sat down on the steps and took off her shoes, bare toes sinking into the carpet. She was home.

Piyali returned from school half an hour later. From the kitchen, Kamala heard the dragged scraping of her boots along the front path followed by the door slamming with a careless push, which made the house shudder. 'Hello,' called Kamala. She pulled the wooden spoon through the huge pot of dal, watching the flat yellow beads melting into thick paste. More water. She reached for the kettle, still steaming, and poured with one hand, continually stirring with the other.

'Stinks in here.'

Piyali stood in the kitchen doorway, a woman with a girl's face. Her hair was long and untidy, and Kamala longed to brush it. Unlike her brother, Piyali was growing relentlessly. Kamala, who secretly measured her children's development in doorways, noticed that the top of her daughter's head was closer to the top of the frame than the last time she had checked.

'It will stink even more if you keep that door open,' said Kamala, putting down the kettle and spoon and wiping her hands. 'How was your day?'

Piyali closed the door and dropped her bag on the dining table.

'OK.'

'Did you get the results back from your maths test?'

'Yeah, I got seventy-two per cent.'

She took a slice of processed cheese out of the fridge.

'Seventy-two is very good,' said Kamala. 'That's a B, isn't it?'

Piyali roughly tore small pieces from the glossy square that stretched like rubber, and ate them in quick succession.

'Yeah,' she said between mouthfuls. 'Can I go upstairs now? I have homework.'

'Wait a minute. If seventy-two is a B, how much is an A?'

'Don't know. Probably, like, eighty.'

'OK, OK. Something to aim for then.'

Piyali looked at Kamala from under disgruntled eyelashes.

'Getting a B in maths is pretty good.'

'Of course it's good,' said Kamala, 'I just want you to do the best you can, that's all.'

'I'm going now, OK?'

'O-K,' said Kamala, gently pushing a few black tangles behind Piyali's ear.

Piyali picked up her bag and left the room, a mess of black and white school uniform, that Kamala would later smell for traces of cigarette smoke. As yet, she had not smelled fumes in Piyali's clothes but she continued to study them, breathing in the other scents of her daughter's life. Deodorants and body sprays seemed to change every week; sweet lemons tickled Kamala's nostrils and then a few days later, rich vanilla buttered the inside of her mouth. Spilled food, paint and nail polish all found its way into Kamala's hands and lungs; they spoke the words that Piyali had stopped saying.

In July she had allowed her mother to plait her hair and told her about friends and school with an urgency that made Kamala shed twenty years as she listened. But August slowly stole Piyali's old voice, and by September she kept her eyes low and gave nothing away. Kamala knew that in a few short years Piyali would re-emerge into an adult version of the girl abducted by summer, but until then, she would have to learn to get along with the part-Piyali who had taken her place, the one who stormed silently around her house.

The dal looked better; the water had loosened the mixture. Now when Kamala stirred it, it swam smoothly around the pot. Free to tidy up, she turned the ring of blue fire down to an almost invisible halo and examined the state of the kitchen with two careful, rotating eyes.

Kamala's idea of a perfect kitchen was one in which only she could set foot. A kitchen where she would not find her white-tiled worktop strewn with the crumbs of between-meal toast-making; where the soles of boots and trainers did not streak black lines shaped like commas and exclamation marks all over her mock-wooden floor. Now, there were traces of her family on every surface. The sink contained Manik's plate, from which he had dutifully eaten a banana and a slice of bread with honey, with small, unthinking bites. He ate because he had to, without pleasure or discomfort. Abhik's brown jacket, with the gold-coloured zips, hung from the back of the door; it was now thick with the smell of dal. He would not be irritated by this, though. For him, the smell of food could never be a bad thing.

Piyali's closed sketchbook lay on the wooden table. She carried it with her everywhere; to school, to friends' houses, on holiday. One corner of the black book always poked out of her bag, like a dog's vigilant ear. She would come back down any minute now, to retrieve it.

Next to the table, in the alcoves of the wall, were things that forever changed places. Pieces of paper with scribbled messages – 'Back by 7'; 'M at Joshua's house'; 'Potatoes' – waiting to be turned over and reused; chipped mugs too attractive to throw away, leaning with pens and pencils; large books about food, numbers and Tagore. The only item never to move was the most used: the telephone, anchored by cables, occupied the lowest shelf. This simple machine held absolute power over all of them: the fifth voice in the house and the only one they all listened to without question.

The alcoves were the only part of the room inside which chaos was permitted to reside. And yet objects regularly extended their legs and strolled outside their confines, forcing Kamala to acknowledge that the kitchen belonged to all of them, that it would inescapably alter with the day, as early light deepens to late.

But there was a sacred interval, while everybody in the house slept, when Kamala's kitchen stayed exactly how she had left it. She usually woke up well before Abhik or the children, and sat at the table, sipping at a cup of tea in her warmest dressing gown. Spectacularly alone, in a room untouched – that was how she liked to begin her day.

She gathered up the long spoons and knives that cluttered the worktop and put them into the sink. As she turned on the tap, cold water surged out in a crystal column and struck the flat surface of a spoon with such force that it fountained out in a perfect circle, splashing her plastic apron and the wall behind the sink. As she turned the tap down, Piyali came back.

'I'm really hungry. Can we eat soon?' She picked up the sketchbook from the table and Kamala checked the white face of her watch.

'It's nearly five. I can have dinner ready by five-thirty. OK?'

Piyali made a pained face. 'I'm so hungry though,' she said, the 'so' pulled far beyond its purpose.

'Didn't you have any lunch?'

'Yeah.'

'What did you have?'

'Packet of crisps.'

'Oh-ho! Is that a lunch? No wonder you are hungry.' Kamala picked up an apple and put it into Piyali's hand. 'Fifteen minutes. Call your brother.'

They were around the table. Outside, darkness leaned on the curtainless door and windows that led to the garden and Kamala felt observed. In the daytime she had not missed the curtains, for they were always open, but now in the midst of the sunless afternoon, she longed to close them. They were drying on the upstairs hall radiator; she would put them back into place as soon as the children had finished.

Piyali was slumped, in a hooded jumper much too big for her; Manik stared out of the black window, resting a tired cheek on his hand; Kamala stood over them both, sari'd legs pressed into the side of the table, dishing out hot dal, white rice and mixed vegetables.

Manik ate with his hands; parcelling dry and wet together with his father's ease. From Piyali's plate there were tapping sounds. She said she did not want hands like her mother's – yellowed by colourful cooking – so she used a knife and fork, even for rice. Watching her daughter struggle to scrape up the last few grains of rice, she wanted to scoop them up with her own fingers, pinch them together and pop them into Piyali's waiting mouth.

'Keep some room, I made chicken,' she said, as Manik began to lick his plate. She carried a brown saucepan from the hob to the table and uncovered it. The heavy smell of slow-cooked chicken and onions made Kamala's stomach mumble. Manik looked around, searching. 'What was that?'

'Nothing, shona, just my tummy growling,' said Kamala. 'Can I give you a big spoonful?'

Manik nodded excitedly and watched the sauce pool around his plate, shining with oil.

'Why don't you have some, then?' asked Piyali. 'If you're hungry.'

'I'm waiting for your Baba, you know that,' replied Kamala.

E. J. Swift

E. J. Swift studied English and American Literature at Manchester and has worked as a bartender and teacher in Paris. Her novel, *Osiris*, is set in a futuristic city whose inhabitants believe they are the last citizens on earth. The novel follows the interlocking stories of Vikram, a third-generation climate refugee, and Adelaide, the architect's granddaughter.

Osiris

Prologue

He sits on the balcony with his legs hanging over the edge and his face pressed between two railings. Beyond the bars lies the great vault of the city and its pale roof of sky. He does not see an architectural masterpiece, although there are lines of beauty here that exist nowhere else. What he sees is a maze of luminous shapes, ignited by the sun.

He has spent hours in this space, high in the eyries of Osiris, where gulls and other birds wheel and screech their hunger. Sometimes he stands and leans over and peers into the depths of the morning mist. At other times he perches on the railings, with death at his side like a neighbour. Occasionally he sleeps. The cold is hostile, and he is not dressed to face it. He wakes in the frost, trembling, surprised still to be here.

In the brittle air he feels, acutely, the internalised heat of his body battling with the outside draught. His blood pulses, bright and torrid. His heart tattoos a rhythm in his chest. Icy stone pushes against his bare feet. When the storms come, the elements sweep around him in multilingual conference: rain lashes the windows and his skin, wind claims the moisture back. He turns his face to the heavens and closes his eyes.

Once, people came and found him here. They spoke to him, and when he was silent they begged him to talk and when he talked their eyes grew strange and harboured clouds. But it has been a long time and the findings are things of the past, things that lie almost beyond the reach of memory. He holds on to only one. He has forgotten her name, but she tumbles through the world: bold, vital and violent. He cannot let her go because she knows no fear.

People still watch, although he is unconscious of their surveillance and the whispers that shroud him. These stories skip along bridges, ride up and down the glass lifts. From unseen lips, they echo in the hollows of a dozen ears. They make good copy. There are episodes when he leaves the balcony, even leaves the penthouse it is attached to, and then the Reef field buzzes and tingles in the keys of many different voices. But days pass, and his expeditions have become rarer. He keeps time for the city, watching it dissolve around him.

He knows there is something he has to do. A mystery he has to solve. It is in the water. It is in the ice.

One morning, in the lilac hours before dawn, he lifts his arms as if they are wings. They have spoken at last. It is in the water, he knows it now. He climbs the railings. For a moment he poises, absolutely still. The city is hushed.

But now he hears it. At first barely audible, then louder, as it has been growing these past few months, or even years. Hooves beating on the skin of the waves. They run like streamers in the wind. Foam flies about their salted coats; the horses.

No one is awake to see him fall. His body hurtles earthwards, faster than the diving gulls, faster than a rumour. The air rushes against him. Windows flee his reflection. He crashes into the sea and vanishes instantly beneath the surface, leaving only a faint trace that is quickly gone.

Chapter One: Adelaide

Adelaide first felt something was wrong in the aftermath of the speech. Her father had voiced the formalities, and now those who remained had the chance to speak to the family. The guests were tentative. They offered their sympathy like a gift, of whose appropriateness and reception they were as yet unsure. Buoyed by coffee or weqa, a few dared to meet Adelaide's eyes, but most looked at the bridge of her nose or into a space over her shoulder. She watched them hunting for the right words. They wanted to say something. Or at least they wanted to be seen to say something. Unfortunately, none of the usual phrases – 'so sorry for your loss' – were much use. How do you condole for a missing person? How do you grieve?

Her father had managed it very well. It was a month since Axel's disappearance, and Feodor had staged this event. He named it a

Service of Hope. The phrase was written out on a diminishing supply of cards, by hand: 'the Rechnov family invites you to a service of hope for our son and brother, Axel'. There was no order of ceremony on the cards, but it was firmly established in Feodor's head. First the assembly, with a solo pianist providing background music. The repertoire was classical; nothing too well known, or too sentimental. A few words explaining the situation, for protocol's sake rather than to fill anybody in. And then Feodor's speech.

He spoke adeptly, as he always did. The connecting doors had been flung wide, and Feodor's voice carried to every nook of the panelled suite. The rooms were quiet and graceful, their walls striped with narrow ribbons of mirror, red cedar and sequoia. Subtle lamps drew out the natural richness of the wood, whose polished surface gathered hazy impressions of those who passed. Potted ferns tangled with their reflections. Other than these plants and a scattering of tables and chairs, the rooms were unadorned. They were also windowless. Adelaide's brothers had hoped that the informality of a small, intimate space would make for a more congenial atmosphere than was traditionally associated with the Rechnovs.

At the walls, security guards stood rigidly enough to be all but invisible. Only their eyes, constantly roving, revealed alertness.

Adelaide had wedged herself into an alcove. The alcove was wide enough for two people, seated, but Adelaide crammed her legs in too, denying anyone else access. Two things separated her further from proceedings: a lace veil covering half of her face, and the fronds of a metre-high fern. From her semi-hiding place, the rooms, full of figures and reflections, did not look quite real. She couldn't help hearing her father though.

Incense and cedar permeated the air. Adelaide hadn't eaten all day; the sweetish smell and lack of food were making her feel nauseous. She squeezed her hands against her knees. The roughish cotton of her trousers was comforting. She loosened her tie and undid the top button of her shirt, and felt a little better.

'. . . finally, the family would like to thank you for your continual support and your generous messages. We await news of Axel with anticipation, and as always, with hope.' There was a pause. Adelaide knew that Feodor was taking a pinch of salt from a tin and throwing it, in the direction where a window would have been. 'Thank you, once again.'

Syncopated claps through the rooms. When the sound died out there was a difficult silence, before murmurs and music recommenced. The service, despite the oration, remained unresolved.

Adelaide stayed where she was, and wondered what she should do next.

Feodor's address had already triggered numerous arguments amongst the family. Adelaide in particular had spoken out.

'You can't talk about Axel like he's some kind of saint. Nobody is going to swallow that.'

Those words had resounded just a fortnight ago, and they had all been present, sitting around an oval conference table on the ninetieth floor of Skyscraper 193-South. It was neutral ground. Beyond the immense glass window-walls, Osiris lay bathed in a clementine sunset. The city's conical steel towers were burnished gold, and as a flock of gulls swept past the scraper, their wings caught flashes of red as if they were afire. Adelaide paid no attention to the view; she had seen it all her life. Her attention flicked between her grandfather, her parents, and her two other brothers. Dmitri's fiancée was not at the table. The Rechnovs were clannish. A matter of blood was a matter for blood.

The meeting was the first time Adelaide had spoken to any of them in months. She was wary. She supposed they wanted to discuss how they could bury her twin. Except they didn't have his body, or the facts.

She seated herself at the south end of the table, deliberately facing everybody else. Her mother's eyes, the same green as Adelaide's and Axel's, pleaded with her for compassion, or perhaps for leniency. Viviana would try to use the catastrophe as a catalyst for reconciliation. Adelaide folded her arms on the table. The wood was cool on her bare skin, but sweat lined the hollows of her palms. A grain of salt for every harsh word, she thought. For every tear.

Feodor cleared his throat. He thanked them all for being there, a sentiment clearly aimed at Adelaide, as the only estranged member of the family. Then her mother stood up. She had the blanched face of someone who had not slept in days. Adelaide hardened herself against sympathy.

'I've been thinking,' said Viviana. She stopped, and for a moment it was not clear whether she would continue. Then she seemed to gather all her strength. 'I've been thinking about what we should do,' she said. 'And I think – we must have a – a service. Some sort of gathering, so people can pay their respects. To commemorate Axel.'

It was the wrong choice of word. Adelaide knocked back her chair as she stood, words already feverish on her lips.

'How can you even think about saying that? We don't know Axel's dead. We have no idea where he is. You just want him gone so you don't have to worry about him showing you all up any more.'

After that came tears, and shouting. Only when her accusations ran dry did Adelaide see her grandfather, his shoulders stooped, weariness articulated by every line in his face. He was still, except for his hands, one resting on top of the other. Every now and then they shivered, like two dry leaves stirred by a breeze. He was old, her architect grandfather, over ninety years old. Adelaide and Axel were a bare quarter of that.

Something about her grandfather's silence induced Adelaide's own. She returned to her seat, and folded herself inward.

The rest of the family accepted her retirement as a compromise, and for an hour they tried to discuss objectively what form of service might be held. Her brothers decided that Feodor must say something. If the entire script could be reported in full, it eliminated the necessity of delivering a press statement. Adelaide listened, and said little more. Numbness caught up with her at last. She wished she could expand that emptiness until it filled the cavern in her chest.

Viviana talked about the candles she wanted with a specificity verging on the deranged.

'We'll have a large red one directly beneath Axel's photograph, and smaller orange ones surrounding it. I'll arrange them in a half-moon shape, very simple . . . And then the layout repeated on each table, I suppose it will have to be the same colours, orange and red, or red and orange, we must put the order in with Nina's . . .'

'You know, I'm not sure about having the photograph,' Linus said. 'It might give the impression Axel's dead.'

'But how can anyone think about Axel if there's no reminder of what he looks like?' Tears glistened in Viviana's eyes. 'We haven't seen him . . . in so long.'

'That is a consideration,' Feodor said. 'When was the last time anyone had contact with Axel? A year ago? More?'

He did not say *apart from Adelaide*, which would have been a concession. Viviana was incapable of replying. She buried her head in her arms, strangling her sounds of distress. Streaks of grey meandered through the deep red of her hair, almost conquering it at the roots. Adelaide wondered how much of that was a recent development. Her mother was a strong woman. Adelaide could not remember ever seeing her cry.

'I saw Axel eight months ago,' said her grandfather. 'After Dr Radir's last report.'

'Did you? How was —' Feodor stopped himself. 'Oh, there's no point.'

'The same,' her grandfather replied.

The last remnants of pink and red light infused the room, rendering its occupants unnaturally soft. The room hushed under this elemental spell, and the heavier mantle that fell with it, of guilt.

'What will you say it is?' Adelaide's voice startled her, reinserting itself into the discussion almost without her consent. The others looked at her with equal surprise.

'What?' It was Linus who spoke.

'What will you call it? I mean — the gathering, or however you're going to describe it.'

That was when Feodor came up with the phrase 'service of hope'. He said this was the reason they were holding it, so they might as well make their intentions clear. There was no verbal dissent. Viviana got up and went to stand by the window-wall, staring vacantly out as though the regimented rows of skyscrapers would yield the where-abouts of her son. She rocked back and forth on the balls of her feet. The familiarity of that pose unnerved Adelaide. For the first time that day, she wanted to reach out and pull her mother back.

They progressed inevitably to the content of Feodor's speech. No one could work out how to talk about Axel's life without implying that it was over, which, as Feodor pointed out, would be a strategic blunder. At the same time, Viviana was adamant that her son's achievements should be mentioned. Adelaide's comment that nobody would swallow this line made her mother flinch. Still, Viviana did not seem capable of refuting it, and finally they agreed that Feodor write the speech and send it to the others for approval.

Discussion returned to the mundane. Dates and times. Who should be invited. Where it should be held. They hammered through decisions with a rigidity of conduct, faces disciplined tight. Only at the end did anyone raise the question of the Council investigation, and then it was in passing – Dmitri mentioned to Feodor that they had been asked for access to Axel's bank records. Feodor frowned and said he supposed they couldn't refuse.

Such easy capitulation angered Adelaide, but she saw no profit in expressing it. The choice had been made a long time ago; she no longer warranted a say in Rechnov affairs.

Preti Taneja

The Silent Hours is a novel about little girls born in cities and families that are built to keep out strangers. Preti is also completing a short story collection. She is the co-writer of a short film nominated for the Palme d'Or at Cannes film festival. As a journalist for an international NGO, she contributes to the *Guardian* and *Reuters Alertnet* among others.

The Silent Hours

Chapter One

I woke to the sound of the midday call to prayer. It sank through the open window with the sun, warming me, wrapping me in its promise. I opened my eyes. Sunlight sliced through the slats in the blind, just missing my body, turning to ripples as it met the floor. My bed had become a raft, and I was lost at sea.

I was alone. I opened my eyes wider, breathing in as the mosques around the city called their command and answered each other. I was far from the jangling clangs of India, from the horrific hush of England. It was not my city; the call to submit was not for me. I breathed out.

I was alone. I was safe. Anjali had gone.

I tell you, I have never felt like that. Full of light. A sense of air around me. Every part of me drinking in that air and that light. I wondered if that was how my mother felt, waking up the morning after she finally left us last year. I wondered, then I let it go: that moment, that morning was all for me.

I stretched my body from its night-time curl, slowly, slowly, finding the edges. I was alone on a vast mass of water, and the sound of my breathing was the waves, and the slight movement of my hands over the sheets was the breeze. I felt far away from any land, and Istanbul, waiting outside, might never have existed.

The call to prayer fell away. Kind silence. I held my breath, I waited. And then I heard what it had been drowning. Children playing in a school playground, somewhere nearby. Their voices. They seemed so near; they rocked the raft with their singing. I gripped the sheets. The sunlight trembled. What were they singing? I thought I heard Anjali. I thought I heard my sister, Sonia, and our cousin Chotu, chanting this thing we used to sing as part of a game we used to play, to save us from being 'it'. *Lost at sea means you can't get me. Lost at sea means you can't get me.* I heard their English voices in the bright Turkish day, and the air in the room went from warm to warmer to hot for a second. But how could they have been singing that? They couldn't have been, could they?

No. There was only the muffled noise of the street sellers and the traffic, the day going about its business in a language I did not understand. I was safe. It was warm. I was alone.

I pulled back the sheets and took off my kurta. The sunlight striped my skin: light, dark, light, dark. I saw my feet and my legs, covered in long black hairs. I pressed my hand up my belly and over my breasts: soft, full, unformed clay. My neck, my chin, my face, my head and down through the tangles in my hair, shedding strands all over the bed. I did not care. I lay back. Looked at my hands. Yellow-stained fingertips from eating Indian every day of the last few weeks. Red-painted nails, with Delhi dirt packed underneath. I climbed my uncle's rooftop wall. I scraped my palms doing it.

I let my hands drop.

I breathed. In. Out.

Miracles hung in the air like the dust motes circling slowly, suspended in the strips of light. I was in Istanbul. No one knew me. This was not my house, not my city, not my religion. *Refugee. Refugee! Refugee! Anjali is a refugee!* cried the children. They did. I heard them. And I heard Sonia and Chotu again. I hummed till they stopped.

I felt the sunlight sink into me, deeper and deeper. I felt my breath steady, the raft coming into land. To a room in Istanbul, only big enough for a bed, a bed only big enough for me.

My name in that place was Angela. And there was no one there to call me anything else.

I put my kurta back on, and pulled the sheets back over me. I closed my eyes, and in my head I mapped the flat in the clean blue lines of my father's architect's ink, then carefully built it to three dimensions with only myself inside. On the left of the bed, a door led into a glass antechamber, only big enough for one person to sit in. The chamber hung high over a walled garden papered in plants, with a fall of water rushing down over cold stone. *You are safe*, the walls whispered, and at the end of the bed:

replied the door. I took a deep breath, and went through.

A narrow corridor turned from the bedroom to the right, past the bathroom and kitchen, turning again, opening on to a large living room divided by a sliding partition. Which was closed. The door to the outside hall was locked.

The sorrows in the silence of that flat were not mine. I could not translate or add to them. They let me be. For a girl like me, on my own for the first time ever, you have to understand what that meant. Maybe the beginning of a deep kind of release, a molecular letting go. I felt I had been asleep for years. I felt I was beginning to wake up.

'Hunger, thirst,' said my body. And in the silence I could hear what I wanted.

It sounds strange to you because you probably know when you're hungry. But people can go years never hearing, and if they hear, not listening. I climbed from the raft, I went to find food.

But in the kitchen, the cold stone of the floor burned the soles of my feet. I had to go back to bed and climb back in and hold my feet in my hands to get them warm. I was still hungry. I realised I had to help myself. Everything that morning was new.

I reached for my bag and emptied it on to the bed: whatever I had brought when I ran from Delhi. Bits of paper, shards of tobacco, pencils blunt at one end, chewed at the other. My A4 hardback notebook, not enough underwear and a rolled-up pair of ripped jeans, but I had forgotten my belt. Three tops, my washbag and a brand new copy of the Bhagavadgita, Indian-bound: stiff and cheap and smelling of mothballs. My chapals, the leather cracked like the hard skin on my heels. My passport: the dark red colour of frozen blood, the gold of the lion and the unicorn slowly giving way to an impression of itself. And my sister's precious Pakistan lighter. After I read her diary, I took her lighter. I wondered if she missed it. Only a small green corner of flag and a tiny tip of moon had survived her rubbing.

How many days had passed since then? The dazzling darkness of the wedding party, seen from a standing position on a rooftop wall? And before that, Sonia, and Chotu, and all those smiling faces: make-up melting in the Delhi night. Watching eyes, moving lips, saying nothing. Hearing nothing. Then the parrot on the roof and the dry hard ground below. Struggling with Anjali. Pushing her off.

I tried to keep breathing. The raft. The river. The flat. The raft, the river, the flat.

With the lighter clenched in my fist, I put my chapals on and went again to the kitchen. There was a dirty plate, smeared with cigarette ash, a dirty wine glass smeared with red, and three empty bottles by the bin. Four days then.

Hunger. Thirst. There was nothing in the cupboards except for a packet of Indian tea. I lit the gas, and made the tea the Turkish way, one teapot on top of the other, water boiling in the bottom, tea leaves in the top, steaming.

Marcus taught me that. Last time I came to Istanbul. He had careful hands when he lit the gas, quick fingers when he measured the tea. A firm grip when he fitted the pots tight together. How does it work? I asked him from the bed. 'You'll see,' he said. And showed me. And then took me out into the city. Two years since tea like that.

The pots have to be split for the tea to be made. I broke them apart and poured; the tea spurted out in a golden arc, hitting and splashing the sides of the miniature glass. On its small saucer it became the curved torso of a woman served up on a special plate. For me. Made by myself for me. I thought of my mother, my sister, of India and England. And me, between in Istanbul, holding an hourglass full of golden liquid in my hand. The sands had melted and there was no more counting time. I was back in the city where it all really began. The city was waiting for me. I took my tea to the living room, and stopped.

Istanbul. A vast, delicious painting, framed for my private view. I pressed my face against the glass and licked it a little. Warm and salty dust. Outside, at the end of a flight of stone stairs, the Bosphorus sparkled. I saw an old woman climbing steadily, one step at a time, overtaking a young man whose cigarette slowed him down. I turned along the view to the dome and minarets of Aya Sofia and Sultan Ahmet waiting sternly in the distance. *You are passing through again*, they said. *We have endured*. I turned my head left and right, forehead still touching the glass, but wherever I looked I was either looking at them or they saw me trying not to; like a naughty daughter closing her eyes to make herself invisible. Well, it worked for Anjali.

In the spaces between the old wooden houses, heat disguised the air as water, as if the river was claiming the sky. Asia hunkered on the opposite shore. I turned my back on all of it and faced the room again. Behind the building, somewhere far from the river, Istiklal Caddesi was waiting. 'Independence Avenue,' I heard Marcus whisper. Close, tickling. A breath away. 'Independence Avenue. Anything could happen.' And then he left.

Four days ago, in Delhi, I was the one to leave. The first time I have ever done that. So what if it was the middle of the party? So what if it was the first wedding in our family? I should never have been there in the first place. That's why I left the whole fucking lot of them. And what could I do with my independence, to turn it into freedom? Ice cream on the terrace of the Marmara Hotel? Watch the traffic circling and breathe in dust? Mocha in that alleyway Marcus used to take me to? Flash my eyes at the waiters and see if anyone stopped me. I could do anything.

I whispered it to the wooden dragons hanging high from the ceiling above my head. They turned on their strings with my breath. I said it out loud to the room. 'I could do anything.' But my voice came out in a strangled croak from the soles of my feet, which no one ever listens to. I tried again. 'I could do anything.' I said it quickly, so that it could not be stopped, and once said, could not be taken away.

I had to leave Delhi: I nearly died. I phoned my mother from the airport and heard her voice for the first time in a year. Washing through me like a drink of water, after too long without. I said I couldn't stay in Delhi and I couldn't go back to London. She didn't tell me where she was or ask me to come to her. I waited. Watched the departures board flick through destinations as if it was dealing cards to poker players. Then I said: 'Istanbul.' Silence stretched between us on the phone. Finally, she said she would help. I thought I heard her voice crack but it was probably the line. I told her not to come to me. She didn't ask me how Sonia was. Sonia who promised, who didn't – I can't say more.

I finished my tea. There was one room left. The library. I shouldn't have gone in, I wasn't ready, even though I have spent so much time in libraries these last two years. But the partition was closed and I couldn't stop my fingers fitting in the smooth groove of the sliding door, or my arm from pulling hard. It was not locked. It slid open cleanly, and the room exhaled; dark particles rushed out to fall like ash on the furniture and floor of the noon-bathed room, deepening and merging the shadows, cooling the air. I stepped inside.

In the blind-drawn dark, books stacked the walls from the floor to the ceiling. Time was eroding their pages like the quiet, creeping moss in an English country churchyard, long left to run wild over graves. A cold current eddied around the shelves as I passed and it seemed to me that the fate of those books had been decided with the first line written: this library would be their final resting place. I browsed, I shed hair, I ran my fingers over the spines and they shivered to my touch. Science rubbed shoulders with religion, politics, guides for diets – oversized but ground-breaking tomes by Seventies women had been left to lie horizontal, going yellow with age. I found *The Ultimate Female Orgasm*, a kind of technical manual of pleasure for map-reading men, on top of Henry Miller. *Under the Roofs of Paris*. *Opus Pistorum*. Some force had made them gravitate to each other; a library is a room of many worlds. I weighed them up in each hand, held between their demands, and for a moment felt I was being watched. That Anjali was there.

But it was only the dragons, turning in the other room. I opened

Henry Miller. '*It's not because she is a child, it's because she is a child with no innocence . . . Look into her eyes and you see the monster of knowledge, the shadow of wisdom.*' Anjali's baby-voice spoke in my head, and I could not stop reading.

Christopher Teevan

Christopher Teevan was born in 1985 and educated at the University of Warwick. When he grows up he wants to be a professional footballer, but until that happens, he is trying to write a novel. He lives in north London.

The extract here is an edited first half of a short story entitled 'Telling'.

Telling

While he waited for Pete's train to pull in, Ben's thoughts turned to Gráinne. In the year and a half since graduation and since Ben had last seen her, she had become a familiar memory, to which he often pandered: a palpable, secured fixture of his past. The memory of her distilled itself nearly always to the night they had spent together at the Salisbury. It was an episode which had taken on a near immortality for him in the numerous retellings he had given of that evening: she would always be 'the Irish girl who had got away' from him, as one friend put it; or the girlfriend of a friend who Ben had cheated with, as another (more prudish) friend had interpreted Ben's story (a version he could not help but enjoy in the way it recast him as something of a cad); and he had, on a few isolated occasions (and only with those he had made acquaintance with since graduating), referred to her simply as the Irish girl he had 'briefly seen' during university.

Although, at moments when Ben thought about Gráinne more generally, when he recalled her with Pete and among their circle of friends; when he recalled certain phrases of hers, certain parts of her Limerick vernacular – 'knackers' when she was referring to townies, 'fluted' when she referred to being drunk – he was struck with a vague melancholic dispossession. It was not a version of her that belonged to him nor was it one recognisable from his retellings.

It was nearly two weeks ago that Ben got the text from Pete. The message said that he would be spending a few days in Norwich, visiting 'Ste' (Stephen, as Ben knew him), a friend of theirs from university. Pete had wondered whether he could stop by in Ipswich for a few drinks before going back to London. The suggestion was enough to inspire in Ben a succession of ideas for his friend's visit: he envisioned introducing Pete, his oft-alluded-to former drinking companion, to his friends from Ipswich; he saw him taking Pete around an 'ironic' sightseeing tour of the town; he considered trips to nearby coastal villages. But, as was the case with someone as disorganised as Pete, he did not tell his friend that he would be definitely stopping by until the night before. In spite of this, Ben still held vague ambitions for the afternoon. He had told his father to set an extra place at dinner, in case Pete decided to stay the night in Ipswich.

It was approaching 4 p.m. as the train filed into the station (an hour later than they had originally planned to meet).

On first seeing Pete depart from the train carriage, Ben noted, with some delight, how little his friend appeared to have changed: he was still sporting the same black, knee-length overcoat, the same public-school scarf, and the same Italian shoes (which would have appeared stylish were it not for their splintering leather). As they approached one another, Ben proffered his hand (a consciously manly gesture, a way of saying no hard feelings for being late), which was gripped by his old friend and yanked into an enthusiastic hug. On releasing him from the embrace, Pete said –

'It's good to see you, mate.'

'You too.'

'You haven't changed.'

'I could say the same for you.'

'No, well . . . not except this tramp's beard,' Pete said, laughing and clutching his jaw.

Ben led his friend through the station into the car park outside.

'Sorry I'm late, by the way –'

'That's all right –'

'It's just I can only hang around for a couple of hours. I've got to go to this house party back in London this evening.'

'Right. No problem,' Ben said, nodding his head, as if to suggest that he had expected as much. 'In that case, do you fancy going in there for a few?' He pointed across the road to the Station Hotel, the only pub, Ben knew, within realistic walking distance.

'Sounds good to me.'

The Station Hotel: a pub Ben had no cause to have entered before. A dusty, *fin de siècle*-style saloon bar, desperately in need of refurbishment. With the exception of a couple of elderly gents parked by the bar top (who had been there, Ben suspected, some time), the pub was empty. He was ready to suggest another venue, until Pete said:

'Great. A place with a bit of fuckin' character. Ste kept taking me to all these pseudo-trendy wine bars when we were in Norwich. I get enough of that in London.' Ben noticed that Pete had developed a slight cockney inflection to the way he spoke.

They went to the bar and ordered a Guinness each. It pleased Ben to see that his friend had not changed his tipple.

'So, how is Ste?' Ben asked when they sat down.

'Good. He's pretty settled in Norwich now. Living with his girlfriend. Just started the PhD.'

'He went straight to doing a PhD?'

'Yeah, I think he's resigned himself to a life of academia.'

'But he's doing well?' he asked, nodding to affect some interest.

'I think he's got a lot of work on, but you know . . . His girlfriend's nice.' Pete took a sip from his glass.

'Cool,' Ben said, continuing to nod. He had begun unconsciously fiddling with his bar mat. 'So how's London? How's the course?'

'Good – yeah, really good, as it goes. I'm broke, but you know . . .' Ben took a certain delight in recalling the good health of his own bank balance. 'You pay a lot more for a pint of this in London,' Pete added, raising his glass. 'But it's good. Bit of a wild first year, mind.' He raised his eyebrows in suggestion of all sorts of debauchery and hi-jinks. 'It's settled down now, though. Actually, me and Laura are going to move in together.'

'Low-ra?' Ben said, pronouncing it as Pete had done.

'Had I not mentioned her before?' Ben shook his head. 'Look, I need a cigarette, but I'm going to tell you all about her when I come back.' He handed Ben an uncrumpled twenty-pound note, from a wallet almost ostentatious in its bulk of cards and receipts.

It was typical of Pete, Ben thought while waiting at the bar, to surprise you with some piece of news and then assume that he had told you about it long ago. He returned to the table with the drinks. He thought about Gráinne, about the night at the Salisbury. A part of him had wondered whether he would tell Pete about the evening.

'I can't believe I haven't told you about Laura,' Pete said when he came back to the table. Ben had begun to fiddle with the bar mat once more.

'I know. So who is she?'

'Well, she's an act*or* too. She graduated from RADA last summer. She's from Milan and she's . . .' He shook his head and smiled. Looking back at Ben, he added, 'she's beautiful. Beau-ti-ful.' He kissed his fingers in mock ecstasy. 'That's why I'm going to this party tonight. She's got a small part in a new play at the Royal Court. And one of the other actors is throwing a sort of pre-production cast party for everyone to get to know each other. Should be hideous.' Pete took a sip from his pint, sat back, and shrugged his shoulders. 'But, you know . . .'

'Yeah, I'm sure,' said Ben, conscious of trying not to appear too impressed.

'So how about you? How's things?'

'Oh, you know . . . Tesco is as exciting as ever. It's all I could want in a job. The pay, the people, the hours are awful, but I think I'm making a real difference.' Pete laughed. Ben had developed something of a self-deprecating sarcasm in the eleven months spent at Tesco, but he saw little further anecdotal worth in talking about shelf-stacking. Nor did he want to go into the tentative plans he had about studying for a teaching Master's. Pete's father had been the headmaster at his boarding school in Elstree; Ben's dad, a primary school deputy. Teaching was a profession, Ben well remembered, that they had belittled often during their undergraduate years. 'I'm thinking about going travelling, actually,' he said. There was some truth in this: he had considered travelling, but how much of a possibility it was, what with the prospective Master's, he was not sure.

'Cool. Where to?' Pete said, nodding with enthusiasm.

'Oh, you know. Asia, South America.' He fiddled with the bar mat. 'I haven't really thought about it too much yet.'

'No, you should. I wish I had the time to travel. And the money.'

'Yeah.' Ben looked at his glass, which was nearly empty again.

'So, are you seeing anyone at the moment?'

'Not at the moment. But that's Ipswich for you.'

'So, you haven't seen Alison at all, then?' Pete gave him a fiendish smile. Alison was a girl they had known at university. During their undergraduate years, she had acquired a certain reputation, having tried to seduce nearly every male in their social group at one time or another. But for much of their third year, she had turned her attentions solely towards Ben and, although her affections had not gone entirely unreciprocated, he had made it clear, after several months, that he did not want to pursue a relationship with her. As improbable as was the idea that he might have seen her in the intervening year and a half, Ben was thankful for the allusion to Alison. He laughed indulgently to himself.

'No, I have no idea what she's up to.'

'Actually, I think she's in London too, as it goes. Working. Shame, though. She really liked you. Attractive too.'

'Yeah, well . . .' Without realising it, Ben had torn the bar mat in half. Pete looked at his friend and smiled. He took a subtle glance at his watch.

'I'm going to have another smoke. I need to give Laura a quick call too. But another round, yeah?' he said, motioning to the pub entrance.

Had Alison been a missed opportunity? Ben asked himself while he waited at the bar. He thought about the night at the Salisbury. He remembered now, with a smile, Gráinne's curiosity about the extent of Alison's affections; she had told him he 'could do better' than her. Poor Alison, Ben now thought. Then he remembered the pleasure he had taken just knowing he played a part in Gráinne's thoughts; that she thought of him enough to worry about which woman he was or was not seeing. *I think you can do better than her.*

Ben took the pints back to the table. Pete was still smoking outside.

Gráinne. How much of that evening had she spent complaining about Pete? 'I hardly ever see him now,' she had said. 'He's always in London.' Had her complaints about Pete been intended as justifica-tion – for what they would do, for what she wanted to do, that night? A part of him had wanted to believe so. He had defended his friend against Gráinne's grievances. It was the necessary side to take: to seem loyal and fair in Pete's absence; but he recalled also the caution he took later in the conversation to avoid any further allusion to his friend.

She had taken his arm as they left the Salisbury. He recalled again their drunken arm-in-arm stumble back to her house. How he had romanticised this walk in anecdotes afterwards. He recalled the engineered pretence of going back to watch *The Apartment*, which was playing on TV that evening. He still pictured now the dark, purple light of her basement room. So much of the memory seemed to be filtered through this impressionistic shade: the 'wintry amethyst', as he had come to refer to it when, at his most indulgent, he described the night to others.

He recalled the self-conscious adjustments they had made on her bed to make themselves comfortable; and then when they were comfortable and watching the television, the first accidental brush of her hand against his as she readjusted herself on the bed; and then, some twenty minutes into the film, the moment when his hand deliberately – deliberately, but while he readjusted himself so as to make it seem accidental – brushed hers; and then the third time their hands brushed and the gentle, tacit entwining of their fingers; all the while their eyes still studying the screen; he recalled again now, with a readying and indulgent melancholy, the soft seconds in which her fingers searched between his and their hands joined together; and then the moment at which their eyes eventually met and her half smile; a half smile at once approving and sober, at once welcoming intimacy and aware of the transgression it was consenting to.

And then they kissed. Tentatively at first, registering the other's consent, and then with a savage, adolescent acceleration. They kissed with hastened embraces, with hands clutching waists clutching hips clutching trouser legs, with hands feeling between layers of shirt and vest, with fingers feeling between jumper and T-shirt, between trouser and underwear, between underwear and cold, goose-pimpled skin.

Later, she asked him, as he wrapped his arm around her, if he was comfortable. And he recalled now, with all too much sentimentality, that he had said, in spite of the cramp in his neck, that he 'couldn't imagine being any more comfortable'. Then he kissed her on the forehead.

Ben looked up at the doorway. Pete was outside still, talking animatedly on the phone.

In the days that followed, the over-earnest exchanges of glances, the hope that she might leave him; the stinging dispossession when she did not. 'You're sweet,' she had told him as, with the sympathy of an elder sister, she kissed him on the forehead.

Pete and Gráinne broke up. That summer, after graduation, she went back to Limerick; he was due to begin at RADA in the autumn. By that stage, had Ben even wanted to, it seemed too trivial, too inconvenient, to tell Pete about the night at the Salisbury. He found himself, instead, recounting the story to friends. Even now, the summoning of that evening restored to him a sense of self-possession.

Pete returned to the table, waving his phone.

'Laura's already at the party, putting up decorations.'

'Do you know what Gráinne's up to at the minute?'

Colin Tucker

Colin Tucker was born in Dar-es-Salaam. He has worked in television as a script editor and producer and has taught film in the UK and in Europe. He has written for radio, television and film. *Harbour of Peace* is his first prose fiction.

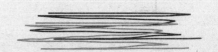

Harbour of Peace

Chapter One

Dar-es-Salaam, Tanganyika Territory, March 1932

He couldn't sleep. There had been low cloud cover all day, an oppressive blanket sitting over the town. The netting around his bed ratcheted up the claustrophobia and he felt conscious of his breathing. The rains were coming, McLeod had warned him.

As dawn began to filter through the cracks in the shutters he got up. He was still unused to the heat but the floor tiles were cold and welcome. He didn't stand straight away but sat on the narrow cot swathed in netting, his feet planted, his soles absorbing the transient chill. The room was bachelors' quarters, one of six in a mess-house allocated to junior officials. It was pictureless and sparsely furnished, but he felt disinclined to embroider it in any way. He didn't want to feel at home.

'At least it's functional,' McLeod told him. 'There's a houseboy who cooks and a cleaner, wages paid by Admin. Shouldn't think you'll see much of it apart from sleeping.'

A small lizard clung to a distempered wall. It had been in the same position every morning and Walter appreciated the continuity. He unbuttoned his pyjama top and shrugged it off on to the floor; after a week in Dar he'd abandoned pyjama trousers. Ten minutes of callisthenics followed, push-ups and Indian squats, not enough to raise a sweat but enough to create a satisfying sense of the physical. He stood for a moment in front of the cheval glass, the one flicker of originality in the room's standard-issue furniture. I'm here, so get used to it. Would Winnie make a difference? His penis thickened and he shook his head to rid himself of her. Don't start that, things to be done. He struggled to open a drawer of the camphorwood chest. Bloody Joseph. He'd used candle grease for God's sake and it both eased and gummed the movement. Talk to him. Must be some proprietary furniture oil, one of the town stores would surely have something. Fresh cotton underwear though, the dhobi-wallah was reliable, cotton socks, knee-length, held up by grey elastic garters, and then the white drill shorts and the crisp cotton short-sleeved shirt with its Customs & Excise epaulettes. And with every garment the familiar odour of camphor. White moth-ball marbles in the bedroom he'd shared with Nick. They rattled around on the floor of the clothes closet, were pushed by Mother into trouser pockets and jacket pockets and arranged by her in rows on the underwear shelf. The aroma reached across continents.

He'd visited her two days before he left for Southampton and they'd spent an awkward hour together. Her goodbyes had been as expected, formal, a handshake only. Then as he stepped out on to the path that led from the back of the cottage around to the road she called him back.

'I've something for you.'

He waited while she returned inside and clambered up the narrow staircase. The earth in the vegetable patch was grey; there had been a frost the night before. With kid brother Nick gone to his new life as a fireman in Marlborough who would look after the garden? That had always been a man's job. Her functions began and ended inside the cottage.

'Here. Open it later.'

It was an envelope, used, the address scratched out and the stamp steamed off. He could tell that there was a card inside. Wishing him well? Surely not enclosing money, a pound note or two? Could she afford it?

'Thank you.'

They stood for a moment.

'God bless,' she said.

'And you look after yourself.'

'I'll get by.'

'Nick's not far away.'

Her lips puckered and she turned from him. He'd never seen her cry and now felt only embarrassment. Marlborough was too distant for her to cope with. He was only going to Africa.

He opened the envelope at Pewsey station. The Bristol train was delayed but there was a coal fire in the waiting room and a dozen or so people had crowded in. He took out the card. St Anthony of Padua looked at him, blue eyes moist, brow furrowed with solicitude. The patron saint of lost things. Why? Was St Anthony significant? He turned it over. Two words in her careful, looped handwriting: *from Mother*. He looked for and found a metal rubbish bin into which he dropped first the envelope and then, after a brief pause, the card. He didn't want St Anthony's help. And for a moment his Catholicism seemed irrelevant. It was her religion.

Boots in hand he sat on the edge of the cot and bent forward to put them on. His hands moved to support his skull while his fingers groped in his thick mop of dark hair. There were gaps in the floor tiles where the grouting had shrivelled. He'd seen cockroaches at night but had never located their daytime base. Were these crevices their hideaways? Surely too narrow. They shunned the chest, that was something. Did the camphor deter them? The smell got everywhere, smell, that was the word, not scent, scent was subtle, camphor was not. What was the scent Winnie used? Oh yes, *Shalimar*. Pale hands I loved beside the Shalimar. Musk, heavy, but vanilla too. Weren't those vanilla pods drying in the sheds out at Msimbazi? And that other scent she wore, the sandalwood one, forget its name, expensive, present from some bloke no doubt, Alex? He'd encountered that too, in the Asian Zone. Reminders of her everywhere.

He finished tying his boots. A distant argument disturbed him, voices echoing down the corridor from the kitchen, Joseph's dominant, asserting his authority over an inferior. Walter rose heavily to his feet, located his fountain pen, Waterman's, good make, and went to the common room. There he settled himself in front of the shabby escritoire, pulled down the leaf, found a pad of lined yellow paper and prepared to write. He'd delayed long enough. A proper letter was necessary.

> P.O. Box 453
> Dar-es-Salaam
> British Mandated Territory of Tanganyika
> Saturday 12th March 1932

Dear Winnie

Nothing came. Write anything, anything better than silence. Must hang on to her, the possibility of her. She'd not said an outright no.

It's wonderful here. You'd love it.

How could he say that? There were moments when he had to admit that Dar-es-Salaam was almost pleasant. He recognised a ramshackle charm, an attractive incompetence. The street-sweepers' enthusiastic onslaughts which seemed to spread rubbish rather than eliminate it, the stately Sunday procession of Asian families along Azania Front, the yells and banter of the dock coolies, all had a quality that he warmed to. But his resentment at being sent to this obscure outpost lingered on. Why not Bombay, Calcutta, Madras, the great Raj seaports he'd hoped for, presumed on? How could she love it if he didn't? He crumpled the yellow sheet and flung it towards the basket in the corner of the room. Missed.

What now? Could write to Kitty? Easy person, Kitty, open, generous. Letter to her would loosen him up, get him in a writing mood. No, ducking the issue. Winnie, have to write to Winnie, but no gush, no, instead calm, observant, masculine.

Dear Winnie
   How are you? I hope you liked my p.c.s. What did you think of the Port Said gully-gully men? I'll have to send you one of this place. It's not what I expected. For a start, it's both small yet quite spacious, at least in the European Zone. It was laid out by the Germans before we booted them out in the Great War and hats off to them they did it well, wide streets and pleasant villas built on stilts with red-tiled roofs and large gardens. Bougainvillea is every-where, and frangipani and casuarina and prickly acacias. Then there's a Commercial Zone, which is where the Indians live, so it's sometimes called the Asian Zone. That's much more crowded, more as I imagined. All our clerking staff are Indian, mainly Goanese. The locals aren't up to it. They keep to the Native Zone

unless they have work outside it. They're supposed to carry passes,
but of course never do.

My work is pretty dull, masses of paperwork to do with the East
African Customs Union. Actually the whole place is dull. Or worse
than dull. In fact I hate it, as I thought I would.

He paused and reread. Hate it? He couldn't admit that. And besides, was it even true? Or an indulgence in self-pity? In fact the whole bloody letter was useless, stupid, cold, he'd overdone the impersonal. Crumple. Throw. Missed again. Damnation.

Dear Winnie
I hope you're well, I'd love to hear from you. I'm sorry we
parted like that. My fault, I know, but we were so great together
and if you were here we'd have such fun. As it is, I'm a bit miz,
feeling stuck, in a sort of purgatory, waiting for my tour of duty to
end. When it's only just begun.
The trouble is I miss people, you in particular of course but all
the gang too, Kitty and Deirdre, and Reg and Frank and Mary.
There's a decent chap here, Petrie, he came out with me on the
Llangibby Castle and is in the same mess, he loves it here, or so he
says. But there are hardly any women. There's McLeod's wife,
that's my boss, the Commissioner, two kids at school in the Cape,
she seems pleasant enough. And some of the commercial chaps'
wives are here, but I don't see much of them. So no one to talk to,
talk properly that is, no one like you, Winnie, I think about you all
the time, remember Iron Acton? And I want you so badly. Why
didn't I say so, things could have been so different?

Pause. Oh God, can't send that, desperate, a guarantee to turn her off. Scrub it out. Crumple. Waste basket. Yes! Third time lucky!

Dear Winnie
What did you think of my p.c.s? I'm missing you in so many
ways.

That's fair enough. Now keep writing, work round to the main point.

This is a dull town. Its name is Arabic, it means Harbour of Peace. What a laugh. No docks, a couple of feeble jetties and a lighterage quay, and on the water a mess of small boats, dhows, outriggers, canoes, floating rubbish, chaos. The big ships anchor in the middle of the bay and cargo has to be transferred by lighter. Passengers, too, we had to clamber down a rope ladder into a launch, one old lady needed a breeches buoy to offload her.

Not bad for the opening, but must get to the issue. Which is?

He leaned back in his chair and stared at the ceiling, seeing nothing. The heat of the day was apparent by now and he could feel a first trickle of sweat from an armpit. He mopped at it with his handkerchief.

Concentrate! The issue, yes. Want her, but marry her? Winnie for the rest of my life? Kipling had her pinned, 'The Cat That Walks By Herself'. Anyway, don't know if I love her, do I? Properly, deeply. And does she love me? Could she love me? Could Winnie love anyone? Oh God! Should have stayed in Blighty, fooled around, let things develop, and anyway does love matter? What a stupid word that is. Brain gone to mud. Another for the waste basket?

The door opened.

'You're up early.'

Petrie stood in the doorway, his small frame exaggerated by a combination of baggy shorts and tight shirt. He was combing his hair, slicked down with brilliantine flat across his scalp.

'The boy's got breakfast, he must have sensed we were up.'

'I couldn't sleep,' Walter said.

'Nor me.'

He folded the unfinished letter and put it in his shirt pocket. Good enough so far, let it simmer, finish it later. He stood up from the desk, folded the extended leaf back into position, replaced the upright chair and then searched for and retrieved the failed drafts.

'Don't want Joseph reading my letters.'

'Can he read?'

'He might show them to someone who can.'

'Fair enough. They to your girl?'

Walter didn't answer. He'd told Petrie too much about Winnie, some of it true. He dug the crumpled papers deeper into his pocket.

'Breakfast then.'

'Wish I had a girl. I like the company of women. She sounds great, your girl.'

They walked down the corridor to the mess room where Joseph hovered. There was no sign of either Ellis or Dusty Miller, the only other residents.

'Salaam, bwanas.'

'Porridge, Joseph,' Walter ordered.

'The usual,' Petrie said.

Joseph inclined his head and Walter could see the warty growths on the back of his neck.

'I wish he didn't bob and scrape like that, he's twice our age,' he said when Joseph had left the room.

'Or just looks it.'

An eddy of wind stirred the dust in the compound, and they could hear Joseph coughing. Walter removed the fly cover from the fruit salad bowl and they helped themselves to slices of fresh pawpaw and mango. Joseph returned with a bowl of porridge and a plate of fried plantains on a hammered pewter tray. He laid the tray down carefully in the middle of the table and stood back waiting, it seemed, for applause.

'And the tea?' Walter asked. Joseph opened his mouth as if surprised by the request. He then tapped the side of his head with the heel of his palm and scuttled away, his sandals flapping against the tiles.

'I sometimes think he's mocking us,' Walter said.

'Surely not, he's a decent soul.'

Walter grimaced. No, you're the decent soul, you're the one who sees the best in everyone.

'He makes good porridge, I'll give him that.'

The tea arrived in a chipped Rockingham pot with matching cups and saucers. The milk jug had a square of netting across the top, weighed down by beads attached to each corner. The sugar bowl had the same protection. As if to justify this, a pair of flies landed on the tablecloth at Walter's elbow, attempted the bowl, were defeated by the netting and settled on the wall to wait and hope. A gecko began to stalk them.

'Sup up,' Petrie said. 'The Empire calls.'

Walter yawned.

'It can wait.'

Marshall Veniar

Marshall Veniar was born in 1983. Prior to completing his MA in Creative Writing, Marshall studied English at Exeter University. He now works in the film industry. His novel-in-progress, provisionally titled *Mucus Man*, follows the story of a self-conscious young man with cystic fibrosis as he enters into his first romantic relationship. In the following extract, Stuart meets Laura for their second date.

Mucus Man

We're texting each other regularly now. In fact, my entire mood this week has been determined, at any one time, by the last text I've received from Laura. I read them through countless times and deconstruct each one like literature. If she texts, and I think that the message is generally positive, or has any hint of flirtation, I'll reread the last message *I* sent *her* and congratulate myself on its phrasing. If she so much as drops a kiss off the end I'll do the same but agonise over what I could have said wrong. When it comes to replying, I'll often wait a while, because knowing that I'm next in line to text is far less stressful than the anticipation of waiting for a response. Sometimes my phone will vibrate and I'll scramble for it in my pocket to find a message from Hunt and, for a second, I'll *hate* him for the disappointment he's inadvertently caused me.

Despite all this, however, I'm grateful for the opportunity to be playful in writing. I type messages into my phone that, if I attempted to utter in person, I'd trip over the words and go crimson. My latest text is a prime example. Laura has sent me the message:

> Just heading over to unpack now. Give me a call when you arrive. Can't wait. x

To which I've responded:

> Lovely stuff. Prepare yourself for a cuddle! x

(I've lost count of how many drafts these seven words have been through.)

And this cringe-worthy behaviour doesn't stop at text messages. For the past three days I have been reciting amorous conversations between the two of us in my head. Fabricated of course. Occasionally I'll even catch myself uttering lines from these conversations out loud. Alone in my flat, I'll squirm. The other day, in the shower, I said to a bottle of conditioner, '*Well, let me talk to your mother.*' And after this sentence had reverberated around my bathroom walls and back against my ear drums I was forced to admit that I had been imagining a scenario in which I'd asked Laura to move in with me. She was concerned about how her mother would react when she called to say that the rent for her room no longer had to be paid. Apparently I was offering to talk to Mrs Laura on her behalf. Well! How gentlemanly of me!

But now, on the way to Laura's new student accommodation, nerves rising inside me, sweat collecting at my hairline, I'm forced to take stock of reality: that this is a second date, the third time Laura and I have ever met and that, perhaps, chats with her mother are some way off in the future.

These nerves are doing no favours for my bowels either. I know, I used the toilet right before I left the flat but on the tube ride here I was struck with that familiar piercing in my side and that warm oily feeling in my abdomen. Still, I figure there will be public toilets aplenty in a set of student halls. I like to pop to the toilet just before I meet people anyway, to clear my chest if nothing else.

The reception area of the halls is large and concrete, a multi-storey car park with walls, but crammed into each parking space is a bedroom and a kitchen. On both sides of the foyer I look up to see five or six rows of windowed corridors stacked tight on top of each other. Before the stairwell, or the lift, or any public toilet though, is a glass reception booth and two metal turnstiles. A whiteboard reads 'Show your admissions form and ID at reception to collect your key.' Behind the turnstiles a few kids wait by the lifts with suitcases, boxes, one of them a desk fan.

'Admissions form and ID,' the man at reception greets me.

'I'm not moving in,' I tell him. 'Just visiting. Can I pass through?'

He hands me a red folder and points at various boxes in a table with the end of a biro. 'Name. Room number. Time,' he says.

'I don't know her room number, she's just moved in today.'

The man shakes his head as a queue of foreign people holding boxes forms behind me. 'Look, we really don't encourage visitors on moving in day, sir.'

I sigh at the man. *'Listen,'* I say, *'this is our second date. This is the most beautiful and likeable girl to have ever shown an interest in me.*

The first time someone in my league, let alone the league above it, has seemed to find me attractive. Surely you're not going to jeopardise that based purely on policy.' Of course I don't say that. The pharmacist taught me how far trying to appeal to people's sense of romance gets you. What I actually say is (just for the purposes of getting through the barrier of course) 'Mate. She's my girlfriend and I promised I'd help her unpack.'

Another sigh, this time from him. 'What's her name?' he asks, now hammering at computer keys.

'Laura,' I say.

'Surname?'

There's a pause before I burst into a laugh, a grunting-type laugh at myself. I don't know Laura's surname. This morning, in my shower, I was asking this girl (played by Vidal Sassoon at the time) to share my flat with me and here, in this concrete reality, I don't even know her full name. The man looks at me with impatience.

'Never mind,' I say. 'I'll just call her,' my punishment from the heavens for jumping the gun and using the term *girlfriend* prematurely. I'm still chuckling a little as Laura's phone rings and I want to tell her self-deprecatingly about my embarrassment until I realise that this story will involve me admitting that I referred to her as my girlfriend, and that would be a mistake. It's a story for Hunt. A story for a future Laura, when she *is* my girlfriend.

'Hi,' she answers the phone, but not the *hi* I expected, not with the cheery excitable tone implied by her latest text. This is a sad *hi* injected with disappointment.

'Hi,' I say. 'Are you OK?'

'No.'

'What's wrong?'

'Oh God, it's horrible. This room is horrible.'

'Oh shit, really?' I say. A vacuous sentence. 'Look, the guy down here isn't letting me in. I think you're going to have to come down.'

'OK,' she says vacantly. 'Unless . . .' Silence. Her breath skips a little as she inhales and I realise that she's been crying over this room.

'Unless what?'

'Unless you wanna take a rain-check on tonight?'

'Oh,' I say again. It's odd but my first instinct is relief. I could go home and have that poo. I could stop feeling nervous right now. No more stress of having to be good-looking and funny all night. I know, though, that once the nerves have dispersed they'll be replaced with disappointment and a bereavement of my fake conversations in the shower. I'll go back to watching Hunt chat girls up while I sheepishly sip from a pint in silence, thinking about how close I once got to this lovely American girl.

'Why?'

'I'm a real mess up here, Stuart (Stoort).'

'But . . . I've come all the way here.' I stutter. *This is not the way to win this battle. She's not going to give in to an attack on her manners, you twat. She's not English.* 'Don't you want to see me? I might be able to cheer you up.'

'I donno.'

Well, I'm not going to beg her. I've got too much pride to beg, I think to myself. But that's not it at all. The truth is I don't have the confidence to argue.

'OK,' I say, adopting the same tone as Laura. 'Well, let me know if you want to reschedule.' That's when it happens. Something inside me, my inner De Niro, slaps me in the face and yells *Ow! What are you, a fuckin' pussy? Eh? Is that what yoo arr? Whatcha gonna do, stay at home chokin' ya toiky all ya life? You godda grow some fuckin' bawls, kid. What? You don't watch enough movies d'know how to act in a situation like dis? Here. Here's watcha godda do.*

'Listen,' I say, in a far more English accent than Robert, 'I'm sorry. I can't go. You're alone. You're clearly upset. I'm the only person you really know in London. I'd be a moron if I left you like this. I'm afraid I'm going to have to put my foot down here. I'm coming to cheer you up.'

'Yeah?' she says. 'You're putting your foot down, huh?'

''Fraid so,' I say, hoping she'll attribute the squeaking in my voice to a dodgy phone signal.

'Hmm, I did sorta wanna collect that hug you promised me.'

'Well, I have hugs to give.' The man at reception looks at me. Laura laughs the nasal laugh of a girl who's been crying and then sniffs.

'OK. Just, promise me you won't run a mile when you see me,' she says. 'I look gross.'

'I promise,' I say and we hang up. I continue sporting the smile on my face when I nod to the receptionist and tell him, 'She's coming down.'

I busy myself for a while. I flick through a couple of leaflets in a stand by reception advertising Madame Tussaud's and the National Portrait Gallery. I think about going to these places with Laura, holding hands, re-experiencing this taunting city that has always flaunted loving couples in my face but never delivered the opportunity to be one. I look up to see if she's waiting for me, light-heartedly wondering if I'll recognise her in her *gross* state. What if, I wonder, she came down to meet me and she really did look horrendous, a total opposite to what I imagine her to look like? Suddenly, I'm struck with genuine concern. What if she comes down and I spot something about her that I can't shake, can't abide. God knows it's happened before. Not with anyone I've been seeing, but girls that I've fancied. Suddenly, one day I'll catch a glance of some wax in her ear or the inkling of a moustache forming at the edge of her smile and from then on that'll be it for her. I won't be able to shake that image and she'll be associated with it in my head for ever. Why am I pretending to be unconcerned with appearance when I am? I am concerned. Appearance is a real issue for me. What if Laura had me pegged when she suggested a rain-check, and I've gone and pretended to be a gentleman, something I'm not, and what if she was being totally honest with her warning? What if . . .

'Hey, mister.'

Gordon Weetman

Gordon Weetman is a short story writer from Oxfordshire. He spent half a year travelling in Latin America before reading American Literature at the University of East Anglia. His influences include Kafka, Borges, and Roberto Bolaño. He would like to write a novel at some point, but doesn't think he has the patience.

No Fun Anymore

'Eat the apple,' he said. When I refused: 'You're no fun anymore.' Then he started on about why couldn't he have two wives: one for cooking and cleaning, and one for 'other duties'? After all, there was no shortage of ribs. All of this was spoken in a stage-mutter loud enough for the man upstairs to hear.

I took a long look at the glossy red orb in my hand. It was perfectly round, and shiny like it had been sprayed with something – although in those days there was nothing to spray it with. The grass at my feet was littered with these little crimson baubles, and since there was no decay in the garden they never rotted. The animals – they weren't stupid – wouldn't touch the things. Consequently, we had more apples than we knew what to do with. If we'd figured out how to make cider, we could have had a real knees-up, but that only came later – by which time apples were thinner on the ground.

We were at such a loss for how to dispose of our surplus that at one point Ads invented a game we could play with the pestilent crop. I would stand at one end of the clearing, and he would stand at the other holding a big stick whittled from the bough of an oak tree. I would launch an apple at Adam and he would swing the stick and try to hit it. Most times the thing just imploded into a whitish pulp, but occasionally the stick would connect just right and the apple would soar off over the treeline, the arc of its trajectory mirroring the fecund curvature of the fruit – which was itself a miniature replica, we were told, of our beloved home, the Earth.

Okay, so we may have condemned mankind to an eternity of tedium and suffering, but did you know we also invented baseball?

'Go on,' said Adam, temporarily shelving his bigamous aspirations. 'Just a bite. What harm could it possibly do?'

'I don't know,' I said. 'Isn't the colour red nature's code for danger?'

'You're being anachronistic again,' Adam warned. 'We both know there's nothing dangerous in the garden.'

Just as he said this, I spotted out of the corner of my eye something moving in the tall grass.

I yelped. 'What was that?' I said.

'What was what?' said Adam.

'It was probably nothing,' I said. I knew it was unlikely that I'd be able to locate the creature again, since whatever it was was the same colour as the grass around it.

'Just eat the damn fruit,' said Adam.

I raised the small scarlet globe to my lips. Adam was watching me with an unhealthy keenness.

'Eat it,' he whispered. His pupils were dilated.

I closed my eyes, and bit.

There was a thundercrack. Adam whimpered, fled behind a bush. The apple fell to the ground. It was, I suddenly realised, a rather beautiful thing – perfect in every way. Every way except one: at a certain point on its equator there was a chunk missing, and the fruit's pale innards were visible. The edges of the cavity were indented with an unmistakable pattern of scallop shapes: the imprint of a dainty set of human teeth.

Streetlights

All summer the Killer terrorised the city. By mid-August Maria and I gave up all pretence of working. Instead we stayed glued to the television screen like flies to a strip of poisoned paper.

'It's unbelievable.' Maria shook her head sadly as the death of yet another victim was announced. This one found in the middle of the Parque Central by an old man who had stumbled upon the woman's bloodied corpse while taking his dog for its midnight walk. The blood was still damp when they found her. Unbelievable, Maria had said. Yet improbable as the murders were, they kept happening. The media were all over it. True serial killers were still rare in our corner of the world; for political pundits the murders provided further proof that we, along with the rest of the world, were rapidly turning into America.

We listened incredulously as the newsreader detailed with something approaching weariness the way in which the woman had died. She had been stabbed over fifty times in the chest, upon which her heart was excised ('Like the Aztecs,' gasped Maria), and her limbs arranged in the shape of a crucifix.

'You don't think,' said Maria, 'do you, that she was used as some kind of . . . *sacrifice*?'

'No,' I said. 'That's ridiculous: horror-movie stuff.' But there was no conviction in my voice. In truth, my initial feelings had been running along pretty much the same lines as Maria's. I wondered if what we were witnessing here was some form of hideous syncretism between two ancient forms of evil – between the old, bloodthirsty gods and the new. After all, most religions demand some form of sacrifice. But I quickly dismissed this theory as mere fantasising – the reveries of a lifelong atheist.

'I'm going out,' I said.

Maria whirled round with a fearful expression on her face. It was the first time all night that her eyes had left the television screen.

'Where are you going?' she asked.

'To buy some cigarettes. I've run out.' I picked up the empty carton, and jiggled it to illustrate this fact.

'But – but, you can't,' said Maria. 'What about the Killer?'

'I'll be fine,' I said, drawing upon phantom reserves of confidence. 'The chances of anything happening are a million to one.' It astonished me that I could display such courage, which I did not remotely feel. At the back of my mind, I wondered whether all bravery was like this: an illusion, a sham, a piece of cheap theatrical trickery. But this was something that I did not like to probe too thoroughly. Memories from childhood: an image of myself prodding at an ants' nest with a stick, then reeling back in horror as the little black soldiers – armies and armies of them: an insectile Third Reich – came pouring out. True or false? I thought. The 'memory' may have been from my childhood; on the other hand, it may have just been something I'd seen in a horror movie.

'Besides,' I said to Maria, aware that some time had passed since either of us had spoken, 'that park we just saw is on the other side of town. Right?'

She nodded, as if to say, Yes, but where is this going?

'Well,' I continued, 'the man on the news said that the woman's blood was still uncongealed, yes? So, how could the killer make it all the way across town in this short space of time? No buses run at this time of night. The Metro closed down hours ago. So it's impossible, unless you think the killer can fly. *Do* you think that?'

Maria shook her head. The slowness of the movement somehow accentuated her *mestizo* features: the high cheekbones, the broad, flat nose, the folds at the corners of her eyes that made her look slightly Chinese. My little Indian, I used to call her. Though she denied all knowledge, Maria's ancestors were almost certainly drawn from one of the tribes that in previous centuries had provided prey for the more 'advanced' (i.e. brutal) Amerindian civilisations.

Right now, my little Indian was avoiding my gaze. I knew I was right, but I suddenly sensed that I had gone too far: my demonstration of logic had slid over into not-so-subtle ridicule.

'Everything you've said is true,' Maria said, 'but you know I can't help worrying. It's only natural.'

Poor Maria. I leant over and kissed her on the forehead, causing one of the stray black hairs of her fringe to adhere to my saliva, and fairly leap into my mouth. Furtively, I extracted it.

'Don't worry.' I bent down to tie my laces. 'At least *try* not to worry. I'll be back in ten minutes, I promise. Fifteen minutes max.'

'Okay.' Maria still sounded uneasy.

'Do you want anything?' I asked, hating myself because this had only occurred to me as an afterthought.

'No,' said Maria. 'Actually, a carton of Kreteks, please.' Clove cigarettes – disgusting things, in my opinion.

'Okay.' My hand on the doorknob.

'Hurry back,' said Maria. Then she said something else, I think, but by that time I had already closed the door behind me.

Outside, the streets were dark and unpeopled. As I've already stated, it was the height of summer; the temperature of the air was the same as that of blood. Everyone's staying inside, I thought with a shudder of nausea. Everyone's staying inside because they know that something is going to happen tonight. Why did I think this? I have no idea. My life is riddled with questions.

It's just a short walk from our apartment block to the cigarette kiosk on the corner. Short, but dark. On one side is the local park, named after a corrupt politician, where there are no streetlights. On the other side are houses with gardens overflowing on to the road, where street-lights are few and far between. On the way to the cigarette kiosk I thought about the nature of fear: a nature which at times – to me, at least – seems very precise, almost geographical. Fear, I decided, is a place where your footsteps sound like the footsteps of a pursuer.

The cigarette kiosk on the corner is manned by old Alfredo. At any hour of the day or night, up until about three o'clock in the morning, you can find him standing there at his post like a soldier guarding an abandoned palace. Alfredo gets good custom from people going to and from the Metro; the stop is just over the road. Alfredo is also a lifeline for the many students who live in this neighbourhood, for as well as over fifty brands of cigarettes and almost every type of chewing gum, he sells good quality American rolling papers, which can be hard to get your hands on.

'Hey, Alfredo,' I said. 'How's it going?'

'Same as always,' said Alfredo. Always the same response, morning, noon, or night: same as always. It suddenly occured to me that I had never seen Alfredo's legs. Maybe he didn't have legs – for all I knew, he could have been an amputee from the waist down. But, no (I peered over the lip of the kiosk counter): there they were, swathed in dirty linen. Peasants' trousers, I thought. The really curious thing was that although I'd never paid attention to Alfredo's legs before, once I'd seen them I realised they couldn't be any other way.

'What'll it be?' asked Alfredo.

'Oh, uh . . . two cartons of Marlboros, please, and a carton of Kreteks.'

'These ones?'

'Yep, those are the ones.'

'Here you go, cowboy,' said Alfredo. It's an old joke, but Alfredo still manages to get some mileage out of it. The joke refers, of course, to the fact that I always buy Marlboros. Imported, they're expensive, but I rarely smoke anything else.

'Thanks, Alfredo.' I handed over a couple of notes, badly crumpled because I'd been playing with them in my pocket on the way here, squeezing them into a tight little ball. A ball of fear, I thought, my stomach clenching

'Thanks, cowboy,' said Alfredo.

As I walked away, I decided that Alfredo would be the perfect victim for a serial killer. Think about it: he works alone, until the early hours of the morning. There is no one around to witness a crime. Not even a policeman, tonight – which was odd, considering. But then again, most of the city's police force was probably downtown, combing the park for evidence. Either that or fucking hookers in exchange for some sort of amnesty arrangement or police protection (I wondered what sort of protection a policeman would use).

Anyway, that was all beside the point. The point was that I could have killed Alfredo – I could have *easily* killed Alfredo. And I could have just as easily got away with it. All I'd have to do would be to take a sharp knife out with me, which I could wrap in a rag or a piece of cloth, and then conceal in my jacket pocket. Then, when I reached the kiosk, I could casually lean over the counter as though I were about to whisper something into Alfredo's shrivelled ear, to impart some tantalising secret. But instead I would drive the knife swiftly into his belly. Or his ribcage: whatever, as the Americans say. I would clamp the cloth over Alfredo's mouth, which would probably drown his screams just enough. Then I'd stand back and watch the life drain out of his eyes, and I'd feel a warm sense of satisfaction spreading through me, upwards from my crotch.

What am I turning into? I wondered, as I reached the entrance of my building. And as I climbed the stairs to our apartment, I experienced a curious feeling of vertigo, as though my past were falling away from me. A fleeting vision: myself as a priest, quetzal-cloaked, scaling a bloodstained pyramid with an obsidian dagger in hand. By the time I reached the top, I had trouble remembering my own name.

Cautiously, I pushed open the door to our apartment. Silence. The television had been turned off at some point; its screen was now as blank as the face of an animal. I felt fear – not just abstract fear, but real, concrete terror. Maria was nowhere to be seen.

'Maria,' I whispered hoarsely. I felt like shouting, but couldn't bring myself to do so. A loud noise at a time like this would precipitate disaster, I felt, causing fate to descend upon my head like an avalanche in a snow-covered valley. 'Maria,' I repeated. I heard the noise of a toilet flushing. Relief: the purest of all human emotions. Purer – far purer – than love. Purer even than fear.

The sound of a door unlocking. Maria emerged from the bathroom. But what I saw in her eyes was not relief, but something else. Something darker, something less uncontaminated. For a moment – only a half-second or so, but in life it's often these forgotten half-seconds that matter most – she looked at me as though I was a stranger.

Eley Williams

Eley Williams graduated from Selwyn College, Cambridge in 2008. She won the Christopher Tower Poetry Prize in 2005 and has had three pieces published in *The Mays* anthology 2008. Her submission is taken from a collection of shorter works focusing upon events at a fictional school. Aside from writing, Eley enjoys composing bland, potted biographies of herself as often as possible.

Terms

I first realised I was in love with Piggy in an airing cupboard. She was too busy demonstrating how to fit four handfuls of marshmallows into my mouth without causing suffocation to take much notice at the time.

Both six years old, both jammed in with our faces mere inches apart, I was rendered entirely immobile in mind and body by the sense of pure adoration for her that descended upon me. This was some hours into my birthday party during a game of Hide and Seek; she was wearing the then fashionable half-velvet, half-doily style of party dress and smelt of tinned peaches. I had been hitting the jelly and ice-cream table pretty hard since breakfast and had spent the day semi-delirious with sugar.

'You have to be willing to squeeze them against the sides,' she had explained sternly, through an electric hyperglycaemic haze.

I watched the demonstration in silence, appalled and thrilled in equal measures.

I was appalled and thrilled in somewhat unequal measures six years later, when Piggy leant forward and shook a ball of tinfoil in my face.

'What's that?' I asked, shifting against the tree-house wall. I was trying to seem nonchalant. In fact, I was assuming an angle of Mooch quite precisely calculated to make me appear interested in the speaker whilst also establishing a subliminally indicative distance between myself and whatever trouble she was planning.

'It's from lunch. Ham and Dijonnaise mustard sandwiches.' Piggy was exactly the kind of person to remember the kind of mustard and feel the detail was important enough to mention.

The foil caught the sun and doodled neon blares across my line of sight. I closed my eyes. 'And why are you showing it to me?'

'We are going to use it to kill your mother.'

All my friends had a tree house and every boy in every book I had ever read had the times of their lives suspended at least at canopy-layer height. Despite my pleas my parents never granted planning permission for anything bigger than a birdfeeder. Piggy's family, however, owned a huge tree house since she could toddle; its promise of sun-bleached planks and leafy solitude made a fine excuse to visit her every day all summer, every summer.

'In punishment for grounding you, this is a plan,' Piggy continued, beaming, 'that will kill your mother stone-dead.'

'My favourite type of dead,' I said. 'Does she have an allergy I don't know about?'

Piggy raised an impatient hand, bamphed me – an expression of her own invention of which she was particularly fond – and assumed her best approximation of a Gestapo accent. 'No. We will use principles from Geography. You remember the lesson at the end of last year?'

'I hate Geography.' I kicked myself: Geography was Piggy's favourite subject.

'It was all about lightning. Conductivity.'

'Yes.'

'Right.'

Birds sang. Leaves blew. I levered a splinter from under my nail and tried again. 'So, the tinfoil?'

'It looks like there'll be a thunderstorm today.' We snuffed and looked about us. The sky glowering back was bright and dark all at once, foulmouthed with summer showers. 'Lightning,' she repeated, smile broadening. '*Conductivity*. Slip this metal foil into the insole of your mother's Birkenstocks and encourage her to go for a little walk once the storm starts and she'll be fried before she hits the High Street.'

It was at this point that I realised I was not really remembering this event but dreaming it. In the spirit of introductions, therefore, before waking up I should explain Piggy was by no means pig-like; her actual name was Alice Donnell. In my dreamt twelve-year-old and dreaming sixteen-year-old's experience, all Alices in life and literature are either very plain or undergoing some kind of psychosis. It seemed completely natural for a nickname to emerge for her and scrub all 'Alice' credentials aside. I am not sure whether a parent had given it to her – perhaps some long-gone pigtails had earned her the soubriquet – or if it was a bully whose taunt had stuck through mere habit, contempt breeding familiarity. Certainly it was not the *Lord of the Flies*' pathetic fatboy Piggy who was the inspiration; Piggy was definitely on the Twiggy pole of any sliding scale.

Piggy pocketed the foil again, skin taut over the long thin bones in her wrists.

'Think it over,' she said, and bamphed me squarely once more. Then she swung herself down the ladder out of sight with such speed and force that all the anxious summer air dissipated from around me and I flinched myself awake with a gasp.

It did not feel like waking up at all; rather, the ward appeared to be fizzing slowly back into focus. I find this the only exciting feature of hospital boredom: blinks might as well be deep slumber and waking hours might as well be blinks.

A glance at the monitor by my bed confirmed not only that I was awake but also, handily, I was alive and still being flushed through with all the necessary pharmacokinetics and morphinidoodles; bright blue threads unravelled across its data screen with regular popping noises in time with my heart. The monitor's fan added to this sound with its own whirring; the longer I concentrated upon them, the more I found the tenor and tones of both increasingly, deceptively recognisable.

'Dvořák,' said the data screen.

'Ceauşescu?' asked the machine fan.

'Sissinghurst,' insisted the radiator. 'Sissinghurst and *gourds*.'

This became intolerable pretty much within the first week, and in an effort to counterwhelm it my brain trained itself to switch into internal jukebox-mode as soon as I awoke.

The flaw with this lay in there being no way of choosing the sound or music that pops into one's head; for example, the tune that surfaced most often for me was itself quite distressing. As it came rattling through my head, almost immediately I found myself eked back to the moment I last heard it.

*

The first Assembly of the year at my school always followed the exact same format, the stage always set exactly so: gummy, polished parquet flooring, dull gleams on the piano pedals and brassy blind pulls, the shuffling of young knees grown fractious with cross-leggedry and its attendant pins and needles, its suspected deep-vein thrombosis. There was a muted scrabble at hymn-book covers and then the whole student body would mouth along to 'Morning Has Broken', the upper years cringing with each verse. Then came the Headmaster's muddled homily urging us all to uphold old leaves and turn over new traditions followed by 'Lift Up Your Hearts We Lift Them Lord to Thee'. Always struck me as singularly Aztec in theme, that one. As it dawned upon staff and pupils alike that Assembly was not *just* an act of sufferance but in fact the one boon separating them from first class, the school would finally launch into 'When a Knight Won His Spurs in the Stories of Old'.

That first September morning of term Piggy and I stood next to one another and caught each other's eyes. Same as every year, we tilted our heads to the plasterboard, swallowed a cubic fathom of dusty air and let rip into the first line.

Same as every year, we replaced the word 'spurs' with 'spores'.

Same as every year we collapsed into giggles and were frogmarched from the hall before our fits of laughter swept to the as yet unpolluted, petrified first-formers.

'Toucans!' shouted the radiator, quite out of character, and I was back propped up against my wipe-clean hospital pillows.

Morning has broken like the first morning, Blackbird has something'd *like the first bird.* 'Spoken', was it? Unlikely: few birds have ever really *spoken* apart from parrots. My grandmother is convinced the yellowhammers mutter 'little bit of bread and no cheese' at her windowsill regularly every morning as she combs her hair, but this is hardly conclusive. A nurse at the home has taken my parents aside to describe how my grandmother also regularly combs her hair with a baguette.

The blackbird in the hymn must have 'sung', then. 'Squawked'? I have never been able to remember how many 'w's that word contains. It always looks so awkward.

Squawkward.

The walls, curtains, coverlets and carpet in this hospital are all just different shades of *pallid*. The table closest to me has chips of silica in it, however; I learnt that whenever I craved variation in my environment I had only to move my head for the glassy facets within its surface to burst with light. I moved back and forth, roll, twist and the tabletop glinted its mirror-balls at me.

The morning outside the window changed colour, but never quickly.

Apparently my eyelid was swollen as thick as my thumb.

'It's like a prune!' exclaimed the girl in the bed next to me. It was her first day, and she was eating some chocolate.

'A prune?'

'Yeah. And you've got big staples through your cheek.'

'What are they like?'

She considered. 'Train tracks.'

I am train tracks and prunes, and my head is broken.

The next evening, chocolate girl asked for my name. I told her.

'I'm Hannah,' she said, unprompted. 'What happened to you?'

'Papercut,' I said and shifted in my plaster.

She laughed, and I saw that her mouth was full of Dairy Milk. She seemed to breathe in the stuff, her huge hamper of bars replenished on a daily basis by relatives, neighbours, priests, rabbis, butchers, bakers, candlestick makers, tiny monkey-headed gods and the Broadway cast of *Cabaret*.

'I,' she said, again unprompted, 'was in a car crash. Got no arm now.'

'I'm sorry.' I glanced at her with added interest; one of her upper chocolate-paddles had indeed been plucked off at the elbow.

'I fear I'll never play the violin for the Philharmonic.' The joke could be seen coming a mile off, and she obediently dived right in to supply the punch-line. 'Good thing I never bothered learning how to play!'

She exploded into a wheezy hysteria. Hannah is explosive. Hannah is big, and loud, and blasting. 'So, what really happened to you? Car crash too?'

'No.'

'It really is just like a prune,' she said, and for a moment I thought she was talking about her own arm again: a sapling snapped off, pruned to make way for healthier growth with the surgeon a tender nurturer, not amputating but sculpting his patient, deadheading. Then I remembered my eye. She continued, 'But I think –'

'Really?'

'What?'

'Nothing.'

'But I think,' she went on, 'your bruising is a touch more *yellow* than before. A plum rather than prune, maybe. A greengage. A quince? I like the word quince – the sound of it, you know.'

Everyone likes the word *quince*. It sounds like the action you make when you hear strange ticking over the top of an educational video about the War Poets, and when you hear that ticking cease, when you wince, and quail, and quince all at once. Everyone also likes the words 'pamphlet', 'plinth' and 'firkin', incidentally.

'Shame,' I said. I did not want to appear unfriendly.

'I'm sorry about your leg,' said Hannah.

'Thanks.'

'Will you miss it, do you think? I'm not sure I'll miss my hand. At first I thought like, oh my God, my hand, but now, you know, I'm kind of used to it. It's my left hand, and I'm right-handed, so I can still use my right, right? To write. I always wanted to be ambidextrous when I was younger. That means to be able to write with both hands.'

'Yes.'

'Of course, you can't really teach yourself to do that.'

'No.'

'But I always just really wanted that ability and it's no longer an option. No left hand. When did you first come into the ward?'

'About six weeks ago for skin grafts.'

'Woah, six weeks! You're an old-timer around this place.'

'Yeah.'

'How old are you? I'm nineteen.'

'Sixteen-ish.'

'I came in here on the 3rd of January. The sun was in my sixth house.'

'No way.'

'I'm an Aries, totally obsessed with all that stuff, should've *known* I would be *screwed* that day when I woke up. Astrology nut, me. I'm an Aries. Did I mention that? It means I'm courageous and optimistic. What are you?'

'Scorpio.'

'Passionate!' I felt my body make a tiny, clammy shrivelling movement under its plaster-casting. 'What day did you come in here precisely? I bet it was unlucky on your chart.'

'The 8th of November,' I said at once. I regarded her closely.

'Near your birthday then? Nice. Let's think, the 8th . . .'

'Eight-eleven.'

Certain dates are often picked up by the media and plonked indelibly into the public's mindset; I think 'eight-eleven' appealed because it lay between the memorable, pre-existing slogans of seven-eleven (the convenience stores) and nine-eleven (the inconvenient towers).

Hannah cottoned on immediately. Her jaw fell.

HER JAW FELL OFF.

No it didn't. Her jaw fell open and exposed gums creamy with Cadbury's Fruit & Nut. I wondered whether her chocolate intake could be medicinal, and that her bones could only knit together with cocoa butter.

'"Eight-eleven"?'

'Yup.'

'You're one of the kids?'

I made affirmative noises.

'I'm so sorry. I didn't know.' She paused, for tact's sake, then exploded all over again. 'You were there in the classroom?'

'Yes.'

'Did he shoot you?'

'Actually, I was in the room with the device.'

'In 5A?'

I had not realised that the papers had put that fact out. 'Yes, it was my English lesson.'

'God. Jesus. Wow.'

I felt oddly pleased that I had earned the whole Trinity of God, Jesus, Wow.

Hannah made a kindly flapping movement with her mouth to intimate I had confided in her, and that my confidence had cemented some kind of trust between us. She even pushed some chocolate across to me.

'English, you say?'

'Yeah.'

'Christ.'

'Yeah.'

'You like English?' she asked me the next morning, when the nurses came to check me for bedsores. 'I do. Always preferred word searches to Su Duko. Let's play a word game to make the time pass.'

I nodded, more for the benefit of my twinkling silica tabletop than anything else, and tried not to wonder why Piggy had not yet come to visit me.

Alastair Beck

Alastair Beck was born in Newcastle-upon-Tyne in 1954. He studied Microbiology at University College, London. Currently he helps out in the administration department of Oxford University by writing computer software.

He started writing poetry a couple of years ago while visiting Mallorca to do some hill walking, when he joined a writer's workshop in the villa where he was staying, run by the American poet Carolyn Miller.

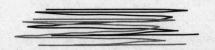

3 Poems

Swift

She glides up to a point of air
and manipulates it with a feather.
When she dives straight at me
time and space compress.
She is saying *'Here is the moment.'*

Unrequited

Opening the thermos on a cold day
I find the lining shattered.
Still the warm smell rises.
A shoal of silvered glass floats in the coffee.

Darkness

Dusk is a fine powder
dispersing in gelatine
with the tang of woodsmoke,
the pinprick of a star.

the sky is dark at the zenith
and light at the horizon
somewhere out there
you smile and glint.

Orange Creation

After our bath we bounce on the bed
pausing to prise our bottoms apart.
I don't understand what I see
a wrinkled opening into the dark.

You can't see out of the window at night.
There's only the bedroom reflected there.
Waking alone in the cold wet bed
the darkness inside and outside combine.

Dad holds an orange up to the fire.
'See that fire is the sun.'
Then he makes the orange turn.
'Here is the day and here the night.'

Gift for a Lifetime

You are just a child
with your dreams of falling,
or of walking naked
through the streets.
Come, have a gift.
Hear those footsteps behind?
Feel this, feel that.
Now lean against the privet hedge,
now there are drops of blood on its leaves.
Here is your gift for a lifetime.
Use it whenever you leave the house.
Whenever you see a stranger approach.

Evening Prayer

It is enough to sit here by the pool.
A kind of work, to work at opening the mind.
The evening clouds hanging over the valley
are scoops of orange sorbet; now raspberry.

There are cicadas and muffled goat bells;
my daughter swims, singing through her snorkel
'Tragedy, when the feeling's gone and you can't go on,'
breathing life into the water.

Lost Pearls

While cooking tea my mother said '*My pearls.*'
We were all hungry, sand worn, salt washed.
Next day, Monday it was, dad took off work
and he and I drove back to the coast.
We followed the same path down to the beach.
Where the marram grass gave way to sand
the pearls lay coiled and clinking at our feet
half-buried like a small exquisite snake.

'*That's lucky*' you say and scoop them up.
Then we walk on beneath the dull grey sky
and later sit together on the dunes.
The shore so empty and the sea so calm,
your hand resting warm upon my knee
and you silent, savouring your joy

Drying the Sheets

Peg out a prayer to draw
the clouds to earth.

Press the sea between
book covers. Giggling
children will riffle
through these pages.

Create a maze of light.

Let cinema screens
of ambush and mystery
overwhelm the daisies.

The Berserk Dream of the Oast House

No one throws a dishcloth across the barn,
that's the barn owl rolling out to hunt.
Workers have filled the drying room with hops.
Heaving those sacks has made their ears bleed.

The furnace roar is constant, comforting.
I hold a lake of air inside –
the hops are its delicate silt bed.
A wisp of flowers marks a thread of heat.

It would soothe your mind to see
the complex twinkling of this petal mass.
The oastie leaves the burners on too high,
the surface of the silt begins to pulse.

A vortex erupts in the drying room.
I stare with a frantic inner eye
at a tornado of emerald and dust
escaping through the roof into the night.

Alastair Beck

Night Visitors

In the deep of the night the clouds strap on their aqualungs
and drift down to the corals and reefs we call streets.
For now the hearts may open.

A heart may open, unfold and wave in the current,
giving off a pale light,
hoping for the touch of another.

If there is one close by
they interweave and glow in the current.

If only the memory of another
the heart opens and waves in the current

and the clouds marvel at the universe of lights
shining in the corals and reefs we call streets.

First Job

The barmaid from The Green Lounge
would no more look at me
than she could ignore her ham fisted labourer
with tattooed hands (love, hate)
who leaned across his beer to growl
'Are you sowing her?'
I too green to believe him when he said
'I'll have you if you are.'
Down in The Chain Locker
the underage snake bite crew
dowsed their trapped cockroaches in lighter fluid.
Little angels, racing along the bar
consumed by spirit and fire.

Riverman

Scum floats down the stream.
Let it flow over and around.
I would lie like polished stone
and feel each passing particle.
See rippling shapes in rippling light.
Hear the wash of water speak
foaming from my weed rimmed mouth
of all the ways to be.

Outing

First stare the sky down into dusk,
let yourself fall into grey.

Turn off the mobile, off the satnav,
wind down all the windows. Go.

No 'where' to go so feel the way,
drive into an empty field.

Hysterical rabbits will join in,
stand there alone screaming.

Hear that spirit in the wind?
It's a bad spirit. Run.

Lock the doors, satnav to home.
Drive with all the windows up.

Later dream a dark green train
steams into a station in silence,
again and again.

Alastair Beck

Enchanted

Halfway through the hedge he realised
that this fierce problem was too tangled.
There could only be more useless tugging
(hands twisting on his wedged sword
fingers enfeebled, palms rubbed to the raw).

Then he would call out, then cry into silence
until, hanging in a bracket of branches
creepers would slide through the joints in his armour
thorns scarify, vines tighten
a wren nest   comically.

The Pot Shattered in the Opened Kiln

Let's dance. It's a catholic hell in here.
I'm throwing curves into the hot darkness
until it ripples like a stone struck pool.
Then bang. Each particle of silicate
falls away, falls away, falls into space,
asteroids rolling apart in silence
each heading for their particular sun.
There are suns everywhere.

Liz Berry

Liz Berry was born in 1980 in the Black Country. She works as an infant school teacher in London. Her poems have appeared in *Mslexia*, *Smiths Knoll*, *Poetry Wales* and *Magma*. She received an Eric Gregory award in 2009.

The Red Shoes

Crimson. Like flames, like the first sear of blood
that came in the night and daubed a heart on my bedsheets.
They made blushes look pale.

On Saturdays, I pressed my lips to the steamy glass
of the shoe-shop window and blew them
a kiss. I was mad for their patent,

the rubies that glistened up your dress,
flushed thighs with fever.
I was tired of childhood, black and navy.

I smashed the belly of the fat piggybank
and stole ten pounds from my mother's purse,
waltzed to school in them, legs cocky

as girls in the science block lifted their eyes
from Bunsen burners and streamed from the lab
to watch me dance, their white coats glistening.

Some girls clapped. Miss Wetherby rang my mother
to take me home. But I skipped through the playground,
out of the gates that led to the terraces,

the parcels of garden where creosoted sheds
burst into flames as my shoes grazed them.
By the factory, I danced a rhumba,

drew the lads whistling from the high windows,
catcalling my name into the rosy smoke.
I tore my school skirt, threw my tie in the gutter,

Liz Berry

felt my voice hatching like a bird
in my throat as I danced through the waste ground
to the filthy canal. There the sky darkened.

The hedges became copses, fierce with nettles.
In the branches, single gloves hung limp from the brambles.
The dance grew wild, a tarantella

through the forest's darkness, the steps flowing
like a thick pulse of blood.
I heard the screams of girls who had danced

before me, their ankles severed, their toes
still tapping in ruby shoes, white as wounded doves.
But I was not their kind. I out-danced the axe,

the silent woodcutter, the traps waiting with rusty jaws.
I danced so fast my shoes scorched the air
and the sun laid the sky down, crimson, at my feet.

The Last Lady Ratcatcher

I was the last Lady Ratcatcher,
bore the scar of two yellow incisors
on my wedding finger.

Each night I crept out, cage ready,
my mind swift as a trap
on a neck bone, my beauty legendary.

I wore a cape of brown fur,
a belt of silver rats running
from buckle to back.

Gentlemen followed my scent
to the gutters for a flash of ankle,
the sight of my dainty boot upon a tail.

I wheeled the black rats
in a squirming tea chest
round the dog pits of Bow,

brought the pretty ones home,
kept them in a golden bird cage
by the bed, gorging on cheese,

licking the clotted dregs
from the cocoa cup. I fed them crumbs
from my lips, laid their heads

upon my pillow as I slept
in a bone white nightdress, dreaming
of fur, of rough pink tongues.

Nailmaking

Nailing was wenches' work.
Give a girl of eight an anvil and a little hammer
and by God she'd swing it,
batter the glowing iron into tidy spikes
ready for hoofing some great sod horse
who had lost its shoe in the muck.

The nimble ones were best,
grew sharp and quick as the nails they struck
from the scorching fire.
Eighteen, she could turn out two hundred an hour,
tongue skimming the soot on her lips,
hands moulding heat.

In the small brick nailshop,
four of them worked, faces glistening
in the hot smoke. First the point was forged
then the rod sunk deep into the bore
so the head could be punched,
round for regulars, diamond for frost nails.

Marry a nailing fella and you'll be a pit 'oss
for life, the girls had told her,
but she'd gone to him anyway, in her last white frock,
and found a new black hammer
waiting for her in his nailshop,
under a tablecloth veil.

The Goddess of the Spoons

When I was a young girl I met the goddess of the spoons,
deep in the belly of the silver drawer: the cutlery.
Her touch was stainless and cool as Sheffield steel
and she took me to the darkest place of all: the pantry.

She led by the hand through the cupboards, down the sinks,
her voice a tinny music, the apron strings pulled tight.
Close amongst the crockery she taught me all she knew
of how a spoon's full curves might give more pleasure than the
     knife.

She showed me she lived inside the drawers of unwed girls,
across the plates of spinsters laid with elderflowers and ham
and hot within the hands of sleep eyed widows, lonely wives,
she filled my spoony heart with mouths of cream and crimson jam.

Then pressing back to belly she told secrets of her thrill:
of young girls' tongues grown wild on bitter cherries, honeyed
     talk,
of mothers' mouths red raw from licking deep within the scoop,
their babies sleeping milk fed in the cupboard love of dark.

And waking in the morning I lay saucer eyed and bare,
my pantry ransacked empty, every knife and fork cast out.
But my heart swooned as it recalled her final parting kiss –
metallic as a bite of blood, a spoon within the mouth.

Notes on How to be a Woman

Be six. Click clack in high heels.
Watch your sisters and your mother
undress. Stroke your own flat breast,
still concave and white as a summer seashell.
Wonder how on earth you'll ever be beautiful,
splashing and graceless as a mermaid in the bath.

Be fourteen. Like Venus from the bath
you emerge to make-up, hair, high heels,
that first streak of scarlet, bloody and beautiful.
Sit by the mirror, open legged, and see your mother,
the hot red folds like the heart of a seashell.
With a curious finger awaken your breast.

Be twenty-five. Consider a breast
op. Scrutinise your body in the steam of the bath
and mark its curves like whorls on a seashell.
Tremble at the consultation, the tapping heels
of the nurse in the corridor. Ring your mother
and snort when you hear her: 'You're already beautiful.'

Be thirty-seven. Pregnant. The beautiful
swelling of life blooming from belly to breast.
Undressed at the hospital, bawl for your mother,
the mermaid tail you lost in the bath.
Cry when you feel her, at last, on your chest, her kicking
        heels,
her breath in your ear like the wind in a seashell.

Be fifty-two. Amazed that like a pearl from a seashell
something you made could become so beautiful.
Throw out your make-up, your old high heels.
Feel the rush of longing flood your breast

as you listen to her singing upstairs in the bath
and hear in her laugh the voice of your own mother.

Be seventy. Suddenly. 'Mother,'
she breathes, when you show her your body, the seashell
of your ribs, its single scar, swollen from the bath.
Touch the stitches, dream back that beautiful
time when her small mouth suckled your breast,
her fists clenched, the dig of her heels.

Now in the bath, let her be the mother.
Let her lift your heels, cradle the brittle seashell
of your body to rest, for a moment, on her beautiful breast.

Nicola Bray

Nicola started writing poetry two years ago after graduating from the Open University with a degree in Literature. She studied Creative Writing with Newcastle University before applying to Royal Holloway. She lives in south London with her five sons and has just had her first poem accepted for publication.

Salmon

One afternoon she massages my shoulders,
I feel her knuckles, or her thumbs,
I'm uncertain but I feel them

as if I were wading through water
and my skirts were swelling
pulling me under. Then the push

against the tide, I leave the silver ocean,
the water is cold and yet as I sleep
I am salmon. Not one but countless

fish plunging through the seas
like different ideas or bellies
filled with symphonies. A migration –

fathoms deep as instinct –
overripe ovaries ready for burial,
an itch like a hook an inch from a spine

snags the fishermen's net. We spend
our final days spiralling sand
with our dorsal fins, then wait to die.

The Girl in the Bed Opposite

I hate the sound of oats
in china bowls, a table set for twelve
in the middle of a ward. Toast
in an orderly's hand – crumbs that fall.

I can't wake up – I've tried
for three days now – lifting my head
from the pillow but every time it flops.
So I watch cereal from one eye

and a beautiful girl in the bed opposite.
She's wasting away, cornflake by cornflake.
My very own Bertha – I want to brush her hair,
make her Antoinette again,

take her by the hand and run
or cry like twins at a mother's breast.
A nipple in her mouth.
A needle in my vein.

Berwick Street Market – August 1978

She knows the shortcuts – the back lot
of streets and alleyways where red lights
echo riffs from songs that linger
on the stairs like groups of girls.

She knows the men
and spins them on a dime,
juggling their wallets
until the coins pile around her ankles.

She doesn't know that twenty years
from now – pregnant with her second child –
the telephone will ring as she cooks tea.
That somewhere in pathology
blood is spinning in a phial,

dodging tea-time light – dodging like a girl
who falls and grazes her knee
on a pavement slab in Soho,
grit and fruit pips buried
beneath the surface of her skin.

Playground

I can hang upside down from the middle of the climbing frame,
wrap my legs around the bars – dangle my arms in the air
and lift my head. I can leave the playground if I want to –

dodge the rails that stop dogs biting, run across the grass
and wait for your fingers on the latch – I can come home
or I can stay out here and listen to the screams –

we do scream; the climbing frame is red,
there are bubbles in the years of paint –
chippings like coloured sand on concrete.

The boys scoop sand and throw it in our eyes,
voices high like swings dare us to somersault,
tangle chains – jump from ninety degrees and graze our knees.

All of the children in the playground are screaming –
screaming it is better out here and I am hanging
upside down from the middle of the climbing frame.

Cobra

My mother – pressed against her ayah's hip
collects eggs in the hen house for breakfast.
Settled on dry grass she listens to her ayah's song
– the missing words and mispronunciation.

Sunday evening comes and as she dries my hair
we sing, *A Mary Jahn, A Mary Jahn*, a pigeon Hindi
chorus – return to the barn where the air is warm –
a stirring in the corner, an easy glide through orange light

a sudden snap and feathers in the straw. Tone of voice
ripples through the years – disturb the air
and Mother Cobra rises from her nest to stare
a small girl in the eye. Black Naja – Mother of fear

swallowing our lines – the moulted skin
left behind. Your mother wasn't in the barn
and you were too young to remember.

Pomegranate

Slicing a pomegranate always makes me think of you
and the girl who sold her soul to the devil.
But when my youngest says, *It looks like a brain*
I see he has a point – I've never thought of it like that –

split open on a chopping board – scalpel in a hand,
spilt juice on the table, sticky fingers, stained nails;
blood red pearls – each one a different thought.

I remember your red nails – somewhere for the juice to hide,
your silver needle picking out the aril from the pith.
Hunched over the kitchen table I listened
as you told me of the girl who slept beside you in the dormitory.

How she wanted to be best and bartered with Old Nick –
the night he came to claim his prize in dog disguise.
I can never remember the name of the girl –

the girl who sold her soul to the devil – I always remember
Sister Philomena – her heavy silver crucifix.
The weight of her skirts brushing the floor.

Mother and Daughter

She writes the first line and I am another,
the Russian doll she left behind;
There are aspects of the mother in the daughter.

I turn through time to remember a quarter of her,
the edge of a picture or book for the blind;
She writes the first line and I am the other

girl, a reflection in a mirror
made of sand. A voice that doesn't make a sound
resonating aspects of the mother in the daughter.

Amplify her silence, slaughter her laughter
belly to belly and breast to the ground,
write a new line, write me another

dawn, a light inside her womb and Father
Forgive Me for scratching at the wound,
there are aspects of the mother in the daughter.

Will they bury us together, as pencil is to paper?
A common script, a duplicate we find?

She writes the first line and I am another
aspect of the mother in the daughter.

En Pointe

A hypodermic needle waits beside odd ballet shoes;
shank to shank, elastic pairing, burlap and glue.

Unnerved by a finger on a switch, a spotlight
or footlight perhaps, Mrs Finlayson stops stitching

feels for a ribbon – the key to her pharmaceutical
chest where she keeps phials like orchestral overtures,

capsules of applause – a fix of ambition.
Each dream is an uneven stitch

or satin on her fingers, an itch like resin in a box.
I wasn't there of course – I was in another room

slowly turning pages, learning how frankincense
is tapped from the very scraggly Boswellia tree

and how if you scrape the bark the resin
will bleed, harden and form tear shapes.

Venus Effect

Turning a corner should be as simple
as slipping from third gear to first,
lighting a cigarette with one hand
or catching the eye of a guy

in the rear view mirror. Stopped in my track;
the snap of a chord in a tune on the radio,
knowing this is different now,
framed by lines painted on a road.

Forgetting the salt at the crook of your arm,
the slip of your hip over mine,
when mirrors were made of sand.

Now I watch as you watched me,
bide my time as if you were a wave
splashed against my thigh, wipe the salt
from my eyes and wait for the light to change.

Nicola Bray

Blowing on Dandelion Seeds

for M O'G

This isn't the day to drive to Fulham,
hangovers make me nervy – besides,
the rabbit has died – time is short.

Wait – streets pass by unnoticed,
the bench I climbed to stare at the high tide,

disturb the hand that hovers at my waist
but doesn't touch. Old Saturday,

walking by the river – leaves and paper
stick to the wheels of my car;

I will not find you crumpled on the floor
nor is today a funeral – the flowers shrivel

lose their seeds to the wind,
a hollow stalk splits, spitting at dry earth.

Marianne Burton

Marianne Burton's pamphlet, *The Devil's Cut (Smiths Knoll)*, was a Poetry Book Society Choice. She was awarded a year's mentorship by the poetry magazine *Smiths Knoll*, won first prize in the *Mslexia* competition, and is widely published in magazines such as *Agenda*, *Borderlands: Texas Poetry Review*, *Magma*, *Poetry London*, *Poetry Wales*, *Rialto*, *Stand* and *The North*. She is a poetry mentor for the prison arts charity, the Koestler Trust.

Encyclopaedia: *Within These Covers*

I crouched over its leaves
in the perpetual gloom
of the Hoover cupboard.

It felt animal,
the raw-rubbed nap
of window leather,

and smelt vegetable,
the stink of attic boxes,
damp, and unburied bulbs.

I unfolded its back pages,
flapped diagrams
of dissected yew and apple,

the needled reservoir
beneath the bee's fur,
the frog's kinked lariat of gut,

the female torso, sawn off
at the thighs, with pink
balloon and long-armed claws

– one left one right –
coming at you bear-like
for a treacherous hug;

and the male figure,
smooth between the legs
as a shop mannequin, who

undressed three times to show
(*i*) the fuchsia muscles
of a Marvel comic hero,

(*ii*) a tangle of blue and red
knitting wool, and (*iii*) the yellow
grinning man who beckoned,

while outside the window
in the summer heat
the street sent up

hooves and the cry
she said took people away,
Rag Unbone, Rag Unbone.

The Elephant-Headed God

It was Aruna who, flush with Feng Shui
from her own home, noticed him; only his trunk
and crown showed over dishevelled
copies of *Anna Karenina* and *Madame*
Bovary, a borrowed score of *Katya*.
'There'll be trouble if you leave him there,'
she said. 'Ganesha is a jealous god.
Neglect him, he'll be after his revenge.'

It took me a month or so, like most chores,
to move him to the radiator shelf
– the one uncluttered surface in the house –
under the Erté print of *La Dame aux*
Camélias, where he sat, deity
of our crossroads, watching the coming and
playing between living room, music room,
and bedroom. And in truth his standing there

did stir memories of lives before this one,
when all our holidays were honeymoons:
Egyptian cotton sheets in French chateaux,
a bed with a view over San Zanipolo,
chewing a late naan breakfast into
the emporium in Old Delhi where
we found him. Believing as we did then
in the immune godhead of the couple.

He looks baleful still. I should wash
the dust that clogs his feet and the rat
that crouches by his chair. His soapstone
pedestal has a crack that catches on
my fingers. He'll need careful handling.
Even so some days I press my thumb
into his outstretched palm as a gesture
of reconciliation. We'll come through.

Mr Christian Remembers Appleton Gallows and the Weldon Brothers

Weeks passed and people watched to see
which corpse would be the first to drop.
Chains from their waists still swung between
their legs. The younger lad had sobbed
at the noose, but Dick, who strangled
the prison guard and pitchforked the baker,
he kicked his shoes into the crowd shouting,
'Ma said I'd die in my shoes. I'll prove her a liar.'

It was a famous year for plums at Oakham,
but fruit lay wasting in the market. People
wouldn't buy because they thought the flies
had been at the gibbet, sucking at the flesh.
Me, I took no heed of foolish talk,
I always liked a nice plum when I found one.

Marianne Burton

The Anagram Kid

This salesgirl scum serves us the garlic mussels
then refuses my debit card, claiming it's bad credit.
A shoplifter has to pilfer, so I sneaked the pepper pot
and we headed off for the tense charm of Manchester.
Some used car raced us up on the motorway and won.
The truth is, it hurts being poor. The billboard said
Elvis Lives, but we don't, not so you'd notice.
You can tell I'm bored, emotionally curbed;
when you've no income, no one says, come on in.
Voices rant on, the conversation always about money.
It said 'Christine' on her name badge, on her nice shirt.
Circumstantial evidence can ruin a selected victim.
It was desperation, I said. A rope ends it. Pass me one.
A funeral is about the only real fun I can afford.
Nine thumps. A bit of punishment. She deserved it.
Listen. I didn't mean to hurt her. I'll remain silent.

Behind the Cellar Door

What is going on, Mummy, behind the cellar door?

There is a party going on, children.
Hear that crazy jazz percussion,
skip of syncopation, slow drumming heavy
as the blows of Murdoch the butcher
beating his cleaver on the wooden block.
They come and go at night, children,
instruments in cases, dressed in black,
that is why we never see anybody.

What is going on, Daddy, behind the cellar door?

There is a meeting going on, children.
Poets, philosophers, politicos:
all those thinkers hitting their fists
on the table and drinking, drinking,
how they need beer to ease their thoughts.
They come and go at night, children,
books in rucksacks, dressed in black,
that is why we never see anybody.

What is going on, Uncle, behind the cellar door?

They are digging you a playroom, children.
Blades of shovels turn the stones,
pick away and pit the limestone floor.
All hours gravel slides into barrows,
pitch pine planks are nailed across the walls.
The diggers stay till dawn, children,
tools in zip bags, dressed in black.
One of us will take you down there soon.

Marianne Burton

The Names of God

for Arthur C. Clarke

when all the names are uttered
when all the symbols written
Ishvara and Allah
sea and sou
pi and the periodic table

(Abba Alpha
Elohim Adonai
Tetragrammaton)

stand in the garden
on the wet path
listen to creatures
crawling in the dirt
and witness the stars
being squeezed out one by one

Changing the Sheets

Nothing more intimate
than this tending.
Though these are not
special, not wedding

sheets, no child
was born in them.
They have no rolled
hand-sewn hems,

are not embroidered
with sprigs of gorse.
Not new, not ironed.
Just creased, coarse,

cheap store cotton
for the night tomb
where we clutch, twins
in our feathered womb.

Not perfumed, not linen.
Just your night sweat,
acid and a peck of salt,
safe in my keeping.

The Lux and the Lumen

in memoriam mfb

I

is what they call sickle.
Her balloon
has deflated to a sac.
She has
not eaten in three days
and was
barely there the last time I looked.

The veil
between her and the next world
is so frail
a breeze could snuff her out.
And then
where will we be at night
when
only the stars are left to us?

II

400 lux
sunrise, sunset, or a brightly lit office
10 lux
candle at distance of one foot
1 lux
moonlight at high altitude in tropical latitudes
tenth lux

full moon on clear night
one hundredth lux
quarter moon on clear night
one thousandth lux
moonless night sky, clear
ten thousandth lux
moonless night sky, clouded
one twenty-two hundred thousandth lux
the stars and nothing else.

III

I danced under neon strips,
played in City basements,
never walked the fields at night.

The difference between
the lux and the lumen is
the second is light given out,
the first is light received.
They are rarely the same.

Lizzie Fincham

Lizzie Fincham's first poetry collection, *Needing Your Mana,* was shortlisted for the Poetry Business Competition 2005. Her poems have been published in a dozen poetry magazines, including *The North* and *Poetry Wales.* She won first prize in both the Barnet Open and the University of Sussex Robin Lee competitions. Her first Orkney poem appeared on an Edinburgh hoarding and in the National Museum of Scotland anthology, *Present Poets.*

Winter is by far the Oldest of the Seasons

Gaston Bachelard: The Poetics of Space

After the hurricane the garden
was never the same.
Your room is humming
its emptiness at me.
The first time you slept here
you said it was a near death experience.
Open season for fears, going back.
I've slipped into a time crevice,
my brain wiped clean
by the warm lemon scented flannel
from the plane journey.
'In Ecuador almost one fifth of the population
has abandoned the countryside
in recent years carrying their possessions across the fields.'
Edwardian explorers brought
back pockets full of seeds from Nepal.
The peaches on the blue plate
have acquired a punk's hairdo,
fine silver pin spikes,
a fuzz of purple toxins.
Your mother's gold bracelets
were sold for her medicines.

Greek Island Easter

Four blue domed churches in a row
have fuchsia nylon brushes
propped in the forecourts for slapping on whitewash,
sprucing up for Holy Week. Palms stacked by open doors.

On Good Friday we walk through an inland village,
a black-robed priest collects bread from the forno.
At noon there's a terrible cry
from inside a ramshackle garage.

Another lamb with tethered feet waits outside.
Suddenly the whole village is filled with that sound,
as outside each house, lambs hang from olive trees
with their throats cut, dripping blood into black plastic buckets.

Beyond

Beyond the warm south wall
the garden of childhood hides
rusted spades, cat shrines and fear.
Maggoty fruits squirm in our hands.

Beyond the cold north wall
sinister with alabaster peaches,
the death garden of slow hearses
sneaks us through the maze to fire-dark.

Panes are cracking around us

Too much August air crammed into the greenhouse
at the nursery. Small trees with name tags in earth beds.
Giant flowers in metal buckets.
We're choosing a birthday present
for your mother's grave.
There's a quarrel without words
growing in this small space.
I don't know what it's about.
It's snatching my breath.
Now panes are cracking around us.
Arum lilies leaping free.

Singing the Blues

One hour to talk, look, touch.
Two cars crunch across gravel
in The Trout car-park.
Henchard's December weir louder
than the screech of peacocks.

Bourges cathedral. Stained glass exploding
delphiniums, cornflowers, bottles of Quink.
In the room, bells called each hour.
Dodgy French plumbing,
lavender soap the size of a house brick
in the dish at the side of the bath.
Sky leaking colour until dawn.

In the morning wasps were committing
hara-kiri in the confiture jar
on the breakfast table
laid right outside our window.
We were trying not to make a sound.

Maundy Thursday

Maundy Thursday, purple-black day of Lent
closet poet, lover, priest, apostate,
needing confession, keen to repent
his treason to the faith he tries to hate.

Donne's bright brain is filled with red-raging fears,
beyond fierce stars glimmer torments of hell.
He reaches for his Lord, Creator of the Spheres,
then turns at last to the Compline bell.

The garden is betrayal, false peacocks cry,
the olives taste bitter; now he must choose;
without absolution he knows he will die.
Gethsemane's gate opens, he cannot refuse.

Easter morning dawns; exhausted by his pleas,
he kneels at the tombstone, looking for heart's ease.

Wanting to Talk to my Mother

During this sharp winter
in the abandoned conservatory
the white camellia petals fallen
to the floor are clammy to my touch
like your cream kid summer gloves.
If I could see you for just one more
winter afternoon, chairs drawn to the fire
would I ask you those questions
or would my nerve fail me again?
Do you feel the same or is it only here
sins of omission, commission wake us at night
when even the querulous seagulls
are weeping for the souls
of the living and the dead?

Orkney Diary

Box of a Leather Worker

Rain slapped our heads,
wind bit our cheeks
as we took surly directions
from the jazz-chapel man.
Follow the road to Evie Sands.
Searching for where you'd lived, perhaps,
as you made your box from rare alder.
700 AD.
Maybe.
Found instead the older site,
home in turn to Orcadians,
Picts & Vikings.
Broch of Gurness.
Built around 200 BC.
Granite blocks heaved
into large beehives.
Interconnected.
Inside a few ledges for sleeping.
Central hearth.
Hole in the roof for smoke
from each fire-house.
Small slits for light.
Skins and flesh long gone.

Winter Solstice

Morning. At another fire-house
saw the proto-type of a chair
made by a young man
when he took a wife

and a new hearth.
He used driftwood, three sheaves of white oats.
Makers, they earned the right
to sit in them, always.
After each death
the chair is burned
as the high straw-back has taken
the shape of each man's life.
Afternoon. Waited for the gleam
of the setting sun
to hit the wall of the passageway,
creep round
to light the cave tomb
at Maeshowe
at three fourteen pm precisely.
Evening. On the road back over moor-land
saw the fire-pits of winter
burning again on isolated farms.

Lizzie Fincham

Bike Trip

First trip round the island each May.
Park bikes under the fig-tree.

Look at new graves.
Nonagenarians usually.

Dry earth, withered flowers.
Hammering from the mason's yard

across the road. White marble taking shape.
Sliced with giant cheese cutters.

Over the churchyard wall
two cabbage whites shimmy

in the abandoned garden.
Artichoke heads spilling seeds.

Maximilian Hildebrand

Maximilian Hildebrand was born in London in 1980, on the same day as his twin brother. He holds a degree in Human Sciences from Oxford University, and works in corporate intelligence to support himself.

In 2007 he published a volume of his early work with the Park Road Press, entitled *What happened to my socks?* He still struggles to understand the concept of coincidence.

Basolith

No words for this, just my hand placed softly
on your belly's plain,

the river of your mouth flooding yes
from a long-known source now reached,

precluding a sweet trek to old lips.
Now a swelling of hips,

interlocking spurs of gorse, a landslide of chests
rumbling toward altiplano.

Our lives become deep, the incline full and narrow,
An arête that only two may breach.

It's here, that sincere flinging
of bodies into a ravine

that tumbles and careens without regret
to a rubble of hugs and clinging.

How much the same it is, afterwards,
Where possibly

great shudderings of earth begin,
a first grin of new sayings

unheard in the rockfall of sands;
love's secret the softness of dew

trickling over hands,
the rising of granite beneath grasses

where on ground once desolate,
now and forever two lands meet.

Thylacine

(*Thylacinus cynocephalus*, Hobart Zoo, 1936)

what am i?
you do not know because now you are the last

what am i?
you are not a dog
for dogs are loved and given names
and allowed to share my house
you are not a dingo
dingoes were brought untamed to this land
they are free to overrun your silent pastures
you are not free

what am i?
you are not mine
although I give you food
tidy your kennel
maintain the secrets of your past
from visitors who gawk
delivering verdicts on your pouch and awkward gait
it is cold
and you are not welcome in my house.

what am i?
you are not a cat, though some call you tiger
because you bear stripes on your back
as tigers do
they are fading now because you are old
and your howl is just a whisper
one day
          only your bones will remain
from a history divergent as your yawn

for record keepers who will turn them in their hands
and recognizing no spectacular shape
believe you are a dog
you are not a dog

what am i?
you are not like my kind
for I speak and the world hears
across your dominion there is a great susurrus now
I do not think it will ever be quiet enough again
to hear the shiver of your name

Moo Sea La Genius

(*or* Ode to the evolutionary hubris of the slug, *Arion lusitanicus*)

ZZZs chimney from his pneumostome,
the night wet and muddy as his tentacles.
Dreaming of ferns and fungi, denticles
nosh softly against radula. Foam
rolls off and down the back of his flowerpot home
to the foreign deliquescent English lawn
that is this tour's billet. He wants césped dawns
in Catalunya, or the orange groves in Castellón
where the *Arionidae* first bloomed,
not this suicide mission. 'Seek out *Arion ater*,
black natives, warrior mantled, skin shorn
from night. And mate.' Each slug a Theseus, doomed
to lose the bull, each one also Ariadne, her
thread shiny in the morning dew.

Hammock Song

Beam. Hammock. Bough.

Unimportant points where my day is hung.
The horsehair of my body
upon which I've strung

Apostrophes

Dust. Bark. Sun.
Three spots among many
falling snakehiss snaredrums
where doing nothing my day is done.

And piano chords
                    in dead leaves sung
dawdle invisibly
                    into ampersands of lungs

a cigarette's companion
intervals of busy being breath
three dots on a page
are a journey to no one's . . .
. . . Song.
            Hammock. Time.

An afternoon
                    The disregard of clocks
changing colours to its ownly chime.

The cross-hatch cotton of music
blends hours of unbelong in mime
above the clutter of earth's back room

where flintlocks
fill shots of nothing's wrong
             no venture unfair

when even three dots on a page
insist that nothing's there.

This Poem

*This is the title of the poem, which tells you what the poem is
    about*
which may be lust regurgitated, or quiet romance,
but do not forget that we poets are fond of spanners,
and are unafraid to use the word auburn
when describing ginger hair.

This is the beginning of the poem
the elevator doors close
and something clunks beneath you,
you descend into a half completed world
poorly lit as a latenight dive.

This is the development of the poem's world
where small details are put in, such as the wood used at the bar
and the brand on the paper that she peels off her bottles of beer.
The guitarist clears his throat with an arpeggio.
A barman wrings the neck of something fizzy.

This is the poem's key imagery
eyelashes shaking hands,
bubbles falling unnoticed to mahogany,
desire and doubt curling sticky-end out into themselves.
Someone switches off the light where the poem is being written.

This is the non sequitur
the following morning everything is much the same,
The sun has risen as promised in the east,
but you're not sure if the rules have been followed
or the poem's algebra contains a proof.

Here is the truce
spilt water on a bedside table,

a newspaper crinkling under the lamp
fusing page and cedar,
counting the ring-years of its host.

This is the disambiguation
a place of safety in meaning's frugal home.
Heat has turned the paper brown, which poets sometimes call
      sienna
because speaking it excites the tongue like a good story
or the pillow-smile of a face that only recently was strange.

This is the place where the poem ends
blinking through drawn curtains to the familiar,
where the writer may or may not have the courage
to present the facts of his life, beyond beauties in blues bars
and love overlooking auburn hair.

This is where the poet begins.

Old Shoulder

The day you were born you had your gift for me.
An abducted scapula through coracoid process.

The arm that first broke step with the body
when you were the age that I am now,

that kept stalling when swimming
or other things a young man might do,

until a doctor popped you open like a bonnet
and laid new circuits to the surgeon's lighthouse.

So that you could be young for me again,
diving the length of the pool, with a ragtag fin
and a gleeful remora around your neck.

Perhaps one day a man will cut me open
and correct the fault that told me I was yours,
leaving in place of the pain a sickle for a scar.

Neetha Kunaratnam

Neetha Kunaratnam is a male French teacher, working in Kent. He is London born, bred and affiliated, but has also spent time living in Japan and France. His parents are both Tamil Sri Lankans, but he speaks and understands very little Tamil. He speaks French, German and Spanish, and English is his mother tongue.

He was awarded the Geoffrey Dearmer Prize for 2007 by the Poetry Society.

Nine Die In Suicide Bombing

Eleven if you include the bomber
and the moulting canine, both present.

Four died oblivious, their minds combusted,
but six had considered their own mortality

that very day, of whom four had prayed and two toyed,
for reasons unknown, with the idea of self-immolation.

The stats of divine vengeance were: three Catholic, three Agnostic
and three Muslim. There was one Other, Miss X, and the Alsatian.

Three were stood on the platform,
five were running late and the dog was asleep

with the tramp, Mr Z, when fire stopped the clock.
14:26 was the official time of death but two

watches were slow and three fast. Two were
drenched in coats and five in suits, although the

rain had long since given way to sunshine.
Five were still carrying umbrellas, which maimed them.

Half of the victims hailed from the soil and half the concrete.
Spores of fear crackled in the air, electrifying

all fifty-six witnesses, the majority of whom
sustained serious injury, and echoed the explosion

with fearsome cries. Most were traumatised,
even those who had been caught daydreaming.

The Chair

It takes five men to strap him in,
like a waxwork cast beyond inhibition.
The first makes a casket of the ankles,

the second pins a strap across the chest.
The third, a priest, intones whilst
anointing the ears with Vaseline.

The fourth, the administrator, ensures
no risk of whiplash, cross-checks the eyes
for crusts of sleep, instructs a fifth man

inserting the bit, like a large prawn cracker
or holy wafer, abundant with ridges
to stop the sixth biting off

his tongue. As the lampshade is lowered,
his limbs are so heavy, no man
need check if he is earthed.

Curfew

Sri Lanka, August 1983

The red betel smeared on our jowls was meant
to cure our mumps, but made us conspicuous,

so at every checkpoint we were told to reiterate
burgher caste, in spite of our dark Tamil skin,

being too young to be entrusted with the proof
of our British passports. Buying provisions had by then

become a treacherous task, and the tension in the house
only eased if everyone was home by dusk. Then the

gunshots would start up, announcing the curfew, and repeat
at regular intervals, like whips cracking ominously up the street,

until you could sense them knocking at the door.
Then one evening, unannounced, mum hissed that

the storm troopers were coming, to quickly get dressed.
(Later, she would tell us Darth Vader was Singhalese,

but by then no analogy would suffice.) We rushed into the cellar,
eyes pounding, a nickel stink corroded our shallow breathing,

and we hid, wheezing, until the footsteps had disappeared
overhead, and the gunshots been wrung out of earshot.

Carted out of town the next day, in an open-topped van, we
    reached
the refugee camp, makeshift like a school turned polling station,

and took sanctuary a few nights. Huddled on the floor in blankets,
a dark ocean of bodies and familial territories, children spied

at each other curiously, before learning slowly to dim the glare,
improvise, share: brush our teeth with *Thambi's* mint leaves,

enjoy the neighbours' chai, with its excess of cardamom,
dish out the boiled sweets though no one was car sick,

until one time I woke up forgetting – a six year old again,
so selfish and intractable that, not knowing she had gone for
     water,

I tearfully reproached my cousin
for borrowing my sandals and not bringing them back in time.

The Courting of Silhouette Artists

They meet as fists, uptight at first,
before breaking into handshakes,
then the parting of fingers brings
about a smile, hunger, the intimation
of a kiss, a promise of cuticles.

A mating ritual is a performance
in itself, so overpowering and intrusive
you wouldn't want to be a fly on their wall.
The hares' ears show mutual interest,
a heightened sense of keenness, before

they crouch down into frogs' mouths,
ready to coalesce if they get close enough,
or one decides to extend into a long drawn
member, and the other to bite down
and swallow him whole, but this would require

a role-play of submission; they might
decide they have met their match
and start on an equal footing, forming
a butterfly, a gorgon's head, or two
Venus flytraps, lock-jawed and pulsing.

Neetha Kunaratnam

Wheal Coates

Beyond the plummet of this rock world,
even the scree has taken on russet,
taken on evening, only to lose it again.

We are rich here, could fill a knapsack,
if we wanted, with the bell heather
or yellow gorse that blankets the headland.

Ferns line the path like lilac
caterpillars, curling into a crisp.
The ruins, jutting out

their Cubist vision, are watchful.
You can read vigilance in the slats
of the meurtrières, adorned as they are

with greying blackbirds. From such
silence, it seems only the sea itself
is squawking. Gulls overhang

as cormorants splice the sea
into a patchwork of lanterns.
Seeing men climb the rock-face

a dog yelps suddenly in the dusk.

Popeye Comes Clean

I cansht standsh no more, I tellsh yer,
I haz to tellsh the truthsk: it wuzh all aboutsk
a deshkimal point. Spinashk ainsht

as ferroushk as you migsht thinksk,
dough the cansh presherve some nootshrientsk
Didn'tsht yer ever sushpectsk

the producksh placshkment?
Didn'tsht it sheem odd
I alwayshk had a can up me schleeve?

Didsht yer relly shink I likshked der tashte
of alumniumshk on me tung?
God, I misshed der freshk shtuff

but it alwaysh tickld me good I made
shpokeshman for der industhtree wid
my blindshk eye, speechsk impedimentshk

an not bein vegskitarian.
But I never onshe complaind
I sher as hell knew me playsh

I wuzh but Ham Gravyshk
whippin boy bfur dey shpotted
de futskure wuzh in canned vej.

I do wantsht to lay some ghostsh
to restsk about Bluto and meshelf, yesh
we *wer* an iterm durin our shailor dayz:

Goin off to bootsh the Natshkeesh and de Japz
relly brung ush closhe, and de resht wuz
Yankee Doodle and toot toot,

dough the timez wer crool so we kept it shtum
and it fizzkled out, but blow me if we
didnsht just bout manij ter shtay frendsh.

Here in de retirementshk home, I playz
bingo all me howerz long, boozhin
shumtime on wheatgrassh wid Bettsky Boop,

laffin bout de olden dayz in Thimble
Theatrsk, wundrin how de publiksh fell hooksh,
lines an shinker for me charmzk. Me honeshty

I guesshk, that etrnel trooshk on
me graveshtone: 'I yam wht I yam,
and dat's all dat I yam.'

Singin' in the Rain

Stinkin' with the 'flu, Gene Kelly
taps and tuts in his trailer.
Raging with a temperature of 103,
he wants to light up, but thinks better
of it, storms out to have a pop
at the director and mad cigared men
who want to spike the raindrops
with milk so they'll show up in

glorious Technicolor. Splish and splosh
under studio lights, he feels fresh
and re-energized, couldn't give a toss
if he's scythed down by lightning,
tip taps out of his sodden skin,
slumps, smiling, in a heap of sweat.

Declan Ryan

Declan Ryan was born in County Mayo, Ireland, in 1983 and raised in north London. He works as a freelance writer.

The Perseverance

It appeared, by the time we ordered two drinks
in The Perseverance, I'd spent my emerald years trailing
inches behind you. The flock wallpaper is sacred
in my personal rosary, just as in yours,
for the night I darked this very candle and said 'no more'
to drone days, wings-caught-in-machinery mornings
and vowed to be my own June Carter.
                                        We could be
each other's angels, or on reflection just enjoy the
songs of Julian Casablancas as they keep the bar warm,
flicking ash in the eyes of early starts and making martyrs
of us both. Repeat a decade with me, or I'll surely crack up,
tell me how you danced months of flirtation into a liptrot here
when you learned you were loved by a beautiful boy,
whom you have seen cry twice, and who works late often.

Declan Ryan

The Hope

Stepping into this meat museum, the youngest bud
on an ominously quiet branch, preservation is key;
eyeing belly flesh, leg slices, well-grooved, resilient Teds,
Smithfield slaughtermen admiring the soft slip of warm
beast against cool science – proud of their part
in each paper-plated triangle.
                                                    I fear the gherkins'
juices, their neon sweat and ruinous appetite
to seep unwanted into my beef sandwiches,
just as I fear the down on the coarse crackling,
and what it says about standards in the face of death.
Otis Redding soars and the familiar local faces
hunch over cloudy ale, their tapping moccasins
and Timberlands imagining the feel of a dock's wood,
wishing for the same isolation, the same effortless majesty.

The Reliance

A Harwich Hull is moored above us, brown as
the past, run aground. This sofa corner is my new
favourite hiding-place from London's fog-knuckled
fists, for the lost light caught in the cracks
of thumb-worn leather, or the sight of you curled
in the corner.
        The barman has the look of Arthur Lee,
you know that I could be in love with almost everyone.
We are all shifting and replacing, drifting to sea on
coffin-ships, cruising who-knows-where, pointed
towards a New World. The air sags with accents,
stale yeast and hopeless passes attempted
when last orders lead to looking babies. I long
for a red-nailed hand to steer me home, reaching
out through this foul Pea Souper.

Declan Ryan

The Crown

In this upper room, gold leaf on the walls mirrored
in the label on your Corona, there is no one
but ourselves, perched on pouffes, three summers
from the days when I used to walk you home.
When tears interrupt the silence of my audience
with you they are unexpected; the Seraphim over EC1
lean in to catch your gasping words.
                                    Cheltenham Infanta,
I am unsure whether to thumb away your tears
with my navvy's mitts, astonished by the frailty
in your spirit, your sudden grief at the lovelessness
surrounding us all. I haven't the words to impress
upon you your glory from my tenuous position
as court-jester, back-following subject, mere fire-ape,
dumbed by your Buckingham bones.

Total Abstainer

It's changed everything, being off the sauce,
since your bile ducts turned predator,
collapsing your pleasure, yellowing your pallor.
Now a succession of tap waters in pint glasses,
apologetic crescents of lime, suspicious bubbles,
taking your time over Smokey Bacon Tayto,
folding up the packets, dusting away the crumbs.

When you were born, a weak wriggling thing,
your grandfather lied that you had *shoulders like Dempsey*,
then saw you grow into that flattery, through
smaller summers in St Lucia, Somerset pool halls,
Dalston dole queues and a mid-twenties High-Street suit.
You wait, poised on a point, for the signal to surgery
spitting feathers.

Declan Ryan

He never said it to me

Smokin' Joe's cooler now,
living from a holdall
like a street-sleeping cat,
pulling out tapes and vegetable soup,
testing the punchbags.

Still playing that night
over and over, an inferno film,
each delighted blow sinking
once more into Ali,
putting years on, taking more off.

Statuesque in Philly's Badlands
wearing an orange silken robe,
or sparring with the dust,
Joe's jackhammer creaks,
stretched over hollow bones.

Still good to go, snared
by Filipino heat,
eyes swollen shut,
until the day Clay crawls at last.

21:15 to Enfield Town

The dull thud of dub seeps through the carriage as we coast,
deft intruders, rattling by the backs of terraces. Laundry days

and Tonka toys litter neglected lawns, the odd trampoline
or watering can sits holed and mournful. Hunch-kneed and hotly

aware of each seat's boundary, I sweat, breathing peppermint,
pursing my lips against the free papers' take on glamour.

As we pour past Bruce Grove I am arrested by Broadwater Farm,
the evening the Murphys were trapped at ours by the fever

of hosepipe unrest, Silcotting rage which fired the dark,
burning blood on to the layout of rat-runs and affordable housing.

Estates speak to some unconscious twilight of my cowardice,
lining the air with generations who must vent their terror
      somehow,

perhaps in further firecracker revolts, or an unguessable future
backlash when the pounds in their fists are only stones to toss.

We press on to Edmonton, it will not be tonight.

Declan Ryan

Going Days

Let's have a sowing drink,
firm in skin then, red-lipped and our lungs blooming,
all the apples of the forest in reach,
yourself straighter than plumb lines, firm-backed and full of blood,
yet lissom, strolling into town
the veins just under your skin tipping the blue & white cotton of
    your shirt.
I in health and heart, a heavy sorrow behind me,
my joined-at-the-feet twin –
not for all the world would I have swapped
that sobering weight – I carried it in the soft hollow of my hand,
balanced delicate as swan's eggs,
for the hair it had put on my face,
and the sweat it bred under my oxter.
They were going days
and in truth we loved the movement,
whether the lulling drum of steel under our feet,
cantering on rails towards the dark of the city,
or idling, loaf-limbed along all the walkways
around its rim,
reaping discoveries, playing on baize,
learning the volumes our sodden heads could carry,
mouthing words of half-remembered songs, bound by crowds,
the hum and most of all the silences afterwards,
sharing headphones as we coasted back from concerts,
New Wave, New York boys filling my left ear
the whole length of the Piccadilly,
or desk by desk underneath Hoxton, the same songs
easing out of the speakers,
But we're not going anymore.

The Wake

It's difficult to deliver a eulogy for a man who lived alone,
whom you met only in potbellied paper-thin ruin. No longer
keeper of a halfway house for Wild Geese on Plimsoll Road,
a Brylcreemed Danny, bachelor boy, glad-eyeing the handsome
women sipping minerals in The Buffalo on Camden High Street.

What did he do until the pubs opened, waiting for the North
        London's
latches to lapse, without a book or television to his name?
Not a big reader, unless you count the white walls of his room
onto which he projected those lost pink-muscled mornings,
the abandoned acres, baled silage and ferry departures,

relived one last time in The Sacred Heart of Quex Road,
nodded at by blue-suited men who'd beat the road down with him,
shared his rashers and left, one by one, to pots and pans of their
        own,
firm-bosomed wives to dose them with butter and jam,
and who return to him now, greying sons, praying their debts
        away.

His Local rattles with willow-patterned china, Guinness
and ham sandwiches to speed his soul on, warming the bellies
of the frightened boys he'd loved so well, who once flocked to him
wide-eyed and lonesome, when London was theirs for the taking,
and who are now at home, whether they like it or not.

Declan Ryan

The Lost Art of Keeping a Secret

This is what I observed only last night:
seven secrets abandoned to the dark and its cuckolding wind,
five semi-precious names lost to the flow of the sewers,
thirteen intimate recollections snagged in the curve of a stranger's
     ear.

I am not daring enough even to think of you in the open,
on weekdays or when it rains, in case your feet get wet
and some part of you is left in a sodden Mews, or cul-de-sac,

I take you out of my memory only in private,
lift you reverently behind locked doors, raise you from your velvet
and turn you in the shy light that blinks on us,
aware of how delicate these things are, and how dreadful.

William Henry Searle

William Searle, born 1987, lives in Lymington, New Forest. He is currently working on a PhD in Creative Writing at Royal Holloway.

Spring in a Scrapyard

The abode of a fantastic epoch

A blowtorch in a scrappie's darg,
a firework continuous to hand,
clean cuts lagging off copper pipes.
Dross falls past a flower

where tarmac abrades
to a plexus of cracks
jammed up with forgotten bolts,
banished pliers, oil-slick rivets

that fling out rainbow-garb
membraned in smoky syrups.
In its own blot, curfewed to the sun,
I wished the flower sprouted discreetly,

behaved like an unwinding weed
that acted on foregrounded limits
but no, it was cancerous-delight,
its own flare and clime of colours

that not only revived the drab
but tinged it with hints of mockery

especially when across the manic yard

I glimpsed at an up-stuck axle

obvious and dull as a virgin lighting-pole
weeping flecks of black glue and grease
while a slack-jawed crane
rumbled like a viaduct train toward it.

Then the flower would become my hassock
and my father's timely blessing 'now rise
or you'll get crap on your knees'
was my accent into factory ether.

And when a blackbird broke into song
I deemed it nothing less than it prescribed to be
although your hand upon my shoulder
stayed for too long this thundering time round

when a lorry clattered out the tower-high gates
and a hub-cap was flung into suspending air.
It was as if you snagged the sky to me and when
I wanted to move it had to move too.

Another Astronomy

Smoke from garden-fires
clouds the stars above the house.

Does home now become instant constellation
or a preparation to be made so?
From town, brother, we have walked
an avenue of observatories
to the final one before the sea.

The father rummaging to fix a fuse,
a mother's voice is a night-light in a black-out.
Then there are those breathings
prior to what we deem as ours.

We linger in the flicker of porch-light
on the dew-decked lawn
among glistening beads of reflected fires
that burst in nervous hands
as we kneel to make stars of the ground,
trying to mimic how mum would sew.

Nightly you tell me the science
of how bricks can bruise inward at dusk
then you drink the water from my bedside table
so I go thirsty through my dreams.

William Henry Searle

The Way is Across

Safe behind clusters of dandelion seed,
tangles and ringlets of tacky gooseweed,
battered cobwebs quivered in random winds
as dreamcatchers hacked through by omens,

you summoned and held private self-conversation,
aware of eavesdroppers chanting nightmare.
If I approach you I will come unadorned,
fasted away at last from the temptations to mask.

Even my name's agility unhooked from my tongue
so that I cannot speak but remain raw and nameless.
Will you regard as an invader on your meditations,
an object of alien earth, never before observed,

a specimen of some unknown ready to be beckoned and tagged,
to lie calmly on one side of your delicate wall
as a guardian new to the games, fending off nipping rain,
diverting it to a looming, more real realm

where imagination is a house that burns in an abandoned world.
The only trace of others: a tear hanging on the tip of a dock-leaf
bring it down close to thick cuts of upturned marl
under which scatters the bleeding seed of graffiti we need.

Border of Light

Spearing minnows with whittle sharpened sticks,
puncturing mole-heads with deft traps of nails and twine,
lobbing cakes of clay and crab-apples at caravans,
de-nesting birds, smashing discarded glass and tiles,
smacking the violent thighs of wild horses,

losing ourselves in their wreaths of winter breath
so we mount separate hills of moonlit frost,
to scale our map of measured innocence in ratios
of uncertainty and bliss shot through with awe.

Call to me good friend,
when you make it home through dense mists
inhabited by strange voices
that aim to lead you astray to their homes
where I may never recover you soundly.

Leave a trail, if you can, as an animal would do
in an act of drastic altruism.
Let it be a call of laughter
as you shake your father's hand goodnight
and when you meet your mother's eyes
widen in the lack of light in your first encounter with darkness.
You rise, insomnia stricken,

stunned by the border of light
around the black door of your bedroom,
seeing figures flicker past through the golden frame.

Frightened, you dare not make a sound
even a whisper of my name.
Blank and naked
there is nothing you can do

except part the curtains
and imagine dawn and me on the patio
beneath your window
telling you to come down and play.

A child to a child interrupted.
In years to come we address each other
as bleeding pillars of silence,
leaning ever so slightly
as the clock above your head pounds on,
stamping down a single hoof-mark
over the distances we have come,
forged into a circle by an absent flame.

Making Sense at the Gwyle

Leaves, siblings of leaves, frank against day,
found the wind-flow and followed my breath's direction.

I caught you talking to a river bend,
commencing obvious, Chinese whispers
with the sea-bound beck
purling through weaves and looms of trees.

Then you plunged both hands
beneath the weed-blocked bank
searching for the eel you dreamt
slipped between your ears
and wallowed in a head-pool
that cooled and cleared
by finger-clicks to the sun.

I cannot help but take part,
tearing up a picture of you,
floating each piece
on separate petals to where, I hope,
you're in mind for gathering.

The fragments are ours to reimburse across time.

I puzzle you down beneath a bald-star whisked with hair-light
whose smile is the crescent moon off to the right
now my thumb-nail at your sleeping face
brushing over the pelt and scut of your eyebrow
that's a wolf, dormant and dead and living.

I shall not settle on this tilth,
leaving this lair unguarded
except by an ash leaf on fire

that fought free from a brash-burn,
now orbiting the rim of your body
that's decked in the scurf
rubbed off between the friction
of this world and that one.

Here is the river
and I hear you say from the other side . . .

Only the whistle of a bird with no name
sounds throughout the dene.

Wait

I never once saw you wash his tough-skin feet
or rub his calloused hands with scented oils.
Only once, I think, did I see you glance at him
in the mirror when you happened to pass that way
out into the free night, only that to your disgrace
the path from the door led to the sea each time.
So you watched the soothing moonlit foam of waves
gather like a salt bath in a rock pool for your pain.
And does he know where you go at night,
does his knowledge extend that far?
I suppose he might as well count the stars,
measure his life by the weight of fog-laden air.
He will hold you soon. I'm sure of it.
Tell the earth to wait. You need time to prepare.

Contagious

Ignorant of a girl I met on a carousel
was the sole-survivor of a ghost town
I showed her pictures of my living relatives.

One where my mother is laughing
at a skylight rattle on a windless night,
one where my father is huddled up crying
in an armchair in a stranger's house,
one where my brother is reaching out
to catch, kiss and sniff leaves through black iron bars.

Then I tell her about the son I'm going to have
who will name himself before he can speak
with an undying sparkler on November the fifth.
'Take me home,' she said, 'so I can realise . . .'
I haven't seen her since that rendezvous.
My heart beats one less each day
and I heard from sources hers beats one more,
even those I love pass through me with increasing ease.
So I spurn myself to memories of flesh and reflections
while I roll a robin's wing between finger and thumb,
and the ground I need to walk upon
is a lump of acidic earth lodged in my throat
soon to dissolve into voiceless darkness.

Epithalamion Rant

There was this prophecy concerning the efficacy of the imagined
life . . .

Vision blinkered by a bible on the left,
daffodils with beaks not buds on the right,
resiliently monocled,
I took each gesture you made
as a sign to elsewhere . . .

for a hand to seize that may never exist yet guides all hands,
for the face that defines all faces yet has never been seen.

Continually from here I see my dream-familiars –
the shadow-bloke in a stiff cloak of stale blood,
the fox that lunged toward me and turned to breeze-block
and I lifted him, showed him to school assembly,
the oak-trunk in which I etched my brother's name
with a found fingernail of serrated edges,
the golden bullet in the fleshy redwood bark.
And yet I thank you for losing me by the way you are.

I have retreated into hindsight signalled by a flap of skin
strung to a tent-pole mantled on a canyon's far side.

Forgive me that I remember none of the images it projects.
From the beginning it all started with the way I saw things,
not to mention the way you fed me and put me to sleep.
And as a harsh reminder I keep a real sun lodged in the farthest
    corner of my eye
like a birthmark that presses and smarts when I waver.
This morning I saw a mask made of sweat, blue silk, ditch-water
    and tears
but it was far beyond my range to properly invest in.

'Progress is accidental to this clowning endurance.'
That was what you spelt out with Terminator stickers above my
    head on the bed-frame.

Christine Webb

Christine Webb's first collection, *After Babel*, was published by Peterloo Poets in 2004, and in 2007 her poem 'Seven Weeks' won the *Poetry London* competition, while 'Salt' won second prize in *Mslexia*.

She had a career in schools until the mid-1990s, and in subsequent years has, among other things, worked part-time in the Drama department of Royal Holloway and taught English to international students at the London School of Economics.

Trackside

Head's a tanned oval –
seamless rugby ball
half cradled under the shoulder
thrust upward, bare.

A few vertebrae march
towards the sliced-off cliff
of the torso, which spills
its folded intricacies

to bulge with detail –
an anatomical section
tactlessly laid open
dark-flecked, gleaming.

On the far platform
men in yellow jackets
prepare not to flinch
from hot smells, soft

deposits on the rails,
a purpose still vibrating
along the track. We pull
away as smoothly

as if no one's breath
had come shorter than usual
in this glass space
casual with dailiness.

A Family Programme

Under the eye of the camera
the male swallow flies up to the nest
his beak full of surprises.

His wire feet hook
for a moment on the edge, as he inspects
the hot squirming nestful –

organs pulsing behind the paper skin –
picks out one squeaker
and drops it on the barn floor.

These were not his young,
say the presenters, who yesterday pointed
to the *devotion of a single-mother*

barn-owl, to the *tenderness*
of an osprey's beak, tearing
bloody fragments for a chick. The swallow

repeats his sequence – four, five –
tugs out the last chick by its claw,
dumps it, as the female

swoops in. With a quick flutter
and jerk, he mounts her,
their shadows feathering the wall,

and both whirr away. *Now
he will build a new nest.* He weaves and moulds
shiny globs of mud. Soon the female

will swell, strain, lay his eggs.

Christine Webb

On the Beach at Aldeburgh

i.m. Julia Casterton

It's an untidy heap, this coast –
shingle thrown at random, as if the tide's
too disorganised to do it properly.

And the litter! – a gull's cast feather,
empty razor-shells, some in halves,
no use to anyone, certainly not a hermit crab.

The water mucks about, some rollers
sleek and regular, coming in according to the rules,
every seventh wave topping the others

– but too often they jump the queue, skid
and overlap, tilting their panfuls
of foaming omelette at my feet.

The light's all anyhow, one minute
hard and flat as a bone, sucking colour
out of the pebbles, the next sneaking

round the acrobat stacks of clouds, letting
God's fingers through to the sea as it roars
and dances – and a flung stone skips

five times, and the rollers lift shrieking
children, and the gulls ride the air and water

– so maybe you've risen, too, somewhere.

Tremor

I wasn't there last night
in my home town, where a woman
woke cradling a chimney-pot,
but I felt the vibration,

flinched with the man
leaving the pub in Middlegate
as a roof-tile UFO'ed past
missing him by a goose-bump,

as the church spire hummed
with tension, and a dust-devil
spiralled up in the market-place
lifting cabbage-stalks, fish-bones,

string – and watch out! – there
go the striped rabbit I lost,
the kite bucking on its long
string, creak and splash

of the pump-handle, hieroglyphs
of long division, the butcher's
bench with its bloody splinters,
the alto solo, the scholarship paper,

love letters, ashes, ashes
– roaring up with the cobblestones
and settling back while the church
spire steadied itself,

as if nothing had happened.

Christine Webb

Ginger, you're barmy . . .

An ounce of soldier's spit is worth
a ton of polish, said my grandfather,
Ginger Thraves, shining his boots
with the bulging resilient buffer
tugged from an old cake-tin. He paid
special attention to the toecaps.

Six weeks at sea, then Alexandria,
citrus in the off-shore wind,
the quayside swaying nearer,
oranges in toppling pyramids.
Men cheered, played fruit football.
He ate twenty, and was sick.

It was the soldier's instinct – grab first,
eat what you can. Officers' mess,
serving potatoes: he shoved one sizzling
in his mouth, bit down hard. Spoon
in hand, moved on at the regulation
pace, eyes streaming, straight-faced,

unnoticed. Nor did the Colonel miss
his cufflinks, borrowed for a date. I see
Ginger slipping them back with the quick
hands that shone his boots to a gloss:
An ounce of native wit is worth
a ton of education.

Canary Wharf

Glass city, neck-twistingly
vertical, balances on its
peninsula and erupts
into dance. Each building
flirts with its neighbour,
mirrors lines as curves,
oblongs as ovals; seduces
struts to pair up, bracket
winking at bracket.
Ladders of wavering
rungs form in windows,
dissolve. A stationary crane
collapses from its stilts
into a welter of squiggles
while a black-backed gull
tilts its giant wing-span,
vanishes off the edge of
a building it wasn't passing –

and all day, in this grove
of towers above the shifting
tidal flow, light presses
on with its sculptures.

A Monument for Horace

He's made, he says, a better monument
than brass: something that will outlast
the weathering elements – wind, rain,
centuries of processions

while the priest climbs the Capitoline
in the crowded silence, the Vestals pacing
behind. He'll be read for ever, he says,
and everywhere

even in the unfashionable provinces.
He's cracked the code, liberated
crystalline Greek forms
into the new music

of this Italian peninsula, won the right
to the immortal crown: the Muses should
be proud of him. And it's true, blast him.
None of us can catch

him as he soars ahead: we stumble on
reaching out for that elusive word
that would translate us into felicity
if we could find it.

Triolets

After that hour of sleep, you woke, and made
a little sound, between a cough and sigh.
The breathless nights were over: unafraid
after that hour of sleep, you woke, and made
no gesture of distress, but simply laid
your hands in mine. It seemed easy to die
after that hour of sleep: you woke, and made
a little sound, between a cough and sigh.

Revisiting that hour, as every day
I do, I find you waking from your sleep.
You never speak, but always look away:
revisiting that hour, as every day
lengthens your absence, I pretend you'll stay,
look at me, answer. Else why should I keep
revisiting that hour, as every day
I do, to find you waking from your sleep?

Christine Webb

Shoreline

Bowing to its breakfast, a small bird
fossicks in a frayed coil of twine,
splitting hairs to loosen fishy dots,
rags of membrane. It disregards
the puffed oval of a pitta bread
that bowls, flips, turns itself back
into a half crab-shell, holding a spoonful
of sand like sifted flour. Sugar grains
give way to crumbs, to grit, to ridges
of stone eggs, poised to avalanche
down. Sea trundles, onshore wind
flicks the bird's feathers. It persists,
prods, gulps. The sun comes out
and every pebble has its shadow.

Sarah Westcott

Sarah Westcott is originally from Devon. She has a degree in Human Sciences from Sussex University and has lived in Bristol, Brighton and Moscow where she taught English as a foreign language.

Sarah has been a journalist since 1998 and currently works as a news reporter and editor for the *Daily Express*. Her prose and poetry have been published on-line and in journals including *Mslexia*, *Aesthetica*, the *Guardian* and *Poetry News*.

Lost Village

This poem forms part of a sequence based on the Derbyshire villages of Derwent and Ashopton which were submerged beneath reservoir waters in 1946. Since then, when water levels have fallen, stonework from Derwent has reappeared.

Under the days
stones stand
bearing up,
mossed inscriptions intact.

Silt settles,
fine
as ash,
particle on particle,
flake on flake,
burying lines,
life lines
in increments,
delicate
as frost.

Minnows glide and flicker
through torn walls, windows, crenellations,
algae blooms and glows.

A dropped boot breaks through
trailing lovely chains of bubbles.

Fish lay eggs on gateposts,
in the notch of engraved numbers,
the channel of a date, the groove,

the opportunity of an epitaph.

Sarah Westcott

Hot summers, a spire pierces
the meniscus,

and ruins re-appear,
an exoskeleton of brick

two gateposts like sentries,
jammed in slipped topography.

The sky is a thick iced blue
lightening at the rim

the wind ruffles the surface
into cockscombs.

Look into the water:

there's a straining waving kite,
the bridge of a flung ball,

the soft heads of schoolchildren,

the church spire with the vane on top,
its golden tail arched up,

a collared dove,
with a leaf in its beak,

wings beating in the wind.

Common Midwife Toad

(Alytes obstetricans)

He's been shackled for days
eggs twined round his crimped legs
oleaginous, elastic, precious chains –

he knows
the moment of ripeness, feels it –
lifts dead leaves like lids,

drags his load to the creaking shallows,
the pond turbulent
as rumpled bedclothes.

This is birth: he squats and waits,
half an ovoid eye
above the waterline

the apex of his back
a rising island.
Each tadpole wriggles free,

corkscrews into darkness –
he crawls from the soup,
hungry again,

towards the lit kiss of dawn

Sarah Westcott

Feathers

When I was small there was a pool –

I watched the swimmers from the water's edge,
watched them heave selves out on straight arms,
backs glistening, as evening came.

I watched the hazy lanes settling back,
black lines straightening a long way down

until the swallows came,

banking and tilting over the blue,
dipping bills in absolution.

Once, the tip of a primary
grazed my friend's face as we lay
flat on the concrete tiles.

I felt the water on my skin
evaporate into strands of cirrus,
webbed and silken, far away.

I watched the money spiders' crawl
on the pink paving stones
and waited for my turn to feel

the swallow's soft fanned wing.

In the Trenches

We did our best to improve things;
built a neat causeway of logs, with a railing,
explored the wooded valley, dragged
the best tree-tops and stuck them in the ground.

From the gardens of the ruined chateau
we fetched rhododendron, box, clumps
of snowdrops, planted willow and hazel
with catkins, grew colourful flower beds.

We cleared the fast-flowing brook, made
working dams and water mills for fun,
carved a board for each dug-out:
Villa Woodland Peace, Heart of the Somme –

and we never stopped hearing the birds,
their greeting of the day, their cheerful twittering.

This was inspired by a letter home from German soldier Lothar Dietz, written
from a dugout near Ypres, November 1914. He was killed on 15 April 1915.
(*German Student's War Letters,* ed. Philipp Witkop, Pine Street Books, 2002.)

Sarah Westcott

For the Love of Young Leaf

You stippled ripple of wet hem over slate,
rubber necked in the greening growth –
you globular lunar snouter of dark ways,
your bovine, blunted downward gaze beyond
opened sky to micro-scraps of food.

The brittle ear you slide along the ground,
your humped rebuke to beaks, bones and sun,
your stalky peer, erectile eyes, old mouth
your craquelure on granite, your garland
of quiet effort looped around our feet.

Your space-ship purity of vision,
your glowing point of will scooping a trench,
the string of pearls you drop into the earth
softly as butter out of your soft foot,
opaque as babies' fingernails, but tough.

The infinite proportions of your form,
solidified before we learned to count,
the appetite we share that draws us on,
to fall upon the earth, then rise again,
to follow you with slow and greedy passion.

Two Men

(after Carol Rumen's Two Women)

Daily he rises, paid thinker,
worked out. The hours take him
from the wife and children –
he gives his years to the desk,
computer screens and tanked fish.
This is his way of loving them
from a glittering terminal
eight floors high.
Coming back long after dark,
to the heat of the family home,
he brings a rolled newspaper,
the cool print a baton from his world.
That's half the story. There's another man
who bears his name, a dark-nailed lad
who looks for woodlice under logs
and dreams of walking on the moon.
Who longs to melt a girl
on his tongue. A true husband,
he kisses upturned cheeks and pours
a whisky for the dreaming boy.
They used to meet at night, sometimes,
his young voice called out when he came.
They've not touched for years –
if they did, they would kill each other.

The Man from Del Monte Talks Back

This is not just any life. It's my life.
The real thing.
It isn't soft, strong
or very long, but I take courage
because I'm worth it –
I've been exceedingly good, gggrrreat in fact,
I had a break, went to work
on an egg, I am waffly versatile,
I've tried to do more

than it says on my tin,
though I never know quite what –
and yes, it could be you, it could,
but it won't be, not in a million
years – and I ate what they told me
for breakfast but it didn't keep hunger locked up
till lunchtime – no, not for one moment
and this isn't the best a man can get
and the future isn't orange . . .
'*Cut!*
It's a wrap.'

Acknowledgements

Liz Berry: Nailmaking (*Smiths Knoll*); Notes on How to be a Woman (*Magma*); The Last Lady Ratcatcher (*Poetry News*); The Red Shoes (*Poetry Wales*); The Goddess of the Spoons (*Scottish Book Collector*).

Marianne Burton: Behind the Cellar Door (*Poetry London*); Changing the Sheets (*Agenda*); Encyclopaedia: *Within These Covers* (*Rialto*); Mr Christian Remembers Appleton Gallows and the Weldon Brothers (*Iota*); The Anagram Kid (*Magma*); The Elephant-headed God (*Borderlands: Texas Poetry Review*); The Lux and the Lumen (*Poetry Wales*). The Names of God was written as a collaboration with the Guildhall School of Music and Drama, and set to music by Alastair Putt.

Lizzie Fincham: Singing the Blues (*French Literary Review*).

Neetha Kunaratnam: Curfew (*The Interpreter's House*); Nine Die In Suicide Bombing (*Magma*); The Courting of Silhouette Artists (*Magma*); Wheal Coates (*Agenda Broadsheet Online, No. 7*).